SOLDIER,
SPY,
HEROINE

SOLDIER, SPY, HEROINE

a novel based on a

TRUE STORY OF THE CIVIL WAR

Debra Ann Pawlak & Cheryl Bartlam du Bois

YUCCA

Yucca Publishing books may be purchased in bulk at special discounts for sales
promotion, corporate gifts, fund-raising, or educational purposes.
Special editions can also be created to specifications. For details, contact the
Special Sales Department, Yucca Publishing, 307 West 36th Street, 11th Floor,
New York, NY 10018 or yucca@skyhorsepublishing.com.

Yucca Publishing® is an imprint of Skyhorse Publishing, Inc.®,
a Delaware corporation.

Visit our website at www.yuccapub.com.

10 9 8 7 6 5 4 3 2 1

Library of Congress Cataloging-in-Publication Data is available on file.

Jacket photo by iStockphoto

Print ISBN: 978-1-63158-103-8
Ebook ISBN: 978-1-63158-109-0

Printed in the United States of America

This book is dedicated to Sarah Emma Edmonds Seelye, a heroic and tenacious woman whose ingenuity and sheer fearlessness on the battlefield not only demands our admiration and respect, but also inspires us to challenge ourselves. May we all have a fraction of her selflessness and bravery when our rights, freedom, and democracy are threatened.

"No war ever developed so much bravery and devotion among women as did the great Civil War. But none of the many instances recorded have surpassed the record for pure, unselfish patriotism and zeal for the cause of humanity, daring bravery, and heroic fortitude as that of Sarah Emma Edmonds, alias Franklin Thompson of Michigan's Company F, in the summing up of whose life, finds an extraordinary amount of patriotic devotion to the cause of her adopted country in the greatest crisis of its history, and nearly her whole life devoted to the alleviation of human suffering and the whole world made better from her having lived in it."

—Colonel Frederick Schneider

Table of Contents

Part 3: Seeking Justice (1863–1898)

Authors' Notes and Acknowledgments

In 1889, American journalist and women's rights activist Mary Livermore estimated that nearly four hundred women bore arms and served in the ranks of the Union Army during the Civil War. Most of their stories have been lost, but none were braver and risked more for the Union than Sarah Emma Edmonds. A remarkable woman she endured hardships most of us will never know. Yet, through it all, her spirit remained unbroken.

Emma's unusual journey inspired us, as writers, and even though this book is a work of fiction, it is based on facts. Where facts were obscure, or simply unknown, we tried our best to fill in the blanks yet remain true to her character. We would also like to point out, that at times, we felt Emma expressed herself best. In these instances and in keeping with her voice, we paraphrased her own words (taken from letters, interviews, her memoirs, etc.); these passages are indicated in italics. In addition, all Civil War battle statistics came from the Civil War Trust website (www.civilwar.org). We hope Emma's story honors not only her life and accomplishments, but all of those who served their country during its darkest hours. Their sacrifices must never be forgotten.

•••••

We would like to thank our agent, Mr. Peter Riva of International Transactions, Inc., for believing in Emma's story and encouraging us to write this book. We would also like to express our appreciation to Mr. Keith Harrison of the Grand Army of the Republic (GAR) Brainerd Post III Memorial Hall and Museum in Eaton Rapids, Michigan who generously shared his vast knowledge about the GAR. Another round of thanks goes to Linda Wells who proofread the manuscript for continuity and those pesky typos.

•••••

On a personal note . . .

Debra Ann Pawlak would like to thank her good neighbors, Doug and Jessica Lapp, for always sharing their computer when her computer wasn't up to snuff. In addition, she gives a nod to her husband, Michael, for his support throughout the writing of this book. She would also like to hail her cheerleaders: son Jonathan and his wife Stacey; daughter Rachel and her husband Jon. Last, but hardly least, she is grateful to her three baby dolls, Madeline, Olivia, and Michael, whose little faces always bring sunshine to even the bleakest of days and looks forward to another one coming soon.

Cheryl Bartlam du Bois would like to thank Sarah Emma Edmonds for her strength and inspirational spirit, which continues to live on through her own written word. Working as a Paracriminologist for law enforcement, du Bois has used her intuitive and otherworldly communicative skills to tap into the ongoing spirit of Sarah Emma Edmonds whenever possible. Having grown up on a historical Civil War hospital property at Fair Oaks, Virginia, where Emma served during the Seven Days Battle and the Battle of Fair Oaks/Seven Pines, du Bois has felt an innate connection to this tenacious and brave battlefield nurse and spy. Du Bois's childhood "house of spirits" intrigued her intense interest in the war and the soldiers who served, and her relic hunting around Richmond, as a child with her father, brought her a closer understanding of the true horrors of the worst blemish on our Nation's history. She would like to acknowledge her grandmother, Winifred du Bois, who passed on her amazing connection to spirit.

PART 1

The Road to Manhood

(1841–1861)

Chapter 1

A Father's Misfortune

Winters on Lake Magaguadavic were cold and bleak, but nothing compared to the even icier chill that permeated the Edmondson's stone-walled farmhouse. There, life was an utter disappointment to an embittered farmer forced to rely on daughters to run the family farm. His wife, Betsy—a fine Irish lass— had given birth to four strong, but unwelcome daughters, Eliza, Frances, Mary Jane, and Sarah Emma. Their only son, Thomas, suffered from epilepsy, which prevented him from helping out on the farm. It was bad enough that the neighbors often whispered about the cursed lad, but the fact that Thomas could not work alongside his father like a man was Isaac's worst woe. Despite a lack of strong male progeny to help him, Isaac made good on the land, growing a healthy crop of potatoes that allowed him to buy a few cows and horses, several pigs, and a gaggle of chickens.

For the transgression of being born female, at their father's insistence, his daughters donned shirts and trousers to work alongside him in the potato fields every day. Even though Isaac didn't believe in educating girls, his long-suffering wife, Betsy, did her best to ensure that her brood could read and write. She sent the children to the one-room schoolhouse whenever they could be spared on the farm, even in the dead of winter if weather permitted. At night by candlelight, she faithfully read the Bible to her children. A meek, subservient, Christian woman, she did her best to avoid her husband's unfettered anger. She kept to herself whenever possible and slaved daily in the austere kitchen preparing food from the fields on a wood-burning stove, striving to make her husband happy. It was a thankless task and well understood that nothing made Isaac Edmondson "happy."

Sarah Emma Evelyn, being the youngest and the last, took the brunt of Isaac's wrath. Thanks to his constant disapproval, she always tried her best to please him by becoming proficient at many things normally attributed to men. She tried to hide her blossoming womanhood behind dingy work clothes, hoping her father wouldn't be reminded of what he considered her major flaw. He wanted a son, and Emma tried her best to be just that. By her teen years, she was a crack shot with a gun, a fine hunter, and an expert rider. She could outshoot and outride all of the locals, but no matter how hard Emma tried, she never measured up in Isaac's eyes. She was never quick enough, never smart enough, and never, ever good enough simply because she was born a girl.

•••••

Summer in New Brunswick was always a welcome respite from the stinging cold of winter. The balmy fresh air embraced the picturesque countryside, leaving no trace of ice or snow or the blustery winds that kept its residents indoors. Summer meant new life— horses, pigs, and cows were bred—potatoes, beans, and corn were planted. Farmers and their families worked hard to take full advantage of Mother Nature's kindness.

As the sun spread its warmth over the panoramic countryside one hot afternoon in the summer of 1857, sisters Frances and Emma, on horseback, pushed a few head of cattle toward a fast-flowing river in an effort to get them to drink. Isaac had sent his girls to tend the cows and to see how the newest calf was faring in the seasonal heat. As the elder, Frances followed directly behind the animals in an attempt to keep them safe. The churning current, however, was merciless and, without warning, swept the unsteady calf off its feet, pulling it under. She instinctively turned her horse toward the desperate creature, as it struggled to keep its head above the water. While she slowly made her way toward it, the rushing rapids knocked Frances from her mount and dragged her under as well.

Seeing her sister in trouble, Emma immediately raced into the river. She leaped from her horse to rescue Frances, who had just broken the surface and was gasping for air. A strong swimmer, Emma quickly caught up to the distressed girl and dragged her toward the safety of the riverbank. The two clawed their way onto shore and collapsed in a fit of exhaustion.

Emma and Frances lay on their backs, winded from their close call, and in a moment of nervous relief, they suddenly laughed.

"Lord, Emma! I thought I was about to meet my maker!"

"Not today, Frances, but I will surely meet the Lord tonight when father finds out about that calf!"

● ● ● ● ●

At the time that unlucky calf was lost, all of the Edmondson girls were old enough to marry, with fifteen-year-old Emma being the youngest. But only the eldest, Eliza, had claimed a husband and moved from Isaac's house. That left three girls and one boy at home to face their father's wrath.

As for Frances and Emma, they were afraid to return home that evening, knowing that when Isaac discovered their unfortunate loss, they would be forced to endure his uncontrollable fury. Most importantly, Emma realized that it would only be worse for everyone if she returned home empty-handed. So, she went hunting with her favorite rifle, managing to shoot a few hares for supper. She even took down two of them with a single shot. Too bad her skill as a marksman would never matter to Isaac.

When Emma came in that evening, her sisters Mary Jane and Frances were setting the table and helping their mother prepare the meal. The usual somber mood prevailed as Emma hung the rifle on the wall rack. Having skinned and gutted the hares outside, she now put them in a pan and placed them in the oven, hoping that this meager offering would somehow lessen her father's impending hostility.

Betsy left the cake she was making to hug and kiss her youngest child in an unusual display of animated affection.

"You are a real hero, Emma! I heard how you saved our dear Frances from drowning today." Her voice trembled with gratitude.

"I figured you'd be glad I saved Frances instead of that calf." Emma grinned, pleased to see her mother happy. It didn't happen very often.

"Not Father." Frances shook her head. "He would have preferred if you let me drown and brought the calf back home."

"You're right, Frances." Mary Jane snickered. "I do believe that father would have cheered for the cow."

"You girls shouldn't make light of such a thing. It could have been tragic," Betsy admonished them gently before turning back to Emma. "Your fearlessness served us all well today, my girl. But I'm afraid there might be a time when your luck runs out, and I worry that someday you just may meet an untimely end."

"You shouldn't worry, Mother, I have guardian angels watching over me," Emma assured her, but Betsy had never understood her youngest child's total lack of fear . . . except when it came to Isaac, of course.

Emma's ailing brother, Thomas, who endured as much paternal abuse as she did, came in from the garden, toting a basket of potatoes. His face, which was almost always ashen, seemed even paler. His worried look alarmed the women. "Father's coming, and he looks fearsome mad." He set the basket down on the workbench in front of Emma so she could peel the spuds.

"Please . . . don't tell him about the calf." Betsy sighed. "If we're lucky, maybe he won't have noticed yet. You know how his temper gets the best of him." She quickly turned back to her cake as Isaac entered from the back door, enraged, just as Thomas had warned.

"Damn you girls!" Isaac lashed out. "Always costing me money! Why couldn't I have good, strong boys to help with the farm?" Turning to his wife, he continued his tirade. "Instead you had to go and have four worthless girls and one poor excuse for a son. Useless . . . all of you! And you, Emma! You'll be going to bed without dinner for the next month. Do you really think you can make up for losing a calf with some measly rabbits?"

Isaac snatched the knife from Emma's hand as she peeled the potatoes and stabbed the blade into the workbench, missing her fingers by nary an inch.

Chapter 2

Meeting Her Hero

Since they were the dirtiest jobs on the farm, shoveling muck in the pigsty and cleaning out the horse stalls were daily chores tasked to Emma by her father as punishment. What Isaac never realized was how much she enjoyed her time with the animals. Emma felt that these creatures understood her and appreciated the way she tended to them, unlike her father, who believed that all beasts were dumb and not deserving of love and tenderness—the same lack of sentiment he had for his family.

Emma was just finishing up with the pigs when her handsome, young neighbor, James Vezey, rode up on his hay-wagon. She had been admiring James for quite some time. His sharp blue eyes and dark hair had stirred a strange feeling inside her. At this moment, however, she was a sight—all covered in mud with excrement staining her green work boots. Nonetheless, she attempted to wipe the dirt from her shirt and tame a stray lock of hair with the back of her hand. Emma didn't realize it, but her quick efforts left a streak of dirt smeared across her left cheek, making James smile. Shyly, she smiled back.

"James! What brings you here?" she asked caught off-guard and just a little breathless.

"I was wondering if you might like to go to town with me on Saturday night." He fidgeted with the reins, hoping she wouldn't notice how nervous he was. "They're having a dance at the pavilion near the park."

Thrilled, Emma was about to say yes when she heard Frances loudly clear her throat. Emma turned toward her sister who nodded ever so slightly in the direction of the barn. A scowling Isaac was in the doorway, leaning on his pitchfork eyeing the youngsters. He must have heard James ride up in the wagon. "Don't be dallying too long there, girls. There's work to be done around here if you want your supper tonight."

Emma had little doubt that her father would never approve of James who had struggled to keep the family farm profitable ever since his father had died. He had nothing to barter for Emma's hand, and as far as Isaac was concerned, it wasn't enough to be rid of her. He expected a profit.

"I'm awfully sorry, James," Emma mumbled, uncertain what to use as an excuse. "But I can't go on Saturday. I . . . I . . . uh . . . have to mind the pigs."

James's questioning look rolled into disappointment, while Isaac's glowering face turned smug. Crestfallen, Emma looked down. She liked James. He was always so very kind, and she found that attractive. This young man was far different from Isaac, and she couldn't help but imagine what a loving husband and father James would probably be. It was a pity that Isaac couldn't, or wouldn't, see the good in him.

After James's unhappy departure, Isaac moved on to tend the chickens so Emma sought solace in the barn. There, she groomed her favorite horse—a white male she called Freedom. Freedom was her confidante, and she always felt better after whispering her troubles in the horse's ear. Freedom never judged her—just accepted her, flaws and all. As she quietly told the animal about James's unexpected visit, Isaac returned with a half-used bag of chicken feed. When he found her taking meticulous care of the horse as it nuzzled her face, his anger shattered Emma's peaceful moment. "Just what do you think you're doing there, girl?"

Emma took a breath. There was no time like the present to let him in on her plan. He was bound to find out sooner or later, even though Emma would have much preferred later. "There's a riding competition in two weeks, and everyone knows I'm the best rider in New Brunswick. The first-place prize is a gold watch, and with Freedom's help, I'm going to win it!" She foolishly thought she would impress her father by boasting her merits. Her confidence, however, just served to enrage him even more.

"You had better get that notion out of your head, right now! They will never let a girl enter that competition! That's for boys and men! Besides, you're not earning your keep around here by sprucing up the horses! Do you understand me, girl?"

"But, Father, you know I can outride any boy anytime!"

"That's enough!" he shouted. "There will be no riding competition for any daughter of mine, do you hear me?"

"Yes, Father." She diverted her eyes so he wouldn't see the tears welling up. "I hear you."

"And if you love the horses so much, you can sleep with them in the barn until I say you can come back in the house!"

•••••

A few days later, Isaac brought home a distinguished-looking older man. His guest was smartly dressed in a dark, tailored suit, but his graying hair needed a trim as it curled along the length of his collar. He wore rimless glasses and carried several bags of books with ease. Emma viewed him as a man of the world, and she was immediately intrigued.

"Betsy! Set an extra place for dinner," Isaac ordered. "This here's Sam Waldron. He's a traveling salesman . . . sells books. Mostly 'Good Books' and I thought it was time we had a new Bible in this house. Maybe the Lord will bless us with some real men 'round here if we pray a little harder."

Emma sat at the table that night with her head bowed, listening intently to all of the tales Mr. Waldron told about his many escapades while on the road. At first, she was afraid to make eye contact with him. Father would never approve of her fascination with a stranger, but as time passed and Waldron's stories grew more exciting, she forgot herself and her interest became obvious as she hung on every word that their dinner guest had to say.

". . . and there I was, standing in the bank, when three robbers came in with their guns drawn," Waldron declared in excitement as any true storyteller would. "I took my deluxe 'Good Book,' and before the first one knew what happened, I hit him on the head with it. He fell into the second one, and he fell into the third one, and they all dropped their guns. It gave us a chance to hold them down until the sheriff got there! I guess it gives new meaning to the phrase 'may God strike me down.'"

Everyone laughed, but Emma laughed loudest of all. "Mr. Waldron, that's thrilling . . . Please, don't stop now."

"Tell us what happened next!" prodded Mary Jane.

"Why, the mayor was so happy he gave me a key to the city."

"A key to the city?" Emma echoed, forgetting that Isaac was watching with his habitual glare. "I can't believe it! To think a Bible salesman could do all that! Oh, I would love to have a job like you!"

"Now don't go getting any more foolish ideas, Emma! You're a girl and a stupid one at that," Isaac chortled, making fun of her. "You could never make it in a man's world, let alone hold a good job like Sam here. In fact, you can't even get a proper day's work done on the farm. All you're good at is losing things like calves that cost me a month's pay."

Totally humiliated by her father's criticism in front of this stranger, Emma excused herself and fled from the kitchen to the only place she felt safe—the barn.

Shortly after, Betsy found her daughter sobbing in the hay as the horses watched over her. Setting aside the worn blue blanket she carried, Betsy wrapped her arms around Emma and stroked her hair in an effort to comfort her. "There, there, child. It's all right. You know your father can't help himself." Betsy took a comb from her pocket and unpinned Emma's hair. It wasn't often that she showed such tenderness due to her constant fear of Isaac, but that night Emma welcomed her mother's soothing touch. "You really are quite lovely when you allow yourself to look like a girl, my dear." Betsy smiled as she gently combed Emma's long hair.

"Father doesn't think so," the girl wept. "Why does he have to be so mean? Sometimes, I feel that he hates me most of all!"

"That's not true, Emma," her mother consoled. "It's me he really hates, not you. I was the one that failed him."

"But how do you stand it, Mother?"

Betsy thought for a moment and then answered honestly. "I accepted my lot long ago, child, just as you will accept yours one day."

"I could never accept a man who treats me like a slave!"

"I know it isn't easy, but like your father always says, 'it's a man's world,' and if we're not cooking, cleaning, or birthing babies, we women don't have much of a place in it."

"Then I wish I were a man!"

"Well, my dear," her mother sighed. "I'm afraid you were born a girl, and there's nothing to be done about that."

"It's not fair, Mother," Emma insisted.

Her mother wisely chose to ignore her daughter's words and not engage in that debate. Instead she changed the subject. "What's not fair is you sleeping out here in the barn."

"But I don't mind, Mother, really I don't. I like being with the horses. They don't care that I'm a girl. They mind me all the same as if I were a man."

•••••

Later that same evening, Emma was alone in the barn, gathering hay for her bed, when Mr. Waldron startled her. "Are you all right, little one?" he asked as he stepped toward her, carrying his bags of books.

"I'd be better if I were a man like you so I could leave this place and go on adventures." Emma shrugged, hoping that he would be flattered and not scold her for such arrogant thoughts.

"What do you mean?" he demanded with a wink. "Girls can do exciting things too!" He looked down at one of his bags, thinking, and then asked, "Can you read?"

"Yes, of course I can! I've been reading the 'Good Book' since I was a wee one."

"Then you might like this." Waldron smiled, removing a small book bound in black leather from one of his bags. "Here." He handed it to the girl.

"*Fanny Campbell, The Female Pirate Captain: A Tale of the Revolution* by Lieutenant Murray," Emma read aloud from the title page.

"Fanny Campbell was a woman who dressed like a man and fooled everyone around her." Mr. Waldron nodded. "I think you might like her."

Emma looked at the book with a newfound reverence. "Did Fanny Campbell have great adventures like you?"

"Even greater!" He winked. "She was a pirate."

"I wish I could be a pirate."

"Emma, you can be whatever you want. There's more to life than this little farm. You just have to make your way in the world to find it." He put his hand in his pocket and removed a piece of cake wrapped in a handkerchief and gave it to Emma with another wink. "I noticed you didn't finish your dinner."

"Thank you, Mr. Waldron." She beamed, accepting his second gift of the evening. "You are very kind, sir."

Waldron then smiled, tipped his hat, and left the barn with his bags in tow. Emma burrowed in the hay, pulled the blue blanket over her, and next to the dim candlelight, opened her book. Besides the Bible, it was the first one she'd ever seen outside school. Fascinated, she turned the pages in between bites of cake, which for some reason, tasted better than usual. As she read, *she felt as if an angel had touched her with a live coal from off the altar. All the latent energy of her nature was aroused, and each new exploit of Fanny Campbell thrilled her more than the last.*

That night Emma knew her problems had been solved and that book became part of her soul. She carried it with her everywhere she went—in the fields, in the barn, even in the pigsty. Reading those words made her feel competent and up to any crisis she may encounter. For with every word she read, she felt emancipated! Like Fanny Campbell, Emma would never again be enslaved to anyone. When she got to the part where Fanny cut off her long, brown curls, donned a blue jacket, and stepped into freedom and the glorious independence of a man, Emma tossed up her old straw boater and screamed to the heavens with glee.

•••••

Knowing that Isaac was probably right when he said that a girl would never be allowed to compete in a horse race, Emma laid out a careful plan. On race day, she offered to go into town with Thomas to pick up supplies for Betsy. Carrying a list of items hand-written by her mother, she and Tom set off on Freedom. They hurriedly bought the requested articles, and while Tom minded the horse and the newly-bought goods, Emma took the pirate's lead. She carefully pinned her hair under her work hat and disguised herself as a boy. It wasn't too hard since she already had on her trousers and boots—like she always did on the farm.

Hoping that no one would recognize her, she approached the registration table and signed in as a competitor under the fictitious name of Franklin Thompson. She was handed a placard touting the number "16" and asked her brother to pin it on her back.

"You can do this, Emma! I know you can." Thomas's words of encouragement cheered her and eased the nervous pitch in her stomach.

"You mean Franklin, don't you?" She winked as she mounted Freedom.

"Yes, of course, Franklin! Ride like the wind and I know you'll win this race!" Thomas could hardly contain his enthusiasm. "I only wish I could be like you!"

"I'll win for both of us," she promised as she spurred her horse and cantered over to the starting line. There, she joined the other dozen or so men also competing for the gold watch. When the gun went off, Freedom leaped and together they catapulted forward like a ball shot from a cannon. It didn't take long before Emma had not only passed the other riders, but gained several rods on them. As they neared the finish line, the horses' galloping hooves thundered down the track and the smell of dust filled her lungs, but she dared not stop to think. She just pressed on until they crossed the finish line well ahead of the pack. Freedom and Emma had done it! They had beaten all of the boys and grown men at their own game. Emma had won the race, but perhaps it was Franklin Thompson that had given her the courage.

Emma's eager brother met her at the awards stand and gave her a congratulatory hug before the gold pocket watch was awarded. It was a good thing Thomas was there because when the judges called out "Franklin Thompson" as the winner, Emma didn't even respond. It took a nod from Thomas to make her realize that it was her they were summoning.

As Emma stepped up to proudly receive her award, she noticed a group of ruffians approaching her brother.

"Sissy boy!" one hollered.

"Sir Faint-A-Lot!" another taunted.

"Let's see if you can fight!" The third moved closer.

Emma accepted the watch, just as one of the boys shoved Thomas to the ground. Bounding from the stage, she punched that lout square in the jaw, knocking him out cold as the other two scattered. No one was going to pick on her brother—she wouldn't stand for it! Winning that gold watch under the guise of Franklin Thompson made her feel just like her hero, Fanny Campbell—invincible.

Chapter 3

Escaping Disaster

Under the soft radiance of a single candle, Frances and Emma laid awake in bed after a hard day on the farm. Both were clad in shabby nightshirts with their long hair draped across worn pillows. Their bare toes chafed against the coarse sheets, which were threadbare from so much washing. While Frances's eyes were heavy with fatigue, an excited Emma read aloud the most thrilling pages from her treasured Fanny Campbell book . . .

> ". . . It was now evident that there was no escape, or at least without fighting first and Fanny determined she would do so, although she had but eight men to oppose to fifty. The sea now ran so high that fortunately it rendered boarding a matter entirely out of the question. Fanny's quick wit understood this full well and she hoped that it might possibly prove to be her safety by enabling her to fight at a distance, where her eight men could work to some advantage over the heavy gun amidships."

"Don't you ever get tired of reading that book?" yawned Frances.

"How could anyone ever get tired of all the excitement?" The girls may have been sisters, but sometimes Emma wondered if they were truly born of the same blood.

"Well, there's going to be plenty of excitement around here if father finds you making eyes at James again!"

"I do like James." Emma sighed, a little starry-eyed, but quickly voiced second thoughts. "But it doesn't really matter. I'm afraid I'm not the marrying kind. I don't want to end up like mother. I'd rather be free and on my own—like Fanny Campbell."

Below them, the front door slammed with a loud bang, startling both sisters and cutting their conversation short. Isaac had just returned from the tavern and, in a drunken tirade, was screaming Emma's name.

"Dear Lord, what have I done now?" Emma whispered as she quickly closed her book and slipped it under the bed. With each stair he climbed, the sound of Isaac's heavy footsteps matched the rhythm of Emma's pounding heart. When her father reached the landing, he paused for just a second. Emma held her breath. Two more footsteps and then Isaac thrust open the bedroom door with such force, the top hinge jolted out of place.

"EMMA!" he hollered. "I have finally found a way to get rid of you!" Despite his whiskey-hazed presence and his loud manner, he looked strangely happy—a smug look of satisfaction just shy of a grin smattered across his face. "I ran into old Earl Harris about an hour ago, and we had a drink. It seems he's been real lonely since his wife died last winter, and God only knows why, but he's got his eye on you, Emma. I told him if he wants you, he can have you and good riddance, I say . . . It'll mean one less mouth to feed around here and one less impossible girl to look after!"

"But, Father!" Emma bolted up from the bed in disbelief. "Earl Harris is an old man! He has children twice my age! I can't marry him! I won't do it, and you can't make me!"

Isaac slapped the girl so hard she fell back on her pillow. "I won't have a daughter of mine dictating to me! You can and will do as I say! I am the man around here, and I give the orders—not you! Besides, Earl has promised me some livestock in return for your hand—it will make up for that calf you let drown."

Alarmed at all the furor, Betsy appeared in the doorway, nervously wiping her hands on her dingy linen apron. Before she even had a chance to speak, Isaac shoved her out of his way, knocking her hard against the wall as he stormed from the room, leaving only fumes of whiskey trailing behind him. Betsy slid to the floor, momentarily dazed.

"Mother, are you all right?" screamed Emma as she rushed to Betsy's side with Frances close behind. "Please get up. Say something, Mother!" As Betsy slowly came to her senses, Isaac's words took hold of Emma's soul, replacing her shock with a mix of horror and revulsion. As she knelt over her mother, a chill so severe spread throughout Emma's body that she was convinced her heart would freeze and soon fail to beat. Right then, however, she would have welcomed an untimely death. What did it matter? She was only fifteen and her own father had sold her off to a hideous old man for a few head of livestock.

•••••

Enlisting Thomas's help the very next day, a desperate Emma sent her brother to the Vezey farm with a message for James. Thomas found James in the fields tending to his potato crop and explained that Emma needed him. James must come to the Edmondson barn after dark—it was a matter of life or death. When Thomas returned home, assuring Emma that James would meet her, she felt hopeful for the first time since learning of her father's heartless pact. Nevertheless, the daylight hours dragged on as she routinely performed her chores, all the while imagining what she would say to James. If he loved her as she thought he did, he would know how to fix this disastrous situation. He had to help her. She had no one else to turn to.

That night, Emma got ready for bed. Dressed in her nightshirt and with her hair undone, she sneaked out of the house and into the barn. She paced in front of the horses hoping that she looked somewhat attractive despite her bare feet and clammy hands. As the darkness deepened around her, she waited, not daring to light even one candle lest Isaac see its glow. Maybe James had changed his mind. Maybe he didn't really care for her after all. Maybe she should go back to the house before her father noticed she wasn't there.

A shuffling noise interrupted her scattered thoughts, and for a moment, she feared her father had discovered her, but to her relief, it was James who emerged from the shadows of the barnyard, not Isaac. Although Emma could barely see his handsome face, she instinctively rushed into his arms and kissed him, catching them both by surprise. James recovered first and held Emma at arm's length. The scared look on her face and the urgency of Thomas's words caused him great concern.

"What's happened, Emma? Thomas said it was a matter of life or death."

"It is, James. My whole future is in jeopardy, and I need your help."

"What's wrong? Have you gotten yourself in some sort of trouble?"

"It's Father that's caused all the trouble! He says I have to marry that awful old man, Earl Harris!"

"But he can't do that!"

"He already has! He's bartered me off for three head of cattle and two fat sows!" The words spewed from inside her, and once they started, she couldn't stop them. "You have to help me, James. Please! I just can't let that disgusting man touch me! We have to run away. Tonight! We can leave and start a new life far away from here . . . far away from Father and that dreadful man and—"

"But it's not that simple, Emma," James interrupted her. "I . . . I have obligations here."

Suddenly silenced, Emma took a step back, bristling over what she perceived as his rejection.

"I have to think about my mother," he tried to explain. "She's been sick ever since Father died. You have to understand, Emma, she has no one but me, and I can't just leave her alone on the farm. She'd never manage by herself."

"No . . . of course not," Emma mumbled realizing how desperate she must have sounded and, at the same time, regretting her decision to even ask James for help. What made her think that James would ever choose a life with her? There was no sense in begging him to change his mind, and if she couldn't save anything else, at least she could salvage her dignity. "You must go home to your mother, James. I'm sorry I bothered you."

"But, Emma . . ." He stepped closer and tried to touch her, but she moved out of reach.

"Just go home to your mother," she repeated. "Earl Harris is my problem . . . not yours. I will deal with this myself."

As Emma watched James leave the barn, Mr. Waldron's words came back to her: "Emma, you can be whatever you want. There's more to life than this little farm. You just have to make your way in the world to find it."

Emma finally understood—no one, especially a man, could ever save her from life's adversities. As Mr. Waldron had told her, only she could free herself.

•••••

The normally shabby farmhouse was bedecked for a wedding—gaily colored flowers filled mismatched vases while white streamers dangled from the ceiling. Betsy had even washed the old flowered curtains, which now looked as if they anticipated happier times. Emma, in her simple, white wedding gown minus the buttons, sat in the kitchen as her mother pinned partially sewn dresses on her sisters. While she waited for her turn at Betsy's skilled hand, she lost herself in Fanny's book. Maybe, if she read it enough times, she might magically find the answer to her freedom.

A knock at the door intruded on Emma's reading. With an air of nervous excitement, Betsy greeted a tall, well-dressed woman named Annie Moffitt—her best friend from Ireland. As young, single girls, they had sailed to North America together with Annie's family in the hopes of making new lives for themselves in Canada. Although, they were no longer close geographically, they had remained friends by writing letters to keep up with each other's good fortune—or in Betsy's case, misfortune. Nonetheless, Betsy glowed as she welcomed her long-time friend. "Girls . . . you remember Annie Moffitt? She owns a hat shop over in Salisbury."

Frances and Mary Jane both welcomed Annie, who stood in the doorway holding an elegant white hatbox. Emma, however, was so depressed she couldn't summon enough motivation to join in.

"Emma, aren't you going to thank Annie for being here?" Betsy gently admonished the girl. "She came all the way from Salisbury just for you."

"Hello, Annie," Emma reluctantly obliged without getting up from her chair. "I'm sorry you came so far to witness what my father calls a 'bargain deal.'"

"Maybe this will make you feel better." Annie stepped closer and offered Emma the white hatbox. Unlike Betsy, her voice still held a hint of Irish brogue. "I made it just for you, dear. Every bride should have something special to hand down to her own daughter someday . . . a family heirloom, as they say."

Hesitant at first, Emma accepted the box and opened it to find an elegant, diaphanous veil trimmed with the most delicate of lace. As her sisters "ooohed"and "ahhed" over the way it shimmered in the light, Emma burst into tears, dropping the headpiece as if it had bitten her.

"Why can't anyone see that I don't want to get married? Father is making me do this! To him, I'm just collateral no better than the cows and the pigs!" Emma rushed from the room unable to bear the sight of any further trimmings or talk of weddings.

•••••

That night the Edmondsons, along with Annie and Earl, sat around the table at what was supposed to be a pre-bridal dinner. For Emma, however, this meal marked the eve of her life's end—much like the last supper from the Bible, she thought. Tomorrow's wedding, like the crucifiction would be payment for her sins. As she studied the old, wrinkled man who sat across from her, she realized with immense apprehension and contempt that he was cut from the exact same cloth as Isaac Edmondson. They both lacked in kindness what they shared in selfishness. They both disdained education, especially for women, and they cared more for their whiskey than their own household. It was as if her father would still have control even after she left. The only differences between the two men were that Harris was older, had fewer teeth, and smelled like liquor all day long instead of just late at night after the local tavern had closed. Trying to shut out all thoughts of the next day's nuptials, Emma's mind drifted to the high seas, imagining what life might have been like if only she were born a man.

"I'm so happy you're here, Annie," prattled Betsy. "It's been so long since we've talked. Letters just aren't the same as a good visit."

"I know." Annie nodded. "I've made lots of friends in Salisbury, but none like you, dear Betsy. We said good-bye to the Emerald Isle together and sailed the sea for days and days with only our wits to keep us from harm. In my heart, we're sisters and like sisters, we take care of each other and our children."

Betsy, moved by her friend's words, squeezed Annie's hand in reply as if they shared a secret—something that may have bonded them as children back in their homeland, Emma mistakenly thought. She tried to imagine her mother's early years, but she just couldn't picture Betsy as a carefree, young girl. She'd only known the beaten-down woman who now sat before her.

"I could never repay your kindness in coming all this way, Annie, and bringing such a fine gift for my Emma." Betsy sounded almost too sincere.

"I have no daughter of my own to spoil." Annie winked at Emma. "So your daughter will have to do!"

"Enough chattering," Isaac pushed his chair from the table. "I think it's high time we men make some merriment of our own. What do you say, Earl? Shall we take this celebration to town?"

"As long as we don't stay out too late." The old man chucked a lecherous laugh with a knowing wink toward Isaac. "I'm not as young as I once was, and I have a wedding night to prepare for. I wouldn't want to disappoint my new bride and fall asleep before she lets her hair down."

Emma's skin crawled and her stomach lurched. The thought of Earl Harris merely kissing her made her insides quake, let alone the idea of fulfilling her wifely duties. Emma took several deep breaths as a fit of nausea swelled inside her.

When the two men stood to leave, Thomas, who hadn't said a word all evening, timidly spoke. "Can I come with you, Father?"

"Drinking is for men, Tom," growled Isaac. "I'll not be wasting money on a boy who can't pull his own weight around here." Disappointed, Tom sunk back into his chair as he watched his father don his hat and walk out of the door with Earl Harris.

Once the men were gone, Annie and Betsy exchanged anxious looks. "Tom, girls, I need you to take the wedding decorations over to the church," directed Betsy. As Emma stood to help them, her mother stopped her. "No, Emma, you stay here. We need to talk about tomorrow and what you may expect as a new wife." Then she turned to the others, shooing them on their way. "Now hurry along before the church is locked up for the night."

As soon as Frances, Mary Jane, and Tom gathered the decorations and left, Betsy pulled a large brown suitcase from behind the old sofa. She handed the worn, but sturdy valise to her youngest daughter. "Now, you listen to me and listen good, Emma. There'll be no wedding tomorrow. Annie's come to take you back to Salisbury with her, but you must leave now! The arrangements have all been made."

Confused, Emma watched as Annie put on her coat, picked up her purse, and walked to the door. It took a moment for her mother's words to sink in. Betsy had never once gone against Isaac before—at least as far as Emma recalled and now that unexpected rebelliousness frightened the girl. "No, Mother, I can't go! Father will kill you if he finds out you sent me away!"

"Nonsense!" insisted Betsy. "I can handle Isaac. He'll be so hungover when he gets home he won't even know you're gone until it's too late. I'll tell him that you must have snuck off during the night. He'll never know the truth. So, go on now, child. I've packed everything you need. I even put your gold watch, your book, and a few dollars inside. I wish I could afford to give you more, but it's all I can spare."

Emma's eyes welled with tears as the reality of Betsy's words sunk in. Her breath came in short gasps as she choked back a sob. Betsy pulled a bright crimson handkerchief trimmed in white lace from her apron and slipped it into her daughter's trembling hand. "Don't cry now, my sweet girl. The angels will look out for you . . . isn't that what you always tell me?"

"Y-yes, M-mother." Emma pressed the soft material to her face and inhaled her mother's scent. Emma was grateful, but at the same time terrified for Betsy's well-being if Isaac ever discovered the truth. Abandoning her mother would be a selfish act on her part, but the thought of Earl Harris's hands roaming over her body made her desperate enough to flee. Tearfully, mother and daughter embraced as Annie anxiously waited at the open door. "I don't know how to thank you, Mother."

"I couldn't bear the thought of my beautiful child marrying that old letch of a man. In my heart, I know it would be against God's wishes. I pray He will protect you and keep you safe once you leave this house."

"We have to go now, Emma," Annie quietly urged. "Don't be afraid. It's going to be all right. The stagecoach I hired is waiting for us at the end of the road."

"God bless you, Annie." Betsy fought back the tears. "You are saving my daughter's life."

"I promise to look after Emma as if she were my own." Annie gently pulled the girl away from her mother. Emma dabbed her eyes with the hankie and stuffed it in her sleeve before reluctantly picking up her suitcase. She then took Annie's hand and walked through the front door. While Annie led Emma down the road, the young girl looked over her shoulder at Betsy who stood alone on the front porch. She seemed so small and frail, but at that moment, Emma realized her mother was every bit as brave as Fanny Campbell.

Chapter 4

A New Life

The two women rode through the night. Emma tried to study the landscape from the coach window, but darkness prevented her from seeing much. Annie sat across from her with eyes closed and her head against the seatback. Unable to relax herself, Emma found it hard to believe that this woman was actually sleeping as the carriage jerked along. She noted how Annie's smooth, unlined skin was in sharp contrast to Betsy's furrowed brow, which made Emma realize just how hard life had been for her mother.

Emma nervously fingered Betsy's handkerchief as her cluttered mind whirled even faster with thoughts that blurred together. She would miss home—especially her mother, but at the same time, she wondered what might lie ahead in Salisbury. Escaping Isaac and the clutches of that old farmer far outweighed any regrets she had for leaving her siblings without a proper good-bye. Maybe someday, she would have a chance to explain her disappearance to them and hoped that they could muster up enough compassion to forgive her for deserting them. For now, however, it was all she could do to face the challenges of building a new life with only a stranger to rely on.

They didn't dare stop at any roadside inns in case Isaac discovered his daughter was missing and came after them. So they continued on until morning, reaching Salisbury at dawn. The city streets were already bustling with people and horses as they rode through the downtown shopping area. Awestruck, Emma took in the activity of merchants sweeping the sidewalks in front of their shops and vendors hawking their goods in the street. Horses waited for their absent owners who may have been tending to some business inside the bank or the local dry goods store. A group of boys shot marbles in front of a barbershop where men waited for a shave. The owner of an apothecary rearranged his window display and stopped to wave as Annie and Emma rode by.

This was the first time Emma had ever been away from Magaguadavic and the first time she'd ever seen a real city. In the future, she would realize that Salisbury was nothing more than a quaint village, but to a green fifteen-year old, the grandeur she perceived that day was overwhelming.

Salisbury wasn't always bustling. It was originally a small settlement established in 1774 by a group of Englishmen from Yorkshire. Located in southeast New Brunswick along the Peticodiac River, the scenic countryside played host to many a prosperous farm. Lumbering also provided many locals with a good income if they were willing to wield an axe. While the land remained an important part of daily life for most residents, the town eventually grew to include a busy saloon, a banking institution, a place of worship, a one-room schoolhouse, a small but tidy hotel, and several shops—one of which belonged to Annie Moffitt.

Annie came to Canada along with Emma's mother when they were just girls. Both had dreams—Betsy wanted to marry a fine man and raise a family, but Annie fancied hats more than children. She wanted to live in a big city where she could make and sell fashionable hats in her very own shop. Both fell a bit short in their goals. Betsy married a hateful man and Annie ended up in this small village despite her intentions of moving to a grand city like Toronto or Montreal. Unlike Betsy, however, Annie seemed content with her life and her circumstances.

At least that was Emma's notion as the carriage stopped in front of an attractive little shop just off the main street. A sign in the window read: "Salisbury Millinery." Emma was incredulous. This woman, Annie Moffit, her mother's own contemporary, had done well for herself—without a man. Then why couldn't she do the same? After the two women disembarked from the stagecoach, Annie handed cash to the driver.

"You must be rich," Emma gasped as they entered the shop.

"Not so much rich, Emma." Annie opened the shutters to welcome in the morning sunlight. "Just a little clever sometimes. That man who drove us here has a wife who's been eyeing one of my prettiest blue bonnets for months, but with a new baby on the way, she couldn't afford to buy it. When I offered to pay him for his services, he hesitated at first, but when I promised to throw in the hat that his wife wanted, he couldn't say no. It worked out for all of us. You are here safe and sound, he has a few extra dollars, and his wife now owns a new hat."

Emma found Annie's shop fascinating. She was taken by the stunning hat displays that surrounded her. Large hats with elegant plumes, small hats decorated with intricate lacework, and medium-size hats with bright flowers flowing across the brims—all bearing matching ribbons and bows.

"You made all of these?" Emma was incredulous and despite the fact that they had traveled all night, she suddenly felt energized by the sight of the most brilliant colors she'd ever seen gathered in one room.

"Every last one." Annie smiled. "Go ahead, try them on if you're not too tired. You'll see how easily the right hat can turn a woman into a lady."

Emma picked up one stylish chapeau that caught her eye. It was dark blue with a small spray of fine-looking white feathers on the side. The least flamboyant of them all, it resembled the type of hat a man might wear. When she placed it on her head and looked in the mirror, she was transformed. Quite possibly, as Annie said, with a little help, she could look like a lady, even if her real wish was to be more manly. For now, she was at least free from Isaac's tyranny and Earl Harris's bed and that was a start.

"You can have it if you like." Annie smiled her approval.

"Oh, I couldn't possibly take it." Emma shook her head.

"I insist." Annie nodded. "If you're going to live in Salisbury, you must wear one of my hats. It would not be good for business if my new assistant helped with my hats, but didn't own one."

Emma smiled as she admired her new hat in the mirror.

•••••

Emma changed her last name to *Edmonds*, and was soon wearing dresses as smart as Annie's with hats to match. She had never looked so feminine. No longer threatened by her father and no longer a prisoner to anyone, she finally felt safe enough to embrace her girlish side. Annie was a kind and patient mentor as she taught Emma how to set up displays and assist with the store's paperwork. For her keep, the young girl cleaned, arranged the merchandise, and helped Annie pick out materials for the hats that she made in the evenings after the store was closed. Annie was a hard worker, but she was her own boss, with no man to tell her how to live her life. Emma not only admired her talent, but her courage to run her own business, earn her own money, and best of all, to live on her own terms in a man's world.

Annie lived frugally in a small apartment over the store. She had a tiny living area sparsely furnished with a flowered sofa and matching chair and two bedrooms that were just big enough to hold a bed and a bureau. The kitchen, which also served as a sewing room, was surprisingly large. Most nights, Emma volunteered to cook dinner, which gave Annie more time to sew. The two women ate together at the end of each day, discussing current fashion trends as well as the latest news. For the first time, Emma felt that she was actually a part of that larger world Mr. Waldron had described.

One afternoon as Emma was straightening up the store, Annie gently tugged her arm. "Do you think you can take care of the shop while I go to the bank?"

"You mean you trust me here alone?" Emma asked.

"Of course I trust you."

"But what if a customer comes in while you're gone?"

"I think you'll do just fine, Emma." Annie smiled as she picked up her purse and walked toward the door. "I won't be very long."

With Annie gone and no customers in the shop, Emma playfully tried on a few hats—a sunbonnet so large, she could barely see her face under the oversize brim, a small boater that reminded her of the hat she left behind on the farm, and then the most garish one in the store—a lime green bonnet with peacock feathers standing at attention around the crown. Looking into the mirror, she placed it on her head and tied the royal blue bow under her chin. Emma couldn't help but laugh at how silly she looked beneath the large green and blue plumes.

The bell on the shop door rang, interrupting her fun, and Mrs. Stroud, an older, rather large lady wearing an enormous purple hat, entered. She had patronized the shop several times since Emma's arrival and almost always bought a hat on each visit. Emma remembered how easily Mrs. Stroud responded to compliments as she returned the lime green bonnet back to its display stand. "Good afternoon, Mrs. Stroud. Are you looking for something special today?"

"Yes, I need a hat, but not just any hat. It has to announce I'm coming, if you know what I mean."

"Hmmm . . . I think I know just what you're looking for. I'll be right back." Emma disappeared into the back room where Annie kept her extra stock and materials. She returned with a bright red bonnet trimmed in large red roses and even larger white feathers. "When Annie made this hat last week, I thought of you. Only a very confident and refined lady like yourself could wear a hat this bold. It makes a statement I think."

"It does?" Mrs. Stroud blinked.

"Of course." Emma held the flamboyant creation out in front of her. "It says, 'I'm someone to take notice of,' and you are the first customer to see it."

Mrs. Stroud seemed a little doubtful as she examined it. "I don't know, dear. Don't you think it's a little overbearing?"

"Oh no, not on you, Mrs. Stroud," Emma assured her. "Put it on and see if I'm not right."

With that Mrs. Stroud removed her hat and tried it on.

"Well . . . I do like it, but I mustn't buy the very first one I try on." She tilted her head toward the mirror admiring herself.

"Of course not, Mrs. Stroud," Emma agreed. "Let me show you a few more."

By the time Annie retuned from the bank, Emma was boxing up three hats for her very satisfied customer. Annie was quite impressed as she watched Mrs. Stroud juggling her packages. "Thank you, my dear!" the older lady called out. "I will certainly be back. My mother always said that it's bad luck to wear the same hat twice in the same month."

"My goodness, Emma!" Annie exclaimed as she closed the door behind their lavish patron. "I've never sold Mrs. Stroud more than one hat at a time and you sell her three the first time I leave you alone! I'll have to put you in charge more often."

"At first I was afraid I would ruin things and that she would never come back." Emma laughed in delight, realizing that for once her boldness had paid off. "But when I showed her that new red hat you made, I saw how her eyes lit up and it just came to me. I knew what to say to make her fall in love with all of them."

"Emma, I think you've just been promoted from assistant to saleslady!"

"Are you sure?" Emma gasped in disbelief.

"I'm positive." Annie smiled with a quick nod. "And I think we should have a sign made up that says, 'It's bad luck to wear the same hat twice in the same month'!"

The shop grew busier once Emma started helping Annie with sales. In turn, Annie made more hats. She even started teaching Emma the business of hat-making. The young girl from Magaguadavic soon discovered that she had a flair for creating some of the most unique hats that Annie and her customers had ever seen.

Business was booming and Annie was thrilled, not only with her apprentice's knack for sales, but her artistic eye as well. Emma's newfound fortés surprised even her. Isaac had long ago convinced his daughter that no one was interested in anything she had to say, but now in Salisbury, people actually listened to her, and wonder of wonders, some of them even liked her!

•••••

Two young women, near Emma's age, came into the store one afternoon to shop for new Sunday hats. They introduced themselves as sisters, Rosela and Henriette Perrigo—the daughters of a local French Canadian farmer and his schoolteacher wife. The girls seemed to enjoy bantering with Emma as she helped them find just the right style. As they tried on bonnets and boaters, all three erupted into boisterous laughter, momentarily forgetting that they were in a place of business.

"Emma, if you're not busy tonight, can you meet us at the county fair?" asked Henriette.

"Yes, do come with us tonight," seconded Rosela. "We would have so much fun."

Wanting to go, but not sure if she should, Emma looked toward Annie who nodded her approval.

"I'll meet you there after the shop closes," Emma promised, knowing that it was her job to stay so that Annie could work on her newest hats.

"You'll do no such thing, Emma!" Annie interrupted with a stern tone. "I'll close up tonight! You go on now with your friends and have fun!"

Henriette, Rosela, and Emma left the shop together in high spirits. They walked through the fairgrounds, giggling and chatting about the curious sights all around them. They watched as several local men tried hitting a large silver bell with one mighty swing of a gigantic hammer. They gasped in delight at a magician as he pulled a dove from underneath a bright red handkerchief.

One mustachioed man even asked if the girls would take turns manning the kissing booth. All three politely declined his offer, but as the disappointed fellow walked away, they screamed with laughter. They ate foods that Emma had never seen before—like chocolate and licorice. They even rode the carousel with its whimsical horses and calliope music. It was truly a magical night to remember as they stayed until the booths closed and the torches were dowsed.

Making acquaintances, other than horses and pigs, was something new for Emma. It turned out that she and Henriette became the best of friends and the Perrigos like her second family. With newfound companions and Annie as her wise mentor, Emma finally felt emancipated from the bondage of her youth.

Chapter 5

A Change of Sex

Emma happily hummed a hymn while she constructed a new bonnet that trumped all of the other hats in the store. She pinned silk violets around the wide brim, and in between the flowers, she placed tiny bows fashioned from a deep purple ribbon that she held in her teeth so her hands were free. Deep in concentration, she didn't hear Annie come into the store with the mail.

"Oh my, Emma!" Annie's voice startled the girl. "You're getting so very good at this. With your eye for color, I do believe you could compete with the best designers from New York to Paris." Annie laid her purse on the table and shuffled through the mail. Excited, she handed Emma one letter. "This looks like news from your mother!"

Thrilled, Emma ripped the envelope open, but as she read, her happy expression quickly faded and her face paled. The letter fell from her trembling hands and fluttered to the floor.

Annie picked it up and read:

"My darling Emma,

'I miss you terribly, and I hope you can forgive me for what I have done. Your father has been enraged ever since he realized you were gone. No matter how much he beat me, I never betrayed you, but when he laid hands on your brother, I had no choice but to give in. Your father is coming to Salisbury and plans to bring you back home to fulfill his contract with Earl Harris—"

Annie dropped the letter as she covered her mouth in horror. "Oh, Emma, what are we going to do?"

After a moment of silence, a sudden calm came over the girl. She took in a deep breath as the color slowly returned to her cheeks. "I will do exactly what Fanny Campbell would do."

"What on earth do you mean?"

"Never you mind, Annie. It's best if I don't tell you. When Father gets here and demands to know my whereabouts, you'll be able to look him in the eye and tell him the truth . . . you honestly don't know."

●●●●●

Emma strode down Salisbury's busiest street and stopped short at a notice board. She eyed the newest posting:

> *"Book agents wanted in New Brunswick to canvas for New Pictorial, Standard, Historical, and Religious works."*

She wrote down the contact information on a scrap of paper. Her next stop was Baldwin's General Store where she paused out front for just a moment. Determined to take matters into her own hands and stop relying on others, she and her newfound courage stepped inside.

That night as the candlelight burned in her little room above the hat shop, Emma sat at her dressing table staring in the mirror. She had never considered herself beautiful. 'Handsome' would have been a better word to define her looks, and that suited her just fine. She removed the pins holding her hair in place and let her long locks fall across her shoulders. Then she picked up a pair of fabric shears and cut off each curl one by one. When she was done, her hair was cropped short like a man's.

Next, she donned the new suit of clothes she had purchased
from Baldwin's and topped off her outfit with a new man's hat that
she had secretly made after hours in her room. She studied herself
in the mirror. Maybe she imagined it, but it seemed as if a fine-
looking young man was gazing back at her. As she clipped her
gold watch to the new vest, the name 'Franklin Thompson' once
again came to mind. That had been her alias the day she won the
horse race and took possession of her prized timepiece. With a
bit of luck, she might actually fool others into believing she really
was Franklin Thompson. She realized, however, that this was more
than putting on a costume—it was a lifestyle tranformation. From
this day forward, she must act like a man, talk like a man, and think
like a man in order for her ruse to work.

After penning Annie a note to thank her for all that she had
done, Emma packed her small valise, with only her meager possessions and, of course, her book on Fanny Campbell. She then
tucked Betsy's handkerchief inside her sleeve before quietly slipping out the back door into the sheltering darkness.

●●●●●

*Although it was illegal to impersonate a man in Canada, she plunged herself
into a world of isolation, where the truth could never be revealed. Even friends
were, by necessity, kept at arm's length. Emma's survival as Franklin Thompson
demanded a high level of self-reliance, an ability to keep one's own counsel, and
a willingness to forego direct intimacy with another person that only honesty
allowed. It meant living a lie, with all the attendant moral and practical burdens
that would entail. Above all, it meant being alone, even when she was not.*

Pretending to be a man wasn't that hard for Emma, since she
had played that role most days on the farm. Having grown up in
trousers and a man's shirt while she did her chores, she felt more
comfortable in men's attire than in women's. She had spent her
youthful years trying to please her father by becoming the best
marksman, finest rider, and hardest worker. She had studied the

boys at school so that she might be more like them than like her sisters. Flat-chested and always a tomboy, she knew exactly how a young man might think and act. She wore the guise of Franklin Thompson like a second skin, and before long she pretty much forgot how to be Emma.

As such, Franklin Thompson became one of the newest Bible salesmen for L. P. Crown and Company as he hawked his 'Good Books' to the rural residents of New Brunswick and the St. John vicinity, always careful to avoid Magaguadavic and Isaac's nearby realm. Franklin's talents as salesman did not outweigh his ability to be convincing in a masculine role. With a deep voice and muscular build, he was welcomed into many of the homes he visited. His dark, trusting eyes and compassionate smile, along with an amicable charm, helped open doors and hearts to the attractive young stranger. In fact, he was treated so well that Franklin surmised he must be considered, by those who befriended him, somewhat of a gentleman.

Successful to the point of supporting himself, Franklin dressed well and occasionally visited a saloon just to keep up appearances. One beer was his limit, as he never wanted to loosen his lips to the point of letting secrets slip, but he liked to watch the men play cards. Every saloon he patronized had at least one game going, and he was often invited to join in, but always declined. Still, there was something fascinating about the way the cards were dealt and the manner in which the gamblers bantered over their dollars and cents. It seemed that there was something more to gambling than money. He noticed some sort of passion that came from the men who placed bets, and this piqued Franklin's curiosity.

One Saturday night in the dead of winter, Franklin broke his own barroom rule and downed a whiskey instead of his customary beer, hoping to warm himself from the biting cold. Then he naively accepted an invitation to play poker with a motley group of four. He could afford to lose one game, after which he planned to call it a night, but to his surprise, he won three dollars so he felt that it couldn't hurt to play just one more hand. Once again Franklin won. Five hands later, he had made an easy twenty dollars.

"Gentlemen, I think I should quit before my luck runs out." Franklin pushed his chair away from the table.

"But you can't quit now," the dealer protested. "You've got too good of a streak going there, young fella. Besides, you have to give us a fair chance to collect back some of our losses."

"That's right." The man to Franklin's right nodded. "A real man stays in the game."

"All right," Franklin assented, much against his better judgment. "You boys got me for one last hand, but then I have to leave. I'm selling Bibles at the early service tomorrow morning." He realized how ridiculous that must sound—a Bible salesman gambling in a saloon—but he couldn't stop himself. Momentarily he wondered what Sam Waldron might think, but then banished the thought to focus on the cards. As the game progressed, the men began to grumble that the cards were not favoring them that night. They assured Franklin that luck must be smiling down on him so the young Bible salesman bet everything, including his stock of "Good Books."

Franklin lost the hand. Breathless for a moment, he realized he had been taken. A man of his word, however, he handed his money and his books over to the four con men who had a good laugh at his distress. When Franklin left the saloon that night, he had but two possessions—his sample Bible, a top-of-the-line gold-embossed book, and his treasured gold watch. Maybe he could get five dollars for the book, and that would be enough to help him leave New Brunswick. He never wanted to pick up a card again or run into someone who might recognize him as the Bible salesman that gambled away God's 'Good Books.'

•••••

Franklin started for the United States in midwinter—the snow three feet deep in New Brunswick. Mostly, he trekked on foot with the occasional exception of a few miles riding in the back of a farm wagon. It was a long, hard journey, but he never complained of his suffering, even if his only listeners would have been the rabbits and deer he passed on the roadside, or the random farmer who took pity on him and offered a bowl of porridge along with a crust of bread at his hearth. During moments when he waivered, it was Betsy's handkerchief that gave him strength. After all, as a young woman, she too, had once left everything behind to begin again in a new world. Perhaps that small piece of red linen had accompanied her and brought her comfort as well.

When he finally reached downtown Hartford, Connecticut, he was in bad shape—hungry and desperate—his feet nearly frostbitten. A stranger in a strange country—a subject fit for a hospital—lacking money and friends. As the snow whirled around him, Franklin stood on the main street before a store window with a sign that read:

"WE BUY WATCHES"

He stared down at his threadbare clothes and worn boots, then with a heartfelt sigh, unclipped his gold pocket watch from his vest before stepping inside the store. As hard as it was to sell the watch that represented his first foray into manhood, he knew what he had to do. He presented the watch to the salesman, who seemed to disapprove of the unkempt lad's presence in his shop. "How much would you be willing to pay for this fine gold watch, sir?"

Suddenly interested, the salesman studied the timepiece with his loop. "Well, it is a fine watch, but I couldn't pay a penny more than ten dollars."

"As long as you are willing to pay me promptly in American dollars." Franklin nodded. "I'll take it."

The merchant didn't answer, but went to the register, took out several bills, and handed them to Franklin. He then made his way across the street through the deep snow to the haberdashery. An hour later, he stepped out onto the street looking like a well-dressed gentleman complete with suit coat and tie. His next stop would be the local boardinghouse for a much-needed bath, a hearty meal, and twenty-four hours of the best-earned sleep he could ever remember.

Once rested and recovered from his arduous journey, Franklin took a few hours to tour Connecticut's capital, which was settled in the early 1600s by Dutch fur traders. The first English settlers appeared in 1635 and gave the town its name. After taking in the sights, Franklin presented himself directly to Mr. S. D. Hulbert of the publishing house Hulbert and Company. The young man inquired whether they had any use for a boy who didn't have much, but was a hard worker and an experienced bookseller.

"Well, son"—Mr. Hulbert looked at Franklin over the top of his rimless reading glasses, which rested snugly on the tip of his bent nose—"we would have to take you on trial, since you have no security to offer, but you look like a fine, honest fellow who could sell our books, especially the 'Good Book.' You say you have experience, so the job is yours if you want it."

Mr. Hulbert even took Franklin home and introduced him to his family. He also gave the young man enough money and books to make his way to Nova Scotia, but this time not on foot. Franklin took great pride in Mr. Hulbert's belief in him and hoped he would never give the man reason to think that his confidence had been misplaced. There was never a cause for concern, however, since Hulbert's newest salesman proved himself successful. In fact, he cleared nine hundred dollars on that first trip alone and roomed in only upper-crust establishments located along his route. Something of a dandy, he dressed well and lived well, but there remained two things he never partook in again—a glass of spirits and a game of chance. Instead, Franklin donated a fair share of his income to various benevolent societies, perhaps to ease a twinge of guilt caused by the deception he so enjoyed, or maybe he looked upon it as penance for being born a girl.

Chapter 6

A Man's Life

By the spring of 1860, Franklin had found great success with Hulbert and Company. He was so prosperous, in fact, he could afford a fine horse and buggy complete with a silver-mounted harness. In addition, he wore fine and dapper clothes like a gentleman of high standing. Between his polished appearance, warm charm and winning smile, Franklin was delighted to discover that entry to any household was as simple as a knock on the door. Of course, the 'Good Book' that he always carried helped convince any hesitant customers not to turn him away.

Living life as the 'enemy' during this time suited Franklin just fine. He relished the freedom masculinity provided. He went where he wanted, did what he wanted, and earned a sizable paycheck without the nagging restraints society placed on unattached women. The publishing company even boasted that in thirty years' time, they had never employed any agent who could outsell the young man from Canada. The men in charge of the home office were more than happy with his earnest commitment and outstanding sales abilities, and more importantly, they were proudest of the keen professional image he exhibited as a representative of Hulbert and Company.

Convinced he wasn't one to settle down, Franklin rather liked visiting distant places and meeting new people. He thrived on change. Besides, permanency meant risking his secret and that would never do. That all changed, however, when book sales took him westward to Flint, Michigan—about sixty miles northwest of Detroit.

Fur trader Jacob Smith founded what would be the city of Flint in 1819 when mostly Native Americans, known as Ojibwas, lived there. By the time Franklin arrived in 1860, however, Flint was no longer a simple trading post, but a major site in Michigan's thriving lumber industry. Located in Michigan's Saginaw Valley along the Flint River, the village had been incorporated into a city for just five years. The busy downtown area surrounded by dense forests and picturesque farms appealed to Franklin, but it was the people he met there that persuaded him to make Flint his home base—at least for a while.

One of the doors that Franklin first knocked on that spring belonged to Pastor Thomas Jefferson Joslin and his wife, Susan. Joslin, a distinguished, middle-aged minister was the man in charge of Flint's Methodist Episcopal Church.

"What can I do for you, young man?" Joslin eyed the well-groomed boy who stood on his front porch clutching two satchels.

"Reverend, sir." Franklin beamed his brightest smile. "My name is Franklin Thompson, and I understand you are the pastor of a very important church here in Flint. I came to you hoping some fine members of your congregation might be needing 'Good Books.'"

"Come into the parlor and let me see what you have." Joslin led his visitor into a large room nicely furnished. The men sat down facing each other in opposing wing-backed chairs upholstered in blue velvet. Thompson laid samples of his books across the low pine table that stood between them. He expertly pointed out the details and differences of each one while Joslin nodded his approval. Before their conversation ended, the minister was so taken by his new acquaintance, he not only bought a Bible, but also invited Franklin to board at his house and promised to introduce him to his well-heeled worshipers after Sunday services that very week.

•••••

". . . And I say to each and every one of you, go forth from this church today and take it upon yourself to extend the work of the Lord to your neighbors be they rich or poor," Pastor Joslin spoke to his flock from the pulpit of his church.

Franklin sat listening attentively from the front row and joined in the group's enthusiastic "Amen!" Afterward, Joslin asked the Bible salesman to stand and then introduced him to his parishioners, adding that Franklin was an outstanding young man, who had come to Flint hoping to spread the word of the Lord with his 'Good Books.' Franklin smiled in his charming, endearing way as the pastor added, "Anyone wishing to purchase a Bible should see Mr. Thompson directly after the service, or just come by the house during the week. He'll be staying with Susan and me for a bit."

Outside the church, trees were in bloom and the aroma of apple and cherry blossoms permeated the air. An attractive couple in their late twenties approached Franklin who stood next to his stack of Bibles, enjoying the fine spring day. "Mr. Thompson, I'm Captain Morse and this is my wife, Mary. We are in need of a 'Good Book.'"

"And we would like a very special one for our home," Mary added.

"I think I have just what you are looking for." Franklin handed the captain his deluxe, gilt-edged Bible.

Morse looked it over as Mary nodded her approval. The captain then pulled out some notes and paid Franklin for the book.

"Thank you for your patronage, sir. Did I hear you say you were a captain?"

"Yes." Morse extended his hand, and Franklin gave it a shake. "I am captain of the Flint Union Greys. We're a volunteer troop of locals."

"My husband is too modest." Mary gently touched her spouse's arm. "His boys are the finest soldiers in all of Michigan. Why, if you plan on staying here, you should join up."

"I certainly would like to meet your men," responded Franklin, his curiosity piqued.

"Perhaps they might be interested in buying Bibles, Mr. Thompson," offered Mary.

"You should stop by our house this afternoon," the captain suggested. "The boys come by most every Sunday."

"I accept your kind invitation. It sounds like an ideal way to spend a beautiful afternoon, but please call me Frank."

"All right, Frank." Morse smiled. "We'll see you around three and be sure to bring Your Bibles. My boys are all God-fearing men and I believe some of them could surely use a new 'Good Book' to help keep them that way."

●●●●●

The Flint Union Greys were no ragtag group. Founded in 1852, they were expert marksmen and riders. The men often gathered at Morse's home to practice their skills and discuss the latest politics. The country itself was seriously divided over the issue of slavery in the South and the talk of secession by those very states that were built upon such a brutal foundation. Most men of the North did not approve of the inhumane treatment of blacks, but the thought of any state seceding from the Union was considered treason and a definite cause for bloodshed.

As Franklin approached on horseback, the men were in the midst of a lively discussion about the upcoming presidential election. Many of them, it seemed, were hoping that the rumpled Republican lawyer from Illinois, Honest Abe Lincoln, would win the office. Morse's men stopped their conversation to survey the stranger and his bag of Bibles. As the young man dismounted, Morse walked over to welcome him.

"I'm glad you and your Bibles made it, Frank." He then turned to the group. "Men, this is the fellow I told you about, Frank Thompson. Maybe some of you saw him at church this morning."

"I saw him," one of the men spoke out. "Thought he looked a little on the scrawny side."

"Now, boys, let's not give Frank a hard time just yet," Morse admonished with a wink. "He may surprise us."

"Where you from, Frank?" another soldier questioned.

"Canada, sir, where my dear mother remains even now."

"Have you ever fired a gun?" a second soldier asked.

"Ohh . . . once or twice when I had to . . . Grew up on a farm, you know."

"Well then, how about a friendly shooting match?" Morse suggested.

"I think I might be persuaded." Franklin smiled knowing that he could most likely outshoot any one of the men standing before him.

The Greys took turns shooting at the target, but not one of them hit the bull's-eye more than once. When it was Franklin's turn to shoot, he split shot after shot, each one hitting dead center and leaving a wide gap where the bull's-eye had been. The Greys were stunned not only by his accuracy, but also his nonchalance.

"That was pretty impressive, Frank, but can you ride as well as you shoot?" Morse asked the question they were all wondering.

"I can usually manage to stay in a saddle, sir."

"Well then . . . let's have ourselves a race!"

Because the path in front of Morse's house was narrow, the men chose two of their best riders to compete against Franklin. All three mounted their horses and lined up along the dirt road, waiting anxiously for Morse's signal. With a single shot in the air, they galloped off. Thompson easily pulled ahead, leaving no doubt as to who was the most skilled rider. Afterward when the men gathered around offering Franklin their congratulations, he downplayed his win with a bit of modesty. "I just got lucky today, that's all."

"Somehow, Frank, I don't believe sheer luck had much to do with it." Morse smiled, giving him a pat on the back. "You're obviously a lot tougher than you look. What else do you have in your bag of tricks?"

Franklin smiled as if he knew something they didn't. "I can't share all my secrets, now can I, sir?"

"I suppose not, but I'm sure my men would agree that we could use a good soldier like you," Morse continued. "What do you say? Will you stay and join up with us?"

"Well, I might be persuaded. I am tiring of life on the road, and I suppose Flint's as good a place as any to settle down for a bit."

A smiling Morse patted his new recruit on the back once again.

•••••

Soon there was even more talk of a civil war between the states. The words 'contraband' and 'secession' became part of the day's vernacular. It was even heard that ladies of the South were sporting 'Secesh' hats in support of the new government they called the Confederacy. Although slavery was an issue that Thompson was not experienced about because it had been abolished in Canada long before his birth, it offended him terribly. And as a woman, Emma could certainly relate to the slavery she had experienced while living under Isaac Edmondson's control. *It seemed that the slaves of the south universally regarded the advent of the Northern army as the harbinger of their deliverance, as much as Emma had once relied on Fanny Campbell to deliver her.*

While Franklin enjoyed the vibrant conversations with his fellow Greys, he had an even more pressing problem. He did not wish to appear as if he preferred men over women so he found it necessary to court a few of the local young ladies. Thanks to the formality of courting etiquette during that era, he was saved from the embarrassing discovery that could have revealed his secret. In those days, wooing involved well-chaperoned outings or afternoon excursions in public places and nothing more intimate than witty conversation, something Franklin excelled at.

Sometimes, however, these friendly jaunts led to expectations that 'Frank Thompson' could not fulfill. In fact, at one point he came near marrying a pretty little girl who was bound that he should not leave Michigan without her. Although Franklin was favored with more than one declaration of undying love by wealthy ladies of class and stature, he greatly preferred the independent privilege of earning his own bread and butter—practicalities aside.

One such lady friend, Miss Lavinia, was an attractive female companion of substance. While riding through the countryside in Franklin's horse and buggy, she continued to snuggle closer to Franklin who began to feel ill at ease with her too near proximity in the seat next to him.

"Now, honey, let's not get carried away," he warned.

"But I thought you liked me, Frank." She turned out her lower lip in a pout.

"I like you just fine, Miss Lavinia, but getting too serious is another matter. I told you I am just not the marrying kind."

"Then what kind are you, exactly?"

"The kind who likes to show off a beautiful woman to his less fortunate friends," teased Franklin, causing the lovely Miss Lavinia great confusion and even greater disappointment.

Chapter 7

Talk of War

As 1860 folded into 1861, Franklin settled into a quiet life in Flint, Michigan. He made good friends with the Flint Union Greys and grew especially close to one member, Damon Stewart. When he wasn't soldiering, the dark-haired Stewart worked at a dry-goods business known as The Old Scotch Store. Stewart's parents had come to Flint from New York, and Franklin spent many happy hours visiting the family's farm. He especially enjoyed the company of Stewart's numerous siblings. Perhaps they reminded him of his own brother and sisters back in New Brunswick.

Nationally, the country remained in turmoil with a new president who came with controversy. On March 4, 1861, Abraham Lincoln had been sworn in as the nation's sixteenth president. At his inaugural address, he warned:

> *"In your hands, my dissatisfied fellow countrymen, and not in mine, is the momentous issue of civil war. The government will not assail you . . . . You have no oath registered in Heaven to destroy the government, while I shall have the most solemn one to preserve, protect and defend it."*

The South was incensed by the gangly man who seemed to threaten their way of life, while many Northerners stood behind him. Warmongers bellowed on both sides, calling for bloodshed that would settle their differences one way or another. Some, who were more insightful and less emotional, knew that a civil war would devastate the entire country no matter who claimed victory. The very topic stirred the soul of all passionate men who proudly called themselves Americans.

The Flint Union Greys were no different as they gathered one evening shortly after Lincoln took office. Franklin was in attendance, since he was in the habit of accepting most invitations extended by the captain and his wife, Mary. Both were quite fond of Frank, as they called him. Aside from Damon Stewart, Franklin had also endeared himself to other Greys such as Lyman Stowe who dabbled in astrology, Milton Benjamin, a carpenter, and Bill McCreery, a strapping fellow of six feet—all fine men who were proud of their association with the troop. They especially enjoyed the company of their newest member, who offered a different perspective on the country's current state of affairs. With no real political agenda, Franklin could be objective and at the same time vehement about where his loyalties lay. That particular evening, the captain had called upon his men for a very pressing reason—the growing unrest between the Federal Government and the southern states, who refused to give up their lifestyle or their slaves.

Morse's well-appointed parlor smelled of tobacco as some men puffed on cigars, while others smoked their ornate pipes. Each held a glass of brandy as they tried to make sense of the bitterness and uncertainty that loomed over the country's future. Only Franklin refrained from lighting a smoke and drinking anything stronger than Mary's coffee.

"Boys, I think there's a storm brewing in these United States and the cessation of the entire South from the Union appears to be as inevitable as the spring thaw," stated Morse matter-of-factly as he drew on his cigar.

"I can't believe the South will actually be foolish enough to secede from the Union." McCreery nervously stroked his beard.

Morse paused thoughtfully before he spoke again. "If they do, it will be their biggest mistake. Father Abraham won't have it and he will surely do what is necessary to enforce the law of the land on the South. He could never allow the country to be splintered in such a way that would endanger the future of this great nation our ancestors fought so hard to win in the name of freedom."

Stowe shook his head, uncertain of the prospects. "I just hope Father Abraham has the courage to do what's right. A war between the states would be a great hardship on the people of this country."

"Being president during these terrible times is not for the faint of heart." Morse nodded with great confidence. "But it is his job to keep this country unified. We are still one nation under God as far as I know and Father Abraham is not a cowardly man."

Mary interrupted their conversation as she passed through the sitting room on her way to the front porch. She frowned at their sudden silence and slipped a hat on her head before bussing her husband's cheek. "Honestly, boys." She studied their serious faces. "War again? Can't you talk about anything else these days? I almost think you're all wishing for some bloodshed."

"Now, Mary." Morse took her hand. "No one here's looking for a fight. We're just talking is all. A man still has a right to talk. After all it is written in the Constitution."

"You must be referring to the fine print, dear." Mary grinned and then turned to Franklin. "Frank, you're from Canada. What do you think? Are the boys here talking nonsense?"

"Well, ma'am, I think we have to be ready for anything. And if there is a war, fighting next to your husband would be an honor."

Pleased with Franklin's answer, Mary nodded. "William does inspire trust and admiration in a person, doesn't he? But why on Earth would you consider taking up arms for a country not your own?"

"While it's true that I am not born American and I am not obliged to remain here during such a terrible strife," Franklin told her. *"It is not my intention, or desire to seek my own personal ease and comfort while so much sorrow and distress fills a land that I consider my newly adopted country."*

"In that case, you are truly an honorable man, Mr. Thompson."
Mary nodded toward the troop. "Gentlemen, I'll leave you all to
your war talk. It's a beautiful evening so I think I'll go out on the
porch and count the stars for a while."

Morse smiled as he watched his wife leave the room but grew
serious once she was out of earshot. "Frank's right." He turned back
to his men. "Despite my wife's misgivings, we have to be prepared
and willing to preserve the Union—at any cost."

•••••

The next day as Franklin drove his buggy through downtown Flint,
he noticed a crowd gathering in the town square. Recognizing
many of his fellow Flint Union Greys, he stopped to see what was
causing the commotion. As he headed toward his comrades, he
heard a young newsboy hawking the *New York Herald*: "Fort Sumter
Falls to the Rebels!"

Charleston Harbor, South Carolina, was a long way from Flint,
Michigan. But the conflict that took place there and the Confederacy's capture of Fort Sumter shook the nation. The reality of
Americans attacking other Americans was staggering no matter
how much talk of war went on. *Civil war with all its horrors was inevitable now, and ready to burst like a volcano upon the most prosperous nation
the sun ever shone upon. As he stood in the midst of the crowded avenue that
afternoon in April 1861, the contemplation of this surreal picture filled Franklin's
eyes with tears and his heart with sorrow, for this heinous act and its aftermath
were destined to blacken the fair pages of American history forever.*

In disbelief, Franklin approached the crowd of men and soon
realized they were gathered around a handbill that had been
posted in front of the Town Hall. It was a Presidential Proclamation, which called for seventy-five thousand men willing to volunteer in a national effort to preserve the Union. Inside City Hall, a
line had formed in front of a long table where men were already
enlisting, and without hesitation, Franklin joined them. Damon
Stewart had just signed up and as he was leaving City Hall, he

noticed his good friend. "Can you believe the gumption of those southern boys, Frank? Attacking our fort and going against everything Father Abraham and the Union stand for?"

"We have to put them in their place!" shouted another volunteer before Franklin could even reply. "They need to be reminded that the Union is sacred!"

"If the South wants war, we'll give 'em war!" thundered another, and a chorus of high-minded men roared their agreement.

The crowded room grew hot as outrage poured from the throng. By the time Franklin stepped up to be measured for height, he was sweating from the heat, as well as his nerves.

"Sorry, son, you need to grow another four inches if you want to join this army," stated the Recruiter as if casting judgment on the young man who stood before him.

"But, sir, I can outride and out-shoot any man here," insisted Franklin, dismayed at the thought of being turned away. But skill set didn't matter that day. The recruiter simply shook his head and motioned for the next man to step forward.

Dejected, Franklin left the town square while his contemporaries celebrated their good fortune of being accepted into the Union Army.

•••••

On April 30, 1861, Flint, Michigan was decked out in red, white and blue while a local band played a lively version of "Yankee Doodle Dandy." Buntings, flags, and a patriotic fervor stirred the crowd that gathered to send their husbands, fathers, sons, and brothers off to war. Some women cried as the men, excited by the prospect of adventure, marched off dressed in their new uniforms, proudly shouldering their new bayonets. Words of encouragement were spoken by Colonel W. M. Fenton followed by a blessing from Reverend Joslin. Several ladies pinned the new recruits with tricolor rosettes bearing the words "The Union and the Constitution!" to remind each soldier what they were fighting for. Finally, each man was given a New Testament inscribed with Oliver Cromwell's words: "My men, put your trust in the Lord—and be sure you keep your powder dry."

Franklin gazed silently as the men paraded by. With a saddened heart, he ached to join them for training at Fort Wayne in Detroit. His heart lurched when Captain Morse, along with his First Lieutenant, William Turner, and the other Greys passed him by. Morse gave his friend a sympathetic nod as a distressed Franklin watched his friends disappear into the distance.

With the clash of arms and strains of martial music almost drowning out the hum of industry, war became the theme on every tongue and the Flint Union Greys, minus Franklin, were a part of it. The young man desperately missed his comrades, but continued to sell books door-to-door, while keeping abreast of current events. He read any papers he could find and he often listened to orators knowledgeable about the war. He kept as busy as possible with various war efforts on the home front, spearheaded by the citizens who stayed behind. He joined the womenfolk and elderly who spent endless hours making bandages, packaging supplies, and collecting donations for those who would soon face victory or death. As important as these activities were, for Franklin, they were not enough. He craved the heady action that only military life could provide.

Franklin hoped that his time would soon come to join those brave and enthusiastic men in defense of the cause they so faithfully supported. Convinced he had a duty to perform, he spent days and nights in anxious thought considering his options and in what capacity he might serve the Union cause.

•••••

Several weeks after the troops left for Detroit, Franklin received an invitation to dinner at the home of Mary Morse. They had maintained a friendly liaison since her husband's absence and with most of the men now gone, Franklin felt compelled to look after Mary. If he couldn't fight alongside his troop, at least he could ensure that their captain's wife was taken care of. He figured he owed Morse that much. The two spoke most Sundays at church and occasionally, when Mary needed help with a stubborn window or a difficult horse, she called upon Franklin.

"My dear, Franklin, I'm so glad you could stop by," Mary greeted him at her front door. "Please . . . do come in."

Franklin bowed slightly and gallantly kissed her hand. "It's always a pleasure to see you, Mrs. Morse. Do you have any word from the captain?"

"Always the gentleman, Frank." Mary smiled as she led him into the parlor, where to his surprise, he found Captain Morse waiting in full uniform.

"CAPTAIN!" Franklin was incredulous at the sight of his friend.

"It's good to see you, Frank!" Morse welcomed him.

"What are you doing here? I thought you were in Washington."

"I was." Morse patted Franklin on the back. "But I left my finest man behind so I had to return. We need you, Frank."

"But you know that I tried to sign up, sir, and I was turned away because I'm too short."

"What's short is the Union Army," chuckled Morse. "Short of good men, that is. It seems that the height requirement has been eased. I am here to personally ask you if you would consider joining your old friends in Company F."

"I would be honored, sir! I have dreamed of serving with you in battle."

"There are more ways than one to serve, Frank," Morse cautioned. "We need military nurses in the worst way, and I think that kind of work would suit you, but after some training, I promise, you will be right in the thick of it. Are you sure you are prepared for that?"

"Captain, I do not wish to sit quietly on the sidelines while there are men suffering on the front."

"Then will you meet me at the recruiting office first thing in the morning?"

"I will be there before you!" Franklin grinned with excitement. "But tonight, I want to hear all about the war. Have you seen any fighting yet?"

"No, not yet. We've been training men in Washington where you'll be trained. I'll tell you more about it over dinner."

"Which is growing colder by the minute," Mary reminded them with a frown. "Please, gentlemen, let's sit down and eat before you talk. I don't think I could bear hearing war stories at the table."

"Of course, Mary." Morse nodded. "I will answer all of Frank's questions over a glass of brandy after dessert."

•••••

That night, Franklin lay awake, mulling over every detail that Captain Morse had told him. He suddenly understood the seriousness of his decision to join the Greys in their mission to uphold the Union. He even wondered whether or not he could maintain his ruse under such harsh circumstances. What would happen if someone discovered his real identity? Would it be best if he served the Federal Government as a female nurse instead of a soldier?

But, Franklin quickly banished that thought. He realized he could best serve the Union cause in male attire. He could better perform the necessary duties for sick and wounded men, and with less embarrassment to them and himself, as a man rather than as a woman. He thanked God that he had been permitted to express the appreciation which he felt toward the people of the Northern States by serving his adopted country in their hour of need. After mentally resolving his own issues, he fell into a deep sleep, knowing that in the morning, he would be counted among the finest men he knew.

At the recruiting office, there were no physical examinations. Had there been, Frank's true sex would have surely been exposed. Instead, he was assigned a Union uniform along with several dozen other inductees who all pledged their solemn allegiance to the United States of America.

After another patriotic send-off by the citizens of Flint that also included the pinning of a tricolor rosette and a presentation of a New Testament, the new recruits headed to Detroit for their basic training at Fort Wayne. Completed in 1851 along the banks of the Detroit River, Fort Wayne was named after 'Mad' Anthony Wayne, the Revolutionary War general who took Detroit from the British in 1796. The fort was strategically placed near the Canadian border just in case war once again erupted with England. That didn't happen. Instead, a peace settlement was reached between the Americans and the British, so the fort remained unused until the outbreak of the Civil War ten years later. It was then designated as a mustering center and training ground for Michigan troops.

For Franklin, Fort Wayne was the place where he not only learned the rigors of soldiering, but also tested his very existence as a man living among the other privates who were eager for battle. Franklin's smaller stature and clean-shaven face caused some of the men to call him "our little woman." It was all said in jest and no one appeared to have taken the moniker seriously—especially when they witnessed Franklin's remarkable riding and shooting skills. Still, he remained cautious in guarding his carefully kept secret, as well as his mother's feminine-looking handkerchief, which he kept hidden in his left sleeve.

On May 25, 1861, Franklin and his fellow privates were officially sworn into the Union Army by Lieutenant Colonel J. R. Smith, Captain William R Morse, and Colonel Israel Bush Richardson at the Detroit Fair Grounds. With their right hands over their hearts and their left hands raised, the group of novice soldiers vowed to serve their country:

> *"I do solemnly swear that I will support the constitution of the United States and bear true allegiance to the United States of America, and to serve them honestly and faithfully, against all their enemies or opposers whatsoever, and to observe and obey*

*the orders of the President of the United States of America, and
the orders of the officers appointed over me."*

With those few words, Canadian-born Sarah Emma Edmonds
entered military life as Private Franklin Thompson with Company
F of the Second Regiment of the Michigan Volunteer Infantry.
That brief moment of triumph, however, held no hint of the horrors to come.

PART 2

A Soldier's Life

(1861–1863)

Chapter 8

The Union Capital

With the declaration of war, the United States found itself a fractured country. The South had affirmed their independence by announcing their loyalty to a new government they called the Confederacy, leaving Northerners divided politically. Some claimed that President Lincoln had dragged the nation into an unwanted war, while others believed him to be a hero for standing firm and upholding the Union at all costs. Families were split over the issues of secession and slavery and even officers who had once bonded as classmates at West Point now picked sides. Border states, like Maryland, were torn over where their allegiance belonged. These divided loyalties came to a head in Baltimore on April 19, 1861—just days after Fort Sumter fell.

In response to Lincoln's call for volunteers, many newly formed Union Army troops headed to Washington, DC by train. The Sixth Massachusetts Militia, on their way to defend the Capital, stopped in Baltimore and attempted to transfer to another train that would take them on the final leg of their journey. The soldiers were greeted by a mob of Southern supporters who not only flung sticks and stones, but brandished guns. In response, the Union men shot at the crowd. Four soldiers and twelve civilians were killed with dozens more wounded before the hostilities ended.

Although the bloodshed dissipated, the city remained in a state of unrest for many weeks to come.

That June when Franklin Thompson and the new Michigan recruits passed through Baltimore via the rails, they did so with trepidation. Dressed in Union uniform, Franklin sat next to a window while the chugging locomotive slowly pulled them southward, away from the streets of Baltimore. Still within the city limits, he watched in dismay as a small, but infuriated mob quickly formed. The jeering group pelted the train with rocks, brickbats, and other missile-like objects, breaking the glass on the railcars, which were all crowded with Union forces. Although they had been cautioned not to shoot, the soldiers felt compelled to defend themselves and fired into the crowd, forcing the rabble rousers to flee.

Just when Franklin thought the altercation was over, a large, flat stone broke through the window in front of him, striking a young soldier in the left temple. Franklin rushed to help as the man slumped forward in his seat. The wound, though not severe, left blood streaming down his face and seeping into the collar of his new uniform. Franklin wiped the blood away and bandaged the gash with a spare shirt taken from his own pack. He felt queasy at the sight, but soon realized that this was just the first, and possibly the least, of an endless stream of injuries that would require his attention.

A kind of absurd panic set in as he wondered how he would ever aid multiple maimed and dying men on a battlefield. Franklin drew a sharp breath at the overwhelming thought of what might be in store. The definitive reality of war had not quite set in for him or the thousands of other men heading toward the unthinkable madness of a country divided. For Franklin, the time would soon come when, after a long day of battle, bandaging a slight head wound would be a welcome relief.

•••••

When Franklin and the other soldiers finally arrived in Washington, DC tired and hungry, after their long, arduous journey, he thanked God that he had made it. Invigorated by the capital city, Franklin felt grateful—he was no longer obliged to view the war as a spectator and welcomed his new life as a nurse in the Union Army. He found the city itself overcrowded with anxious soldiers, demanding politicians, and unsavory civilians who sought to profit from the war. As more and more soldiers poured into the capital, sickness prevailed. Typhoid fever along with malaria and dysentery threatened thousands, but there were few hospital beds available and a definite lack of well-trained medical staff. Food, drugs, and other much needed supplies were also limited.

To accommodate the sick, makeshift hospitals were set up in various churches, hotels, and schools. Even the US Patent Building, as well as the Capital Building, with its famous dome currently under construction, sheltered ailing men. It was here that Franklin first worked alongside other military nurses, female aides, surgeons, and medical stewards. He most certainly crossed paths with the eccentric female surgeon, Dr. Mary Edward Walker, who received the Congressional Medal of Honor for her work during the war only to have it revoked more than fifty years later when she was eighty-four years old. The medics set up cots and stocked empty bookshelves with bottles of ether and other drugs. They also laid out supplies such as bandages and gauze in anticipation of serious battle wounds. The medical team even positioned large, wooden doors for use as temporary operating tables and organized a gruesome assortment of knives and saws.

There were many such temporary hospitals set up in this manner, but none of them offered suitable or comfortable accommodations for those who required medical attention. Doctors and surgeons were also in short supply and many men had to wait nearly a day to be seen by medically trained personnel other than a nurse or assistant. The congested city became a hotbed of chaos and disease in the dead heat of that turbulent summer.

Before he'd even finished his training, Franklin was charged with caring for scores of delirious, helpless men whose bodies were failing from high fever, acute diarrhea, and rampant infection. Aside from cool, damp rags to soothe sweating brows and quinine pills to ease the symptoms of malaria, little medication was available to help relieve the suffering caused by the unsanitary conditions. Unlike the pharmaceutical supplies, however, malaria-infested mosquitos that inhabited the Virginia swamps just across the Potomac River were plentiful, causing the medical staff to quickly fall behind in their professional duties.

Franklin worked side-by side with the military chaplain, Major Butler and his striking, dark-haired, blue-eyed wife, Kate. They were a handsome and friendly couple in their early thirties, dedicated to their mission of caring for the sick. Major Butler did what he could to comfort those terminally ill soldiers who needed mostly spiritual care, while Mrs. Butler assisted Franklin with the men's physical needs.

Franklin's patience and excellent penmanship made him a favorite for composing letters when the men wanted to send word back home. Many of them couldn't read or write, while some who were literate were just too weak to hold pencil to paper. One such soldier who had only hours left to live, was desperate to contact his new wife in Ohio with a final declaration of love. After Major Butler prayed for the man's soul, he asked the stricken soldier if he had any last requests.

"I need to see Frank," the man answered through labored breath. "He promised to write a letter to my Sadie. If she doesn't hear from me, she'll worry so. Dying doesn't trouble me, but I want her heart to be at peace when I'm gone."

"I'll find Frank for you, soldier," the Major promised.

Leaving the building that hot afternoon, Major Butler spotted Franklin emptying bedpans into a freshly dug latrine behind the hospital. It was a job that many of the staff balked at, but Franklin never seemed to mind despite the stench.

"The men sure do love you, Frank." Butler rolled up his shirt-sleeves and picked up a soiled bedpan.

"They inspire me." Franklin paused, bedpan in hand. "I only wish I could do more."

"We do what we can to comfort those we can't heal," the chaplain reminded him as he poured the receptacle's contents into the ditch. "It's important work."

"I just wish things were different. These men came to fight a war. If they have to die, it should be a hero's death on the battlefield, not languishing in a hospital from disease."

"No matter how they go"—Butler reached for another bedpan—"they are all heroes and deserve the finest care we can possibly give them—on or off the battlefield. You go on in now. I'll finish up here. That young private from Ohio, the one with blackwater fever, asked that you help with his final correspondence home. And you need to hurry. He's slipping fast, I'm afraid."

"I'll make sure he gets word to his wife." Franklin paused, saddened that his patient had taken a turn for the worse. "I know men are dying, Major, but until now, I haven't lost a one."

"That's something you must get used to, Frank. This is war, and he surely won't be your last patient to go on to glory."

"No," Franklin sighed. "But he will be my first."

•••••

The Federal Government had not yet formed the Sanitary Commission and the need for proper food for all of the soldiers, sick or healthy, was a serious issue—one that hadn't gone unnoticed by Franklin. During a brief break one sweltering afternoon, he approached the chaplain's wife, Mrs. B., as he preferred to call her. "I'm worried about our men. Hardtack and bacon grease is hardly fit food for soldiers suffering with dysentery and fever. We have to do better if they are to recover."

"You're right," Mrs. B. agreed as she rolled bandages before placing them in a box. "Maybe we should try a little begging with the ladies of Washington. What do you think about knocking on a few well-to-do doors, Frank?"

"Why, Mrs. B." Franklin smiled, intrigued by her suggestion. "The only thing wrong with that idea is that I didn't think of it first!"

And, from that day forward for as long as they remained in the nation's capital, Franklin and Mrs. B. visited stately homes throughout Georgetown and the Washington DC area on a regular basis. Their philanthropic requests garnered a multitude of goods from the fine ladies who lived nearby. The two industrious partners often returned to cheers from the ailing men as they welcomed generous baskets of food and various bottles of rum and brandy, all donated to numb their pain and lift their spirits. Even one local clergyman's wife supposed that a little blackberry wine might be a good contribution to the cause.

•••••

On July 15, 1861, Captain Morse found Franklin with a patient. It wasn't a friendly visit that prompted him to call, but his job as Franklin's superior. "Frank, I'm afraid it's time to prepare for battle. The regiment is headed for Manassas where we'll meet our enemy for the first time."

"You know that I'm ready and willing to follow you anywhere, Captain." Always pleased to meet Morse, Franklin was especially invigorated by the thought of finally seeing action. Daily life in Washington had now grown humdrum and a restless feeling had begun to consume him. Tending the men was fulfilling, but he had signed up for war and defending the Union was most important. "When do we leave?"

"At first light, Frank. Are you sure you're ready?"

"As ready as I'll ever be," Franklin answered. "The hardest part about leaving will be saying good-bye to my patients."

There wasn't much time to waste, since he had many men to visit one last time before his appointment with the enemy. As he expected, his patients were saddened and distressed by the news of his imminent departure.

"But you can't leave, Frank," insisted one sick soldier. "Who'll look after us like you do?"

"It's time for me go to battle, boys," Franklin reminded them with pride. "That's why we're really here, right?"

"But, Frankie, you don't even shave yet," joked another. "How can they send you to the front?"

"That's what gives me the upper hand." Franklin laughed. "The enemy won't see how fearsome a threat I am."

"Don't go and get yourself killed now," pleaded one young man just recovering from the ague.

"Yeah, son . . . Remember to keep your head down and your powder dry like Cromwell says," chimed in a fourth man.

"Not to worry," Franklin assured him. "I will follow Oliver Cromwell's advice to the letter and put my trust in God. I have no doubt that the Almighty and his angels will look out for me."

"We really hate to see our little woman go," teased a man from New York. "We'll have to go back to eatin' sawdust and gruel."

"Oh, it won't be that bad." Thompson laughed as he shook their hands. "Sawdust served at the right temperature could pass for steak!"

That night, before the Flint Union Grey's were to march south to what would later be known as the First Battle of Bull Run, Franklin sat in his tent preparing his weapons. Outside, men could be heard yelling and cheering.

"On to Richmond!"

"Those Rebs will beg for mercy!"

"The Union will not be made a mockery of!"

As Franklin calmly worked by the light of the oil lamp, his tent-mate and friend, Damon Stewart, paced back and forth much like an expectant father. "Why is it, Frank, that you don't seem the least bit nervous about tomorrow?"

"Like I keep saying, my destiny lies in God's hands, Damon. If I'm meant to die in battle, so be it. The Lord has never failed me before and He won't fail me now."

By this time, Franklin had grown quite comfortable as a woman in soldier's clothing and felt led to this new life by some divine guidance or destiny. *He may have been a little ambitious and a good deal romantic about what was to come, but his endless devotion to the Federal cause made him forget the uncertainty of his fate and the unpleasantries that awaited. Perhaps a spirit of adventure was important, but patriotism would prove to be the grand secret of his success.*

At dawn, Franklin and the other men packed their saddlebags and readied their horses as the artillery and foot soldiers commenced their march to the beat of the Drum Corp. It was all as Franklin had imagined it to be—brave men marching to battle for a noble cause, their bayonets reflecting the sun. Emma's time spent reading Fanny Campbell's adventures had fueled her imagination and her last few years of posing as a man had paid off—no one had yet questioned her masculinity.

Along the journey, the men, eager to meet the enemy, exchanged anxious words about the upcoming battle. *While Franklin listened to their banter, he couldn't help but think that many of those enthusiastic men would never return to their loved ones or relate their tales of success or defeat. Should victory perch upon their banners, it would be at the cost of many noble lives.*

Chapter 9

The First Battle

On the three-day march south, the troops found it difficult to obtain water, and due to the searing heat, many of the men suffered from heatstroke and exhaustion—some needing to be carried back to Washington in ambulances. The occasional sharp volley of shot could be heard as the anxious soldiers attacked anything that looked suspicious. Eager to finally face the enemy, the words 'On to Richmond' echoed throughout the ranks. Many mistakenly believed that the war would be won and finished with this single battle, resulting in the capture of the Confederate capital.

Along the way, Franklin, Mrs. B., and a black cook named Jack, stopped to buy butter, milk, and eggs from the homes and farms they passed. When necessary, they weren't above raiding a hen house or two, contrary to Brigadier General Irvin McDowell's direct orders not to steal. Hefty cattle were also tempting. Whenever the regiment passed a large herd of bovines, a few stray shots rang out, ensuring that the pleasant aroma of fresh steak searing over a sizzling fire, would permeate camp that night.

Upon arriving in Manassas on July 20, 1861, Franklin, Mrs. B., and Major Butler worked with the surgeons throughout the hot afternoon, setting up makeshift field hospital tents, cots, and operating tables. They established a crude medical facility in the Centreville Methodist Episcopal Church, also called the Old Stone

Church by the locals. Built in 1854, the building was strategically situated between Washington and Manassas Junction—an ideal spot to care for the wounded. A number of soldiers were digging latrines and cutting wood logs to set across them to be used as a ledge for the men to sit upon while performing their business. Other soldiers dug trenches along what would soon be the volatile front line. All sweated profusely as they labored under the humid summer sun.

Having finished his duties in the hospital that first evening, Franklin helped Jack prepare the men's last meal before battle. The menu included chicken, steak, and johnnycakes made from the cornmeal, eggs, and milk gathered along the way. As the men enthusiastically collected their chow, they expressed their appreciation of the evening's feast.

"A fine last supper." An older soldier smiled as Franklin served him a piece of beefsteak.

"Our little woman's in the kitchen now and we're all saved." Another grinned, referring to Franklin.

"At least our bellies are," added a third.

Franklin flashed a knowing smile with just a hint of mischief and then quickly turned serious as an unamused Colonel Israel B. Richardson approached the food line.

"Jack, where did you get that beefsteak and those chickens? You know I do not tolerate stealing in my regiment."

"No, Massa, I ain't no thief, I ain't." Jack shook his head and grinned exposing bright white teeth against his jet-black skin. "I'se carried dem all de way from Washington, thaugt I'd cook 'em 'fore dey spoilt."

"Jack has been telling me for days now that he had planned a special meal on the eve of our first battle, sir," fibbed Franklin.

Still suspicious, yet somewhat satisfied as he noted how much the men were enjoying their dinner, the colonel nodded. "That will do, Jack. Carry on serving the men and make a plate for me, if you will. I'll take an extra Johnnycake, too, if there's enough to go round."

"Yes, suh, right away, suh, and de men dey sure do enjoy der meat 'sted of dat ole hardtack an' descate vegetables."

As the colonel carried his heaping plate away, Franklin couldn't help but smile to himself as he remembered just how that chicken came to be part of the evening's fare. That very morning he had ridden up to a small farmhouse in time to see Jack rushing out of the nearby hen coup with two fat and squawking chickens under each arm. A cloud of feathers surrounded him. The lady of the house was close behind him hollering. "You there, darkie! Get back here with my chickens!"

Nonchalantly, Franklin approached the middle-aged woman as she continued yelling at Jack who was now well down the road and out of her reach. "Did you see that fella? He stole my chickens!" Hands now resting on her ample hips, she was out of breath and her face was flushed from her futile effort.

Without a word, Franklin leaned over and handed the outraged lady a dollar. Just as suddenly as it started, her tirade ceased as she slipped the money inside her pocket and smiled.

"Nice doing business with you, ma'am." Franklin tipped his hat. "The Union Army is forever indebted to you and your generosity." He cantered off toward camp, but turned back momentarily. "And I'll see to it that Father Abraham hears how you sacrificed for the cause."

Her jaw dropped in disbelief as she watched him ride away.

•••••

That evening after the last Johnnycake was but a memory, Franklin along with Damon Stewart and Bill McCreery wandered through camp. The night air was still heated despite the absence of the brutal sun. Many of the men were meticulously preparing their weapons for battle. A few were fast asleep while some wrote letters by the light of their campfires; still others played cards, conversing in hushed tones as if they might disturb the dead from their eternal sleep. The surreal scene only deepened the ominous feeling that settled in with the darkness. All appeared completely unaware of what was about to befall them when twilight turned to day.

The three men paused to listen as a small group of soldiers joined together in prayer. Frank's heart suddenly ached for Betsy as the men, led by a reedy young lad no more than twenty, sang a hymn. "O, for a faith that will not shrink; though pressed by every foe; that will not tremble on the brink of any earthly woe . . ."

Franklin absentmindedly stroked the sleeve that held his mother's handkerchief. Consumed by his own memories, as well as the emotional chorus of voices that echoed in the night air, he scarcely noticed Major Butler approach him.

"It's all right to feel anxious, Frank." The major gently laid his hand on Franklin's shoulder. "We are all human and have our own fears and maybe some regrets to face during these uncertain times. That can't be helped. But together, and with the Lord's blessing, we can travel the most difficult road."

"I understand that, Major, but how does a man do it?"

"Faith, my boy. Take Willie here, it's hard to believe that someone so young can bear witness to a faith so deep. He's truly been chosen by the Lord and we can all learn something from him. No matter how tired he is, he never fails to carry on his regular prayer meetings."

When the song ended, Willie bowed his head and spoke just loud enough for the men to hear. "I pray to our Savior above to protect us in battle on the morrow. I pray for protection of our loved ones we've left behind; and for those of us who should give our lives in the fight, I ask that God will comfort and support our families, especially my dear widowed mother if I should fall."

Franklin returned to his tent where he and Damon Stewart lay awake in anticipation of the unknown.

"I miss the farm." Stewart's voice had an edge.

"So do I," Franklin sighed. "I especially miss your mother's good cooking."

"Do you think we'll be home soon, Frank?"

"I think we should leave that in God's hands."

"You're a good one, Frank. Faithful. Honest. I just hope you don't take offense when the men call you 'their little woman,'" Stewart nervously chattered. "They don't mean nothing bad. It's said with affection because you're always taking care of everyone."

"I take no offense from their teasing when they compare me to a woman." Franklin simply grinned. "In fact, my sisters and my mother are the finest people I know. Besides, I've been called much worse."

The men shared a laugh, but after Stewart fell asleep, Franklin remained awake, contemplating his situation and the frightening unknowns waiting to be revealed as a new day dawned.

•••••

When the sun rose on the battlefield at Bull Run, the two armies stood within sight of each other like players on a stage. Three Union divisions commanded by Generals Samuel Heintzelman, David Hunter, and Daniel Tyler were ordered forward by General McDowell while two others, led by General Theodore Runyon and Dixon S. Miles, stayed back in reserve. Spectators from Washington and other nearby towns, anxious to see what they hoped would be a thrill-filled spectacle, sat at a distance with their buggies and picnic baskets. Some even brought their children to witness what they saw as a defining moment in their country's history. The deafening sounds of cannons signaled the commencement of battle and before long the roar of gunfire was only rivaled by the moans and cries of wounded men and horses. The fighting was chaotic and aggressive with enthusiastic Union and Confederate soldiers pushing forward, all anxious to claim victory. Everyone wished to be done with this messy business so they could go home and get on with their lives.

Mrs. B. joined Franklin on the battlefield. She was a sight with her leghorn hat made of fine Italian straw, a silver-mounted seven-shooter secured in her belt, and a canteen slung over each shoulder—one filled with water and the other with brandy. She also carried a large knapsack with bandages and other provisions, as did Franklin. Her husband, the chaplain, sat upon his horse, stone-faced, taking in all of the action. All three were on high alert, ready to provide aid alongside the medical team as necessary.

When a gunner was shot down near Franklin, he clambered to the fallen man's side. Rolling the soldier over, he recoiled when he recognized young Willie from the previous night's prayer service. Franklin felt as if the wind had been sucked from his own lungs as he lifted Willie's head. The young man struggled to pull a blood-soaked envelope from inside his jacket pocket. "Please . . ." he rasped choking on blood. "Get this to my mother."

Franklin took the letter with a nod as Willie gasped his last breath and died in Franklin's arms. A moment later, Major Butler arrived with a stretcher.

"Dear God, not Willie!" The major reeled momentarily, but quickly regained his composure.

The two men gently placed Willie on the stretcher and together they carried him from the battlefield amid the chaos and mayhem. Franklin was horrified by the hundreds of wounded and dying men strewn across the field—both Northerners and Southerners, but all American men and boys. As the bright sun of the holy Sabbath morning shined down, crushed and broken legs, arms, and bodies littered the now crimson ground that, just a few hours earlier, had been lush with greenery.

Losing all color, Franklin stopped to collect himself, drawing short, quick breaths in a fit of hyperventilation. Feeling nauseous, he bent over as a sense of panic and anxiety rippled through him. No matter how hard he tried, he could not shut out the constant, heart-wrenching cries that accompanied the stifling stench of death. Major Butler noticed Franklin's struggle and put an arm around the young battle nurse for support. "It's all right, Frank. Take deep breaths. One at a time."

"Thank you," Franklin gasped, trying to stand tall, hoping that no one else had noticed what he perceived as weakness. He wiped his sweating brow with his shirtsleeve as he attempted to regain

control. "I'm fine now. Go help the men who really need it." After
one more deep breath, Franklin stumbled to the aid of another
wounded man.

•••••

Confusion reigned with hundreds of injured men begging for help,
allowing the medics no choice but to leave the dead on the battlefield in order to attend those they could save. There was no escaping the terror, mayhem, and death. Now distressed and no longer
interested in lunch, the civilian audience scrambled away, drag-
ging their children from the danger. Many brave soldiers turned
their backs on the enemy and sought refuge in the woods only
to be found later that day torn to pieces by shell and cannon ball
fire. At first, Franklin was appalled by the many deserters he witnessed fleeing for their lives. Soldiers were supposed to fight, not
turn tail and run. He thought maybe they deserved death for their
lack of patriotism and the way they abandoned their comrades in
the midst of battle. Yet, he also realized how terrified these boys-
turned-men-overnight must have been when facing their own
untimely demise.

As the battle raged on, Franklin and Major Butler steadily carried wounded men from the field until Franklin was ordered to
help Army surgeon Alonzo B. Palmer with an amputation. He and
the assistant surgeon held down a young soldier while the doctor
used a saw to amputate the man's leg without benefit of anesthesia.
Choking back bile, Franklin turned his head from the gruesome
sight as blood spattered and the stricken man screamed, wept, and
pleaded. "Stop! Please stop! Please . . . Noooo don't take my leg,
noooo! Ahwwwww!"

The agonizing day seemed endless as Franklin worked to the
point of exhaustion. Besides carrying men from the battlefield, he
set broken bones and made splints along with countless tourni-
quets. The knife he kept strapped to his side became his instrument
of choice. He used it to slice away clothing and expose the wounds

for the surgeons to tend. When all was finished, he cut bandages to bind the stumps of what had once been strong arms and legs.

Soldiers who were wounded in the head, neck, or stomach were not treated, as the field physicians were unable to properly care for them. At best, they were simply made comfortable; at worst, they were left to die. The most common surgery, amputation, primarily resulted from minié ball wounds that shattered bones in the extremities upon impact. The surgeons had no alternative but to remove the damaged arms and legs. Those gruesome operations went on and on as Franklin watched death claim soldier after soldier. All the while, the grisly heap of discarded limbs piled next to the surgeon's table grew higher and higher.

Late in the day as Franklin and Major Butler worked in the field, Mrs. B. rode up leading two horses. "We have orders to collect fresh water from the spring for the men."

The three quickly gathered canteens from among the bodies—Rebel or Yankee, it mattered not—that remained scattered across the field. They rode hard toward a nearby spring where they filled their canteens even as the Confederates tried to keep them away. Enemy Minie balls whizzed past them, but somehow the daring trio escaped injury as they returned to the battlefield with their precious liquid load. They delivered the filled canteens to the exhausted but grateful men who still managed to fight, desperate to hold their ground.

The three returned again and again to the spring until the Confederate Army overtook it, forcing them to abandon that important water source. As they attempted to reach another spring farther downstream, the major's horse was struck in the neck. Forced to take cover behind the wounded animal among a hailstorm of Minie balls, Franklin tried to stop the blood that gushed from the horse's wound. Despite his best efforts, however, the horse bled out within minutes. Franklin removed the canteens from the saddle-horn and pushed Mrs. B. toward his own horse as they made a run for it. He jumped onto his saddle, pulling Mrs. B. up behind him in one smooth stride. The chaplain climbed on his wife's steed and they raced off toward the battlefield, returning just in time to see Colonel Cameron dash along the line on horseback, shouting at the troops. "Come on, boys! The Rebels are in full retreat! PUSH FORWARD!" His last words were garbled as a bullet pierced his heart, knocking him dead from his mount.

Franklin was the first to reach his side. He respectfully closed the colonel's eyes, folded his arms across his chest, and then moved on to tend to the next wounded soldier. Mangled men were dying, some alongside their slain horses, as the stench of heavy gunfire mingled with the odor of dried blood. The morbid rattle of death—both human and animal—shook the air, along with cannonading, until an unidentified Union soldier galloped through the pandemonium repeatedly barking, "Our batteries are now in the hands of the enemy!"

The news quickly spread like a plague from one soldier to the next, causing entire regiments to break and run. Panic and adrenaline replaced exhaustion as the men dodged bullets, bodies, abandoned cannons, overturned wagons, and terrified spectators—all racing back to the safety of Washington. Rebel artillery thundered, as enemy cavalry rushed in, adding a deepening terror to the bedlam. Franklin spotted the Major and Mrs. B. tending a fallen man directly in the path of the charging horses. He shoved the couple to safety just as the stampeding hooves dashed by, trampling the wounded soldier and crushing all else in their wake.

•••••

It was dark by the time the three made their way to the hospital at the Old Stone Church in Centerville, only to find piles of dead bodies, alongside abandoned arms and legs laying near the building. The macabre scene that greeted them, however, paled in comparison to what they found inside. Dozens of maimed men lay in the aisles awaiting death.

One man moaned, unaware that both of his legs were crushed from ankle to midthigh. Next to him was a fellow shot in the face—unrecognizable and barely breathing. A third had taken a bullet in the stomach. He held a rag over his own wound in an effort to stop the bleeding. Others were nearly insane with pain, screaming and thrashing until their energy wore out. As she tried to decide just what to do first, Mrs. B.'s eyes were drawn directly to the altar where a drummer-boy, who had been shot in the back, laid calling for his mother. She knelt down and touched the boy's brow, hoping to soothe him.

"Mother, is it you?" he gasped.

"Yes, son," Mrs. B. spoke quietly. "I'm right here."

"I can't feel my legs, Mother," he whispered.

"It's all right, my boy, you just need to close your eyes and sleep," Mrs. B. sighed. "When you awaken, all will be well. I promise."

The boy clutched at her arm. "You won't leave me, will you, Mother?"

"I could never leave such a fine son," she assured the lad. "But you must rest so the angels can bring you home where you will walk again."

"Angels . . ." the boy repeated softly and closed his eyes for the last time.

Nearby, Franklin aided a dark-haired soldier who too was dying. The man had taken a bullet wound in his chest just above the heart. Franklin couldn't help but think it would have been more merciful had the bullet struck just an inch lower. He motioned for the major to join them in prayer.

"You think I'll die before morning?" asked the soldier as blood bubbled from his lips.

"I believe you will soon be with God," answered Franklin honestly.

"And we will pray for your soul." Major Butler took quiet note of how candidly Franklin responded to the man's question.

"Has death any terrors for you?" Franklin continued.

The stricken soldier managed a smile. "Oh no, I shall soon be asleep in Jesus, which is more than I can say for some."

•••••

Being all-consumed with the pain inside the church, the three caregivers had no idea how the Union Army fared outside. Concerned, Franklin slipped from the church later that night under a steady shower of rain. On the main street of the town, he recognized a laundress from one of the Union camps wandering alone in the dark.

"Ma'am, have you seen where the soldiers went?"

Her long white hair was flattened and soaked from the rain, but she seemed unaware of her disheveled state. She fidgeted awkwardly, chattering to herself as if she was busy making something with her hands that Franklin couldn't see. "I have to fix my husband his dinner. He'll love the chicken I'm preparing, don't you think?"

The lost look in her eyes told Franklin that the woman was mad—yet another casualty of the war. With a deep sigh, he left her and walked to the top of the ridge as dawn was breaking to the east. He surveyed the valley, which was now still, with no living soldiers in sight, only the bodies of men and horses cluttering the field as the downpour continued. There were indeed neither Yankees nor Rebels standing. He couldn't believe that the entire Union Army would have retreated toward Washington, leaving the wounded and dying in the hands of the enemy, including himself and the Butlers.

From his perch upon the ridge, he spotted movement as enemy cavalry rode up to the crazed old laundress. After a brief conversation, she pointed in Franklin's direction. Afraid of being spotted, he quickly crawled under a thicket of brambles. He held his breath as the enemy approached and one of the horses nearly stepped on his boot. Quietly, he waited, drenched through to the skin, until the Southern soldiers rode off. He then rushed back to the church to break the news and warn the others.

Once inside, he called for the Butlers who were still tending the wounded. "Mrs. B.! Major Butler! You must leave now! Our army has retreated and the Confederate Calvary is on its way. You will surely be captured if you stay here."

"But what about the wounded men?" inquired Mrs. B., desperate to save them all.

"There's no time or means to remove them. I'll stay here and do what I can. You both go on now and try to make it to Washington where you'll be safe!"

"But, Frank, you will be of no use to the Union Army in the enemy's hands." Mrs. B., reminded him. "It would be far better to continue your work in freedom than to be confined as a prisoner of war. There are so many who would benefit from your skills and your kindness."

Somehow he knew she was right, but he was torn. *To escape meant he was deserting these poor men when they needed him most. Yet heading north, where the Union troops had set up camp, he would find even more wounded men needing his help.*

With a heavy heart, Major Butler spoke to the injured loud enough for all to hear. "My dear brave men. The Rebels are on our doorstep, and I am saddened to say that there is no possibility of moving you to safety."

With his free hand, the man holding his stomach wound waved a gold locket at Franklin. "I don't want the Rebels to find this. Please . . . take it to my wife. Tell her it's from her loving husband, John Rawlings." Before handing it over, he pressed the photos inside to his lips. "Tell her I will do my best to make my way back to her."

The definitive trampling of Cavalry horses could be heard outside the church as Franklin snatched the locket from the dying man's hands. "I give you my word, John. I will send this to your loved ones, and I will tell them of your bravery. Godspeed, my friend."

The soldier smiled and closed his eyes, seemingly at peace. For one final moment, Franklin observed these helpless, yet brave men, who *just lay there, calmly, awaiting the approach of their captors, apparently prepared to accept their bleak fate. Oh how brave they were! He silently asked*

*God to show them mercy and to grace the Rebel Army with compassion. The
reality of war was now clear and any early thoughts of grandeur and glory
receded back into a time where innocence once prevailed.*

The major and his wife escaped out of the church's back door.
Franklin followed just a few steps behind. The three somehow
managed to stay ahead of the Rebels as they slipped away, seeking
safety.

The First Battle of Bull Run had been disastrous. Union deaths
and casualties numbered almost three thousand while Confederates
suffered close to two thousand. One civilian was lost—eighty-five-
year-old Judith Carter Henry, an invalid shot in her own bedroom
by artillery fire. Father Abraham was so disappointed in his Army
that he relieved Brigadier General McDowell from his command
and replaced him with Major General George B. McClellan. It
was the president's hope that McClellan could turn the muddled
military into a fine-tuned force.

As for Private Franklin Thompson, he would look back on his
own lost innocence. *For what he witnessed would be etched upon his memory
forever and the great horrors of the battlefield would be his waking nightmare for
the rest of his life.*

Chapter 10

A New Assignment

After walking all the way from Centerville across open fields and through dense woods, making sure to avoid the roads, Franklin arrived in Alexandria late the next afternoon. Exhausted and hungry, with his army-issue shoes nearly worn from his feet, it took him several days to recover enough so he could continue on to Washington, where the hospitals teemed with the sick, wounded, and dying.

The entire city of Washington, DC was in a state of depression over the shocking Union loss at Bull Run. Stragglers from the battle—some still armed, some not—wandered into the city searching for their regiments. The streets were filled with mud due to the heavy rains and the population reeked of a hopelessness that made officers and enlisted men find refuge in local barrooms. Others, who did not imbibe, wanted to hide their faces in shame. They may have been ill-prepared for battle, but they were never primed for defeat.

While the troops lacked military discipline and focus, private citizens no longer cheered for war. The city melted into a tumultuous sea of mayhem as politicians scrambled for answers. Even Father Abraham was shaken by the loss. And to make matters worse, the Rebel flag boldly flew over Munson's Hill, within plain sight of the Federal Capital.

Amid all the uncertainty, one thing was for sure—General McClellan had his hands full. 'Little Mac,' as he was called, was a Philadelphian by birth and had graduated from West Point—ranked second in the class of 1846. He fought in the Mexican-American War and ultimately resigned from military life in 1857 to work for the railroad. At the onset of the Civil War, he rejoined the army, and after winning some minor skirmishes in West Virginia, he was called to Washington to take command of the now-broken Army of the Potomac.

At the time of McClellan's arrival, the hospitals in Washington, Alexandria, and Georgetown overflowed with casualties from both wounds and disease. It seemed that the *grueling march from Bull Run, through rain, mud, and chagrin, did more damage than the actual battle. After the retreat, measles, dysentery, and typhoid fever ran rampant through the ranks.* Even Mrs. B. became a patient when she contracted typhoid fever.

Upon his return to Washington, Franklin resumed his nursing duties and made the hopeless cases his first priority. Most had but one request—send their most precious possessions directly to their loved ones, along with a final letter telling of each man's bravery both on the field and in the face of death.

Franklin also accrued many anxious letters from home intended for soldiers who had passed on. He felt it was his duty to answer each devoted mother, proud father, or newly widowed wife with details of their loved one's fate. The hardest one of all came from Willie's doting mother:

My Dearest Son,

I continue to pray that the good Lord will keep you safe until you return home to me. The younger children miss you terribly—especially Sam who has taken over your chores. He says you should hurry home so he doesn't have to clean the henhouse anymore. The chickens peck at him and seem to lay less eggs now. I guess they miss you, too. We are all keeping busy with the farm, but you are always close in our hearts. We pray for you every single day before supper and we leave your chair empty hoping that one day soon this terrible war that has taken our finest men away from us will be done with. Then you can come home and reclaim your rightful place at our table. I promise to fix your favorite meal—rabbit stew with lemon cake for dessert. We'll have a real celebration! Stay strong, my son. Keep well. Find your way home and ease the ache in my heart caused by your absence.

Your Loving Mother

•••••

In between his nursing duties in Georgetown, Franklin traveled by foot from hospital to hospital, hoping to learn of the fate of his friends and comrades. Occasionally, he discovered a familiar face, but more often than not, he was left disappointed when only strangers greeted him in the wards. On or off duty, Franklin witnessed men in delirium shouting at the top of their lungs—one going through the entire manual of arms as if he were in the ranks. Hundreds more required constant attention, overwhelming the limited number of medical staff as fevers worsened and infections spread. Outwardly, Franklin remained stoic and unemotional, but inwardly, his soul ached as he watched the countless men suffer and *the 'Soldier's Cemetery' quickly fill with newly made graves.*

Regardless of his surroundings, Franklin always maintained a cheerful demeanor with his patients, hoping to raise their sunken spirits. Most who faced death, however, could not be uplifted. In those cases, Franklin felt it was his duty to talk openly about dying, for it was a brave man who faced his own Judgment Day with grace and dignity.

Although many were lost and others were sent home minus a limb or two, some grew healthy again, eager to take up arms once more. Under McClellan's direction, the army of the Potomac now focused on training maneuvers and sharp military discipline.

The once ragtag group began to take on the appearance of a well-drilled, but restless infantry. McClellan explained to his army of nearly 250,000 that he had purposely kept them away from conflict, so that he might turn them into a formidable army:

> *"I have held you back that you might give a death blow to the rebellion that has distracted our once happy country. . . . The army of the Potomac is now a real army, magnificent in material, admirable in discipline and instruction, excellently equipped and armed. . . . I will bring you now face to face with the rebels, and only pray that God may defend the right."*

•••••

Better trained and anxious to put their newly acquired skills to work, the northern troops eventually became impatient and bored with daily camp. The men craved action. There was great speculation that their next destination would be Richmond, but to their surprise, they were ordered to Fortress Monroe in Hampton, Virginia. Construction of the fort began in 1819 due to a long-term need for coastal defense once the War of 1812 ended. The stone and brick structure was not completed until 1834 and was named after US President James Monroe. It was the largest stone fort ever built in America and positioned in a critical spot where the Union could best defend the eastern seaboard.

In March 1862, nine months after their loss at Bull Run, the troops finally left Washington. The Union Army had come a long way. They were now one of the most highly trained and well-armed military groups in the modern world. Father Abraham and Congress had high hopes for these men as they marched to Alexandria where a fleet of ships with the Stars and Stripes hanging from every masthead, awaited them. The music of the nation drifted across the waters of the Potomac as they set off toward the southern tip of the Virginia Peninsula. Upon arrival, the troops were intrigued by the sight of the recently constructed *U.S.S. Monitor*.

The iron-hulled steamship lay in the waters not far from the fort. Its unique revolving turret became a topic of interest among the men who wondered just how this odd black brute would fare in battle. If it were anything like the once charming village of Hampton, it would not do well.

A blackened mass of ruins, the previously picturesque city had been burned out several months earlier by the rebel General John Bankhead 'Prince John' Magruder and his men. While the state of Virginia was primarily Confederate, this small area was known to have many Federal loyalists. Magruder, it appeared, preferred to destroy the place rather than see it in Union hands. In addition, many former slaves now considered 'Contraband of War,' fled to the area, hoping for deliverance by the Union troops. These runaways then established the Grande Contraband Camp just outside of Fort Monroe. Affectionately called 'Slabtown,' the community was the country's first self-contained African American settlement complete with churches, schools, and businesses.

Upon arriving at the fort, Thompson and Mrs. B. wasted no time in setting out to visit the contrabands and tour their camp. *Grateful to the Northern army for their limited freedom,* these black men worked hard at the docks, loading and unloading supplies from the ships. The Negro women cooked meals and washed clothes for the soldiers. Franklin was inspired by their unbroken spirits and tremendous contributions to the Union cause despite their own many hardships.

•••••

Soon after they had settled in their new surroundings, Captain Morse came looking for Franklin. He first stopped at the Fort's hospital facility, but was soon redirected out back where he found Franklin propped against a tree with his eyes closed.

"You there, soldier." Morse prodded him with the toe of his boot. "You wouldn't be sleeping on the job, now would you?"

"Oh, no, sir!" Franklin jumped to his feet. "I was just contemplating what advice I might give Little Mac in case he asks me for help."

"I see this war hasn't dampened your sense of humor, Frank." Morse smiled.

"Not yet, sir." Franklin nodded. "But it has sapped some of my energy. My work here is fulfilling, but time spent in camp does become stifling. I wouldn't mind a little adventure if you know what I mean."

"I know exactly what you mean, and I just might have a remedy for your delicate condition," Morse offered with a grin. "I'm afraid our mail carrier was robbed and murdered in broad daylight two days ago, and we need a replacement. We are all aware of your superior riding and shooting skills, so I suggested to Colonel Poe that you would be more than competent in the position, and it seems he agrees. If you are willing to take on such a dangerous job, it's yours, effective today."

"By all means, Captain!" Franklin pumped Morse's hand in excitement. "I'll be the fastest mail carrier this army has ever seen!"

"Just be the safest." Morse smiled. "It is not my intention to lose one of my best men."

"Don't worry about me, Captain," Franklin assured him. "I can take care of myself and the mail."

After Morse left, Franklin gave his new assignment some serious thought. It was dangerous work indeed, but he had no idea his skills would be put to the test that very night while on his maiden run.

Knowing he would be safer on the road surrounded by darkness, Franklin readied his horse after supper when most of the camp grew quiet. He strapped a full mail-carrier's bag to the saddle horn and galloped into the night, alone. He rode hard to get to the next mail post—about three miles west. Upon reaching his destination and gathering the mail marked for Hampton, Franklin rested during the daylight hours. As nightfall set in once again, he strapped a bag filled with incoming mail to his saddle horn and began his return trip. He had only ridden a mile or so when he spotted two men on horseback lurking among the trees on the roadside.

The two men wore dark cloaks and hoods, which immediately roused Franklin's suspicions. Instinctively, he laid flat along the neck of his horse to present a smaller target, just as the men began to fire. When they missed their mark, Franklin, with his adrenaline pumping, spurred his horse forward. He thought about the day he and Freedom had won that gold watch. Like then, the pounding of his horse's hooves echoed in his ears while the wind blew against his face and the dust choked him. This time, however, was different. Now, he was riding for his life, and despite the danger, he felt exhilarated as the two men gave chase. About one-half mile down the road, it quickly became clear to the outlaws that their intended victim was by far the better rider, and they retreated, most likely to wait for an easier mark.

Franklin rode into camp at dawn where a few dozen soldiers were busy with early-morning chores. He dismounted and removed the heavy mailbag from his saddle. The men quickly realized that he had brought word from home and gave him an exuberant welcome—gathering around in excitement, each anxious to find a letter or package from a special someone.

"See to it that this mail gets distributed," instructed Franklin as he passed the bag over to one of the younger soldiers.

"With pleasure." The boy grinned with admiration as he watched Franklin draw a long drink from his canteen.

After replacing the cap, Franklin turned to tend his horse. Before he could remove the saddle, however, a familiar face caught his eye. Franklin squinted in the morning sun and held his breath. In all the time since he had left Magaguadavic, he had never run into anyone from home. Throwing caution to the wind, Thompson hesitantly approached the soldier and extended his hand. "You must be new in the regiment. I'm Franklin Thompson, but most everyone around here calls me Frank."

"Nice to meet you, Frank," the newcomer shook his hand. "My name is James . . . James Vezey."

"Where are you from, James Vezey?" Thompson questioned, knowing full well who he was.

"Michigan . . . and before that, Canada . . . New Brunswick to be exact."

"What a coincidence," declared Thompson. "I'm from New Brunswick myself!"

"Thompson . . . Thompson." Vezey thought hard. "I'm afraid I don't know any Thompsons."

"That's probably because my family moved to Michigan quite a while ago." Franklin quickly covered his tracks.

Vezey noted the enthusiastic soldiers who were busy opening envelopes and small boxes from home. "You're a brave man, riding the mail, and a popular one it seems."

"Not brave . . . only fast."

Vezey laughed. It was a familiar sound that Emma remembered with a pang of longing. For a moment, the woman beneath her disguise ached to tell James the truth—to confess her secrets and throw herself into his arms, risking everything that she had worked so hard to hide. Lucky for Franklin, however, a peddler appeared in camp, hawking his wares. His booming voice distracted the men from their mail with the lure of treasures like tobacco and hard candy. Vezey excused himself and left Franklin to see exactly what goods the peddler had to offer. Franklin took note of the man's black eyepatch and wondered just how he had come by it.

While Franklin unsaddled his horse, he watched with curousity as Vezey bought cigarettes. He had never remembered the boy to smoke. His mother wouldn't have approved such a frivolous expense. He must have picked up that habit after he left the farm. Franklin's mind wandered back to the night Emma had begged Vezey for help. He couldn't help her then, but now those old feelings she had squelched rekindled without warning. What were the odds of finding James again like this? It was so unexpected that Franklin had to catch himself when Captain Morse approached, distracting him from his memories. "Frank, I'm so pleased to see that you made it back safely."

"Safe and sound to be sure!"

"Did you encounter any trouble on the road?"

"Nothing I couldn't handle, sir."

"Which is why I recommended you for the job." Morse understood the unspoken implications and patted Franklin on the back. "If you're not too tired from the ride, would you be interested in another mission today? It would mean a lot to the men."

"Of course." Franklin nodded. "Anything to help our soldiers."

"Then I have a new assignment for you. The men need some good food. There's a remote farmhouse about five miles east of here. It's said to be well-stocked with provisions. See if you might locate that house and bring back whatever you can from the landowner." Morse handed Franklin cash along with a list of the required items.

"I'll see to it just as soon as I switch horses, Captain." Franklin smiled, pleased that Morse trusted him for such duties. "This one here has earned a good rest, and I promise I won't come back empty-handed." Besides, the lone ride would give him some time to think hard about James Vezey and how he might handle this startling turn of events.

•••••

As Thompson rode through the woods, he savored its serenity and took advantage of the time to consider his options. He could continue his charade and hope Vezey would not notice, or he could reveal the truth. Honesty, however, meant putting everything at risk. Could Vezey be trusted? Was he worth taking that chance? Perhaps not. He may very well reject her, but more importantly, would he keep her deepest, darkest secret?

Still agonizing over his personal dilemma, Franklin soon noted a large, traditional white farmhouse in the distance. Putting thoughts of Vezey aside, he rode to the hitching post in front of the home, tied up his horse, and cautiously walked up the steps to the front door. He rang the iron bell that hung from the ceiling of the porch and within moments a fine, stately woman with honey-colored hair, swept up in a disheveled bun, answered. She wore black mourning clothes, and her eyes darted nervously as if she didn't want to look directly at him.

Franklin tipped his hat, extended his hand, and offered her the list. "Afternoon, ma'am. I understand that I might be able to obtain some much-needed supplies from your farm."

Looking a bit relieved, she let him enter as she studied the list of requested staples. "Wait here. I'll prepare a basket for you."

Franklin remained in the parlor, standing near the front window where he could see his horse, as she disappeared into the kitchen. She struck him as nervous due to her constant chatter from the other room.

"The boys are out hunting." Her high-pitched voice grated on Franklin's nerves. "If you want to wait I'll have them catch some chickens for you."

"That won't be necessary, ma'am." Franklin grew uncomfortable, suspicious of her motives. He nervously checked and rechecked to ensure that his horse was still outside. "I'm afraid I don't have time to wait. I'd like to pay you for whatever you have and be on my way."

The woman returned to the parlor, carrying a basket filled with bacon, cornmeal, eggs, and coffee. "If you're sure you don't want to wait—"

"No, that's quite all right," Franklin pulled the money from his pocket. "You've been more than generous and the Union Army is grateful."

"Oh, but it is of no consequence about the pay."

"Father Abraham insists." He rolled the bills into her hand and took the basket. "And I thank you, ma'am, for your kindness." With a quick salute, Franklin exited the house. He tied the basket to his horse and as he rode off, a sense of danger took hold. For no particular reason, he laid low against his horse's neck, just as the woman fired a pistol directly at him—the ball taking his hat as it flew past. Franklin immediately turned his horse and took aim with his own revolver. The woman panicked. Her arm jerked upward, and her second shot went wild. She then dropped her pistol and extended both hands above her head. Franklin did not trust her, but he certainly had no desire to kill her. He took deliberate aim and in an effort to immobilize her in case she changed her mind, he sent the ball right through the palm of her left hand.

The woman fell to the ground with a shriek, fainting as Franklin dismounted, picked up her pistol, and placed it in his belt. He unfastened the end of his halter strap and tied it tightly around her uninjured right wrist. He then bound her left wrist with some gauze from his supply kit in an effort to control the bleeding. Grabbing his canteen, he poured a little water on her face until she came to, screaming. "Please! Please, sir, have mercy on an old lady," she cried, tugging at her restraint. "Release me! I won't cause you any further harm! I promise!"

Franklin pointed his pistol at her as she rose to her feet. "If you so much as utter another word or a scream, you will be a dead woman!" He then picked up his hat, climbed into his saddle, and spurred his horse forward, forcing the woman to walk alongside him. By the time they reached the woods, she was too weak to continue on foot. Franklin dismounted with an offer. "You may ride if you wish."

The woman gave a slight nod. Franklin then helped her into his saddle and the two continued on with him marching alongside, holding tight to the reins.

"Do you have a mother, my boy?" she inquired quietly and for the first time made eye contact.

"I do, ma'am," Franklin answered as he inconspicuously reached for the red handkerchief tucked safely in his sleeve.

"What is her name?"

"Betsy, ma'am. Her name is Betsy."

"How long since you've seen her?"

"A very long time," Franklin sighed, thinking again of home, his family, and James Vezey. "What is your name, ma'am?"

"I'm called Nellie." Her tired voice no longer irritated him. "And I'm sorry I tried to shoot you, but I recently lost my husband, father, and two brothers in the Rebel Army. I'm all alone now, and I am afraid my grief had turned into anger. You were the first Yankee I have seen since I received the terrible news last week." She took a deep breath and, with the eyes of a penitent, placed her good hand on his shoulder. "Please, sir, I beg you, do not deliver me to your military superiors. I've had enough bloodshed to last a lifetime. Saving lives is what's important now—North or South, it doesn't matter. Let me do for your men what I couldn't do for mine. Take me back to your camp and let me nurse your sick and wounded."

"How do I know I can trust you to keep your word?" Franklin demanded.

"Because I am truly sorry," the woman sobbed, once again on the verge of hysteria. "And I have nothing else left. My son, if it was your mother asking her captor for mercy, would you not hope that he show her a little kindness and grant her request?"

"My mother would never have tried to shoot someone."

"Nor would I, one week ago, but it was a moment of madness, I assure you, and that moment has now passed."

"Then if you are truly sorry, I forgive you and what happened today will stay between us."

"Yes . . . yes." She rocked back and forth. "Oh, thank you, thank you, my boy! I will not forget your compassion, and I vow not to disappoint you."

Franklin took Nellie directly to Mrs. B.'s tent, telling her that the woman was shot by one of their own, but she had pledged to nurse the Union's wounded if they would grant her mercy, as well as medical aid.

"I thought it best to put her in your care," Franklin explained to Mrs. B. "She'd lost a lot of blood when I found her." Kate Butler was no one's fool, however, as she silently took note of the extra pistol in Franklin's belt. Franklin gave her a hopeful look, trusting that she understood.

"I'll personally make certain that the surgeon tends to her hand, while you take your provisions to the cook." She then turned to Nellie. "May I look at your hand, dear?"

"Yes, please, and as soon as I'm able, I promise to help you with your men."

The very next day, Nellie returned to her house in a Union ambulance and brought back all of the available provisions her farm had to offer. As soon as she was well enough to work in the infirmary, she devoted herself to the men. No one ever knew exactly how that Secesh woman came to be a Union nurse, but all welcomed her as one of their finest.

Chapter 11

The Secret Service

"I dunno how ya do it, Frank!" Jack grinned as he prepared the johnnycakes. "Ya not only bring back da goods, but ya change dat Rebel woman into a Union lady! Mebbe Little Mac oughta send ya to de odher side sos you can transform a few more o' dem damn Rebs."

"Maybe you can suggest that to the general when you serve him supper tonight." Franklin laughed.

"He probly already knows 'bout Nellie! She's da talk of da camp today . . . and you right along wid her! Tell me somethin', Frank . . . did ya shoot dat lady or did ya really find her with a hol' in her hand?"

"What's the difference?" Franklin shrugged. "No matter how I tell it, we all get johnnycakes tonight!"

"And da finest batch I ever did make if'n I do sa' so myself!" Jack nodded toward a dark-haired man carrying a batch of firewood. "Put dat down next to da stove, soldier." Franklin turned toward the newcomer, letting out an involuntary gasp as he recognized James Vezey.

"You all right, der, Frank?" Jack asked.

"I-uh-I just-uh remembered something," Frank stumbled backward, but remained staring at his former paramour.

"Will you be needing more kindling, Jack?" Vezey knelt to neatly stack the wood branches.

"Why yes, suh, I tink so! Thanks to Frank, here, I have a lot o' johnnycakes to cook. Say, maybe you both could collec' some wood fer ole Jack . . . That way there'll be twice as much. Go on now, the both of ya. An', soldier . . . try ta get de truth outta Frank 'fore ya get back!"

"The-the truth?" Franklin stammered.

"Bout Nellie." Jack rolled his big, dark eyes. "Make Frank tell ya how she really got dat hol' in her hand."

Franklin felt more than a little uncomfortable heading off into the woods alone with James. At the same time, however, he was excited by the chance to be near him once again. Along the way, Franklin contemplated his situation, still unsure of what to do. For the moment, he chose to say nothing lest he end up saying too much, but his silence led James to the wrong conclusion.

"Frank, if I have done something to upset you, I am genuinely sorry. It was never my intent to—"

"No . . . it's nothing you did," Franklin interrupted him. "It's what you didn't do."

"I'm afraid I don't understand what you are getting at."

"Let's walk a little farther where no one can hear." Franklin quickly made his decision. He had to take the risk. He could keep his secret from everyone else, but not from James.

The sun was setting fast as James followed Franklin to a secluded area near a fast-running spring, where a doe and her spotted fawn were drinking. Startled by the soldiers, the animals bolted away leaving them alone.

"There's not a lot of kindling here, Frank." James's voice carried an uneasy tone.

"I didn't come here for firewood." Franklin was blunt.

"But Jack said—"

"Jack can wait." Franklin faced James directly. "Right now, I have to confess a secret, but first, you must pledge to keep this to yourself and not betray me."

"If this is about Nellie's hand," James murmured, uncomfortable and confused, "I can assure you that I have no interest in what you did or didn't do to that woman."

"This is not about Nellie or her hand!" Franklin was near bursting now. "It's about me. I am not who you think I am, James. My name is not Franklin Thompson. You do, in fact, know me and my family from New Brunswick, but telling you the truth could jeopardize my mission here and that's why you must swear to keep what I am about to say to yourself."

"Fine!" Vezey seemed impatient, but curious. "But what exactly is 'your truth'? And just how do you think I know you?"

"I'm . . . Emma Edmondson . . . Isaac and Betsy's daughter."

Shocked at her claim, James took a quick step back.

"That's not possible!" Vezey shook his head in disbelief, then quickly looked around to see if anyone was watching. "Is this some sort of joke? Did the men put you up to this?"

"I am dead serious, James, and I realize that this may shock you, but I am truly Emma and I can prove it."

Franklin quickly unbuttoned his shirt as Vezey took two additional steps back still not comprehending the situation. "What are you doing?" He stared as Emma removed her shirt and unwrapped the binding that concealed her breasts. She stood facing him naked from the waist up clutching Betsy's handkerchief in her hand.

"Do you recognize this James?" She thrust the crimson cloth in front of her. "It belonged to my mother and as God is my witness, I swear I am who I claim to be. I am the same young girl who vowed her love to you not so long ago inside my father's barn. Do you remember that night, James? I begged you to save me from my father and his contract with the devil, but you left me to be sold off for a handful of livestock!"

"No, Emma, you're wrong," James finally understood as his words tumbled over each other. "I went straight to your father the very next morning. I had a plan. I wanted to walk away from New Brunswick, start a new life somewhere else . . . take care of you and my mother. I offered Isaac my entire farm for your hand, Emma, but he wouldn't accept it. He told me that he'd rather see you dead than married to me, but I still didn't give up. I came for you the night before the wedding, but you were already gone. Mother died shortly after, so I sold the farm and went looking for you."

"What?" was all Emma could muster.

"After my mother's funeral, I begged your mother to tell me where you were, and she finally gave me her friend's address in Salisbury. I went to the hat shop, but the woman there had no idea where you'd gone to. My God, Emma." He embraced her. "I thought I'd lost you forever."

"But I had to flee New Brunswick." Emma's old resentment toward James began to lift. "My father was coming to get me, and my only chance at freedom was to fight for it. When I left Salisbury, I took on this new identity . . . someone my father would never find. I've dressed as a man and called myself Franklin Thompson ever since."

Stunned at his good fortune, James held her tightly and kissed her with an urgency that neither of them had felt before. She cried in his arms relieved to finally unburden herself. Together, they fell to the ground as Emma returned his passion and began to undress him. There in the forest, they made love for the first time. Afterward, they lay on their backs, looking up at the stars, nestled against each other.

"So will you keep my secret, James?" Emma asked again, knowing the answer.

"I will take your secret to the grave." He kissed the tip of her nose, making Emma smile. "But we'll have to come up with a story for Jack. He must be wondering where we are by now."

"Let's tell him that we discovered we were old neighbors." She grinned. "And that we lost track of time reminiscing about farm life in New Brunswick."

"That wouldn't be far from the truth," James agreed. "We'll just make sure to leave out the part about your real name . . . and this." He caressed her nude body.

Emma closed her eyes, relishing the moment. She had traveled a very long road from Magaguadavic, but here at last, for the first time in her life, she was truly happy to be a woman.

•••••

It was 1862 and Franklin's regiment was still stationed outside Yorktown, Virginia. Franklin kept busy nursing soldiers in their makeshift field hospital and continued to ride the mail, despite the many difficulties in being a young woman inhabiting men's clothing. Her monthly cycle certainly complicated things and during that time she found it necessary to rise well before dawn. This gave her the privacy to bathe naked in the river and dispose of the blood covered bandages from her menstruation. She would dig a hole to hide the evidence of her womanhood, put on clean underwear, and rewrap her breasts in order to maintain her masculinity.

The downtime from battle also allowed Emma and James a chance to deepen their relationship through carefully planned, but clandestine meetings. They, of course, always took precautions to prevent an unwanted pregnancy. In between their sequestered physical encounters, the couple made sure to avoid each other at camp, lest they give away the sweet secret they worked so hard to keep—afraid that the men would notice how they looked at each other.

Late one night, while Emma and James lay under the stars, they dreamed of a future life together. "As soon as this awful war is over, we'll get married and buy a little farm of our own in Michigan," James proffered. "We'll start a family. I'd like three children . . . maybe more. What do you say, Emma?"

"Our own place, our own farm, and our own family." She smiled. "I say that sounds like heaven."

"Then you must stop this charade, "James warned. "Go back to Michigan now and let the men take care of the war. It's far too dangerous here for a woman, and I couldn't bear to lose you again."

"And you know I feel the same about you." She sat up next to him. "But I would never ask you to desert your post and you must never again ask me to desert mine. It wouldn't be right. The men need me. Besides, I always told my mother that angels watch over me. I believe it now more than ever. After all, they led me down this path where I found you, and we've been apart so long I couldn't bear to be away from you again. I plan on staying right where I am and there will be no changing my mind about that."

"Stubborn and headstrong as always." James kissed her forehead. "And I can't say I like the idea, Emma, but if you insist on staying, I promise you this . . . I'll not leave your fate to the angels. I will do whatever it takes to keep you safe myself."

•••••

Several days later, Franklin rode into camp, lugging a full mailbag. Despite the early hour, the place was deserted, but the sounds of a nearby skirmish could be heard. He quickly secured his horse and the mail, then grabbed his gear before rushing toward the din. Upon seeing Franklin, several wounded soldiers called for help. As he knelt to aid the nearest fallen man, he heard rustling a few feet away. Looking up, Franklin found a Rebel soldier leveling a gun squarely at him. Frozen and awaiting certain death, Franklin's eye caught James as he pointed his gun at the marksman. Franklin's sideways glance tipped off the Rebel who then took aim at James.

Both men fired simultaneously. The marksman dropped with a bullet hole just above his right eye, and James fell backward, having taken a bullet in the chest. Without thinking, Franklin left the man he was tending and rushed to James. It was Franklin, the medic, who tightly applied pressure to James's chest, in a futile effort to stop the spurting blood, but it was Emma who cradled the dying man she loved in her arms. James couldn't speak, but his eyes remained focused on his inconsolable lover. Emma watched, helpless, as the life fled from James's eyes and he gasped his last breath in her arms.

Emma dragged him from the field and placed his body beneath a giant oak tree—out of view of the battle. Kneeling next to him,

Emma's feminine emotions surfaced, and she wept openly. *"Oh, God! Is this my punishment for deceiving my father and running away from home?"* She kissed James's eyes and nose. *"I'm so sorry, James! This isn't fair! We only just found each other here in the midst of a conflict that is not even ours!"* She pushed back the dark hair from his face. "You saved my life . . . but I couldn't save yours," she whispered. "You are my angel, and I will always love you!" Emma kissed James one last time and then fled into the woods in order to hide the bitter tears of loss that she couldn't control.

That same night, once the conflict quelled, an emotionally distraught Franklin stumbled from the woods, dabbing at his red, swollen eyes with his mother's handkerchief. The worn cloth never failed to remind him of Betsy, and that gave him some measure of comfort. Still in shock from the day's events, however, Franklin never noticed the lone soldier who stood in the shadows. The man quietly observed Franklin's agitated emotional state and the woman's handkerchief that he pressed to his lips. He then watched as Franklin slipped into Mrs. B.'s tent, desperate to confide in someone.

Startled, Mrs. B. looked up from the correspondence she was writing. "I'm so sorry, Frank. The chaplain told me about James."

The young soldier burst into sobs.

"There, there, my child," Mrs. B. tried consoling him with a hug. "Is there anything I can do to help you?"

"I'm sorry to burden you," Franklin choked out the words. "But if I don't confess to someone, I think my heart will stop beating from the pain! You are a friend, and I trust that you will not betray me."

"Of course, Frank, you know that any secret you have is safe with me."

"I am a woman," Emma cried out, unable to say another word.

"Yes, dear, I know," Mrs. B. said softly. "And I also know that you were deeply in love with that fine young soldier whom we laid to rest today."

The shock of her words stopped Emma's tears. "But how did you find out?"

"My child," sighed Mrs. B. "I could tell you were a woman by the measure of compassion you show the men. Only a woman could be that sensitive and caring."

"How long have you known?" Emma wiped her tears with the back of her hand.

"Almost from the beginning." She smiled. "And, in the midst of all these men, I was glad to have you as my friend."

"Who else knows?"

"Just my husband, but there's no need to worry. We've told no one. Besides, we don't even know your real name."

"Emma. My real name is Emma."

"I declare, Frank, I mean, Emma, this is too heavy a burden for you to carry alone. It's time you had a real friend, and I would be honored to have that distinction. Do you want to talk about James?"

Relieved to have a much-needed female ally, Emma collapsed against the chaplain's wife and wept, releasing the pain and misery that filled her heart. "It's all my fault that he's dead. James was try-ing to save me."

"This was not your fault, Emma. We are at war. Death is the chance we all choose to take every day. James knew that."

"But he took a bullet intended for me," sobbed Emma.

"Because he loved you, Emma, and he did exactly what any real man should."

"But we planned a life together—after the war. How do I start over without him? What would you do in my place?"

"Should something happen to the chaplain, I don't know how I would go on, but go on we must. It's what our men would want, and you mustn't let James's death be in vain. You may not realize it now, but you are stronger than you think and you will survive this. First, however, you must take some time to grieve and then you will find your purpose again."

"After all my lies and deceptions," Emma squeezed her friend's hand. "How can you still be so kind to me?"

"Because if I were your age, I might have tried the same fool thing myself."

Outside the tent, the lone soldier lit a cigarette and walked away. The two confidants inside had no idea he had been there listening to their private conversation. For now, he would keep what he learned to himself, but a time would surely come when this titillating bit of information might just serve him well.

•••••

In the wee hours of the morning, when all was still in camp, Emma sneaked from her tent. Under the light of the moon, she visited James's freshly dug grave, which lay at the base of a magnificent pear tree covered with brilliant white blooms. There, she placed a cross, carved with 'James Vezey' in the dirt. "James," she whispered. "I vow to avenge your death, and as God is my witness, we will love again in heaven."

Now that James was gone, Emma was left alone with a deeper sorrow in her heart than she had ever known before. But her grief was soon replaced by anger. This war between the states had now become personal, and the disquieting rage that settled in her bones would drive her to new adventures that even Fanny Campbell could never have imagined.

•••••

Early one morning in the spring of 1862, scouts from the Thirty-Seventh New York regiment entered the Union Camp at Fort Monroe with two Confederate prisoners. The Rebels claimed to be from a Richmond brigade, but they were most likely spies who came to Yorktown looking for Union intelligence. Knowing that they would either be executed or sent to a prison camp, they gave

up information about a Union spy who had recently been captured in the Rebel capital and was about to be hanged.

"It must be Webster," sighed Major Butler when he heard the
news. "He was given orders to infiltrate Richmond. We have lost
an important asset to the United States Secret Service, as well as a
good man. He'll be hard to replace."

Before the war, Timothy Webster was a policeman in New
York City until he met Allen Pinkerton. He then joined Pinkerton's private detective agency in 1856. When the Civil War broke
out, Webster turned Union spy and, during his many missions,
obtained essential documents along with critical information that
aided the Union cause. Unfortunately, he had taken ill in Richmond and was caught. Unable to rescue him or exchange him for
a Confederate spy, Union leaders were devastated to learn of his
imminent execution.

When Franklin heard about Webster's demise, *he wondered if he
might actually be capable of replacing him. Could he act with as much honor to
himself and advantage to the Federal Government like Webster had? The subject
of life and death was immaterial. He had always left that in the hands of his
Creator, feeling assured that he was just as safe in enemy territory as he was with
the Union Army.*

Once his decision was made, he sought out Major Butler. The
two had not spoken privately since Franklin's confession to Mrs. B.
He found the chaplain in his tent, reading his Bible. "Frank!" Butler looked up, closed his 'Good Book,' and smiled. "How are you
doing? Kate tells me you have been troubled lately."

"I'm still mourning." Franklin felt a bit uncomfortable in the
major's presence. "But I was hoping you could help me, sir."

"You know I'll do what I can, Frank. Tell me what's on your
mind."

"Well, sir, I'm feeling restless, and I think I should be doing
more for the war effort. Nursing the sick and delivering the mail is
just not enough for me anymore."

"What is it you would like to do, Frank?"

"I want to be a spy for the Union."

"That would involve immense danger and require vast respon- sibility." The chaplain seemed surprised at Franklin's request. "Should you be captured, it could even be deadly. Look what hap- pened to Webster."

"I've thought long and hard about the disadvantages, but it's a chance I'm willing to take."

"Of course, there is a great need for brave young men willing to infiltrate Confederate lines and spy for the Union, but are you sure about this?"

"I am positive."

"Then, given your circumstances, I think you would be a per- fect candidate for the job."

"Will you help me, sir?" Franklin asked.

"If you'd like, I can write a letter of recommendation to Wash- ington." The major nodded. "Although the thought of you being put in harm's way by my own hand is troubling."

"I can assure you, Major, that the angels watch over me. You will have no cause to regret this, and I give you my word that I will not disappoint the Union Army."

●●●●●

The major and Mrs. B. accompanied Franklin to Union head- quarters in Washington where he was ushered into the presence of Generals George B. McClellan, Samuel P. Heintzelman, and Thomas F. Meagher. During the interview, the generals questioned Franklin's *views of the rebellion and his motives in wishing to volunteer for such a perilous undertaking. He vowed his loyalty to the Union cause and explained how he felt compelled to serve the Federal government in a more vital capacity.* His answers must have pleased the officers, who then asked him to demonstrate his shooting skills. Duly impressed by Franklin's outstanding marksmanship, the generals ordered one final exami- nation—a phrenological assessment.

Phrenology consists of feeling bumps on the head to determine an individual's personality traits. Popular in the 1800s, phrenological examinations were conducted by physicians who were expert at "reading" the size of various parts of the skull, which then related to specific organs. For Franklin, doctors determined *that his organs of furtiveness and aggressiveness were highly developed* and in accordance with the requirements of a successful spy.

While doctors analyzed the bumps on Private Thompson's head, General McClellan met privately with Major Butler. "Your young man appears more than qualified, but I hesitate giving so dangerous a position to such an inexperienced lad."

"I have something I must confess to you, General," admitted Major Butler. "There's something about Private Thompson you do not know."

"And what might that be, Major?"

"Private Thompson is actually a woman."

"That's not possible!" McClellan fell back in his chair. "He may be a bit effeminate, but a woman! I would have known."

"With all due respect, sir"—the Major shrugged—"if SHE was able to fool the entire Union Army, including three generals, don't you have to conclude that HE is more than competent for a position involving subterfuge and espionage?"

"I suppose you're right," McClellan choked a little, still trying to take this news in. "Secrecy and covert behavior obviously come natural to this soldier."

"But now I have betrayed Private Thompson's confidence and I must beg you to keep this matter to yourself, General—for the good of the Union Army."

"Yes, yes, of course." McClellan nodded. "His true identity is as classified as his position in the Secret Service—for the good of the Union Army."

Chapter 12

Becoming Contraband

Franklin's first order as a Secret Service spy was to cross over into enemy lines and procure information about the Confederate troops stationed just outside of Yorktown. He had only three days to come up with a believable disguise. As luck would have it, however, an unexpected event occurred, inspiring him that very night.

After darkness crept upon the Union camp, a rumble of thunder could be heard in the distance. A light drizzle began to fall, accompanied by an occasional lightning strike. Before long, the rain and wind picked up, while the lightning and thunder intensified, turning the gentle shower into a furious storm. In the midst of the tempest, a large group of contraband fugitives approached the Union Picket who was unfortunate enough to draw guard duty during the heavy downpour. The desperate Negroes—men, women, and children—were thoroughly drenched. Their tattered clothes, no better than rags, clung to their damp skin as they shivered in the night. The eldest, a tall black man with no hair, spoke to the Picket on behalf of all. "Please, suh, I beg ye giv's protection an' food."

Uncertain what to do, but touched by their plight, the Picket ordered the group to wait at the line while he obtained permission for them to enter from his superior. "Captain McGuire, sir, there are at least forty slaves at the picket line asking for help." He stood shivering and wet inside McGuire's tent.

"Send them away!" McGuire callously ordered. "There's no help for them here."

"But, sir, if I can be so bold," the Picket tried again. "They are truly in need. Most of them have no shoes and their feet are bleeding. Several are just children."

"Son, its best you remember that we are not running a charitable institution here."

"I know that, sir, but maybe they have some information about the Rebels that can help us. After all they ran away from somewhere or someone."

"Have you questioned them?"

"No, sir, they are in no condition to be interrogated at the moment, but maybe if we give them a good meal and some dry clothes, they'll feel like talking."

"You make a good point." The captain nodded. "Let them in and see to it they get some food and medical attention. Call the medics and Major Butler to tend to them and have old Jack cook up some chow. And get yourself some dry clothes."

Once the travel-weary slaves entered the camp, they fell to their knees, thanking God and the soldiers for their deliverance. Shouts of "Glory to God!" rang through the air, replacing the boom of thunder and the crack of lightning as the storm subsided. The ruckus aroused the curiosity of the soldiers, who rushed from their tents to witness the contraband slaves huddled together praising the Lord in both prayer and song. Franklin, Mrs. B., and Major Butler built a large fire, which the former slaves eagerly gathered around. They then put on a large kettle of coffee, while Jack prepared hardtack and johnnycakes. The exhausted men and woman gratefully accepted the modest meal, making sure their children ate first, and then they prayed yet another word of thanks before filling their own bellies. Afterward, the leader who had first requested entrance to the camp, stood and spoke. *"I tell you, my breddern, dat de good Lord has borne wid dis yere slav'ry long time wid great patience. But now he can't bore it no longer, no how; and he has said to de people ob de North . . . go and tell de slaveholders to let de people go, dat dey may sarve me."*

Many hearts were moved by the man's speech, especially Franklin's. He thought of Fanny Campbell and how she had darkened her skin in an effort to disguise herself as a foreigner. Maybe this might work for him, too. He could disguise himself as a darkie and go behind enemy lines without raising an eyebrow of suspicion. No one paid attention to contrabands or slaves. They were practically invisible. Besides, he had become well-practiced at being a man. Now he just had to master being a Negro man.

"Soldier!" Captain McGuire's gruff voice caught Franklin's ear. "See what you can learn from these contraband slaves. They may have intelligence about the Rebels. When you're done, send them on to Slabtown."

"But, sir"—Franklin thought the officer cold and heartless for sending these distressed people away—"maybe they could be of help to us right here."

"You would do well to remember that these slaves are not our concern, Private," snapped McGuire. "We cannot waste valuable rations feeding them."

With a sigh, Franklin turned his attention to the fugitives who were now settling in for a much-needed rest, while Mrs. B. and the major tended to their torn feet and aching souls. Fascinated, by the tales they had to tell, Franklin immersed himself in their stories of life on the plantations, their break from captivity, and the hardships they faced as runaways. He studied their mannerisms and speech, duly noting their cheerful demeanor in the face of all that suffering. He watched their interaction with one another and discovered a unique comradery that they shared among themselves, which most likely grew from their common misery. They also spoke freely of the Rebel camps they had seen during their flight, giving locations and detailing any activities that they witnessed, hoping to help the Union cause, and ultimately themselves.

By the time daylight peaked over the horizon, the exhausted slaves finally stretched out around the campfire and slept. Franklin left them to meet with Captain McGuire. He informed the officer of all he had garnered from the refugees concerning the troops in

Yorktown and promised to prepare a full report for him that very day.

"You've done well, Private Thompson." McGuire nodded.

"Sir, I'd like to request once again that the slaves remain here with us." Franklin made one last attempt to sway the Captain. "They are more than willing to work, and we could really use the help around here."

"Private, I've given you an order." McGuire glared. "Send a rider to make certain they get to Slabtown as soon as they have had some breakfast. I do not want to see one contraband left in my camp after noon. If I do, someone will pay dearly for his insurrection."

"Yes, sir." Franklin hung his head and left the officer's tent, disheartened by his superior's lack of compassion.

•••••

Two days after the former slaves had been escorted to Slabtown, Franklin sat in his tent in front of a mirror. His reflection was that of a stranger. He had just returned from the barber where his head had been methodically shaved. Now that his hair was gone, he darkened his skin with liquid silver nitrate, careful to completely cover his hands, face and neck. He donned old work clothes then placed a dark, wooly wig on his head, topped by a worn, black hat—all used items he requested and then purchased from a trusted merchant. He loaded a revolver and concealed it in his waist, pulling his shirt and coat over it. He hardly recognized himself, but the real question now was whether his disguise would fool others. Confident in his ability to masquerade as a man, he was unsure if anyone would accept him as a man of color.

Christening himself with the name Cuff, Franklin stepped to the entrance of Mrs. B.'s tent. "Hello der, ma'am. You be needin' any hep wid ur werk today? I'd werk a week fer a nickel."

Mrs. B. looked up from the report she was writing, but did not recognize Franklin in his new disguise. "Are you are willing to work hard?"

"Yes'm!"

"Then I might be able to help you." She led him to Dr. Evan J. Bonine, the Regimental Surgeon, who also knew Franklin from his work in the hospital.

"This here is Cuff, doctor." Mrs. B. nodded toward Franklin. "He tells me he is looking for honest work."

"*Well, Cuff, just how much honest work can you do in a day?*" the doctor asked kindly.

"*Oh, I reckon I kin do heaps o'work. Will you hire me, Massa?*"

"*I may if you can cook.*"

"*Yes, Massa, I kin cook anything I ebber seen.*"

"Well, I think you should start in the kitchen with old Jack. He's a fine cook and an even finer man. You could learn a lot from him."

"Yessuh." Franklin grinned. "I'd be grateful fer da chance."

Mrs. B. then took Franklin to the galley area and introduced him to Jack, who grinned in satisfaction at being the 'boss' over the 'new cook.' He gave his charge the task of baking biscuits. Now feeling quite confident in his new disguise, Franklin used a stick to stir the dough so the coloring wouldn't wear off of his hands. Jack did not approve. "If ya wanna werk in dis kitchen, boy"—he pushed Franklin aside and began to knead the flour mixture with his fists—"ya can't be aferd to git yer hands dirty."

Franklin smiled to himself as he watched Jack prepare supper. The Federal Government's newest spy was finally satisfied that those who knew him well didn't recognize him. Even a man of color accepted him as one of his own. Still, he carried some guilt about deceiving Mrs. B. and felt obliged to tell her who he really was. After polishing Dr. Bonine's boots, he found Mrs. B. folding linen in the hospital's storage area. With no one else nearby, he removed his hat and wig. "Frank?" She blinked in disbelief. "Is that really you?"

"Yes." He grinned sheepishly. "I guess I fooled everyone tonight, but I didn't feel right keeping the truth from you."

"Well, I'll be." She laughed. "You must be preparing for a mission."

"I am." Franklin nodded. "And I'm leaving tonight. Will you keep my secret?"

"Of course I will," she agreed. "But what should I tell Doctor Bonine?"

"Tell him that poor old Cuff was bewitched by a pretty little girl in Slabtown, so he won't be coming back." Franklin's eyes sparkled with mischief.

•••••

After most of the camp had retired, Franklin, with nothing more than his loaded pistol, crossed the outer picket line of the Union Army. By midnight, he was within enemy territory near the Confederate Camp at Yorktown. He had managed to go unnoticed by any sentinel before he laid down on the cold, damp ground without so much as a blanket to keep him warm. His sleep was restless as he repeatedly mulled over his risky situation. In the morning, he would have to face the enemy and hope that his disguise—with the help of his wits—would fool them all. A little luck wouldn't hurt either.

He remained hidden in the woods until dawn broke. It was then that he spotted a group of Negroes carrying hot coffee and provisions to the Rebel pickets. He quickly made their acquaintance and was rewarded with a piece of cornbread and a hot cup of coffee laced with a nip of whiskey. Normally, darkies were allowed a moderate ration of spirits, but rarely were they given meat or coffee. Franklin considered this a good omen. He was grateful for the alcohol that warmed his chilled bones and calmed his frayed nerves.

Franklin, as Cuff, blended right in with these men who had been conscripted by the Confederates to help build their fortifications.

Thanks to the contraband slaves he had met, he understood their plight, as well as their nearly invisible presence to the soldiers. He easily fell into step with them marching to Yorktown, without raising any suspicion. Once at camp, he was given a pickaxe, shovel, and wheelbarrow before setting to work next to his companions in bondage. He labored alongside them, hauling building materials near the Rebel camp constructing the breastwork, or low wall that served as cover during battle. It was arduous work, even for the strongest man, but for Franklin, it was grueling. At the end of the day his hands were covered in blisters, his feet ached, and his back throbbed, but that did not deter him from his mission. He kept his eyes and ears open, learning all he could about the camp, the troops, their munitions, and their military plans.

In the evening, he was free to amble around the fort where he took meticulous notes on scraps of paper, carefully sketching what he saw when no one was looking. Afterward, he hid the papers in the soles of his shoes. He also witnessed the arrival of that same one-eyed peddler, who regularly visited the Union camp. Franklin recognized him by his black eyepatch. He watched as the peddler and the Confederate Officers huddled together, whispering among themselves. Franklin moved closer so he could hear their conversation and watched as the peddler used a stick in the dirt to draw the location of the Union Army encampment.

"There must be a good thousand of 'em," the one-eyed peddler offered. He even brought out a map. "And this here gives McClellan's exact position. I told ya I'd get ya what ya wanted. Now, let's see those gold coins ya promised me." The captain handed a small brown sac to the peddler-turned-Rebel-spy, who pulled out a gold coin and bit it with a satisfied smile.

•••••

The next morning, Franklin, still wearing Cuff's clothes, remained exhausted from the previous day's efforts. Nonetheless, he once again joined the contraband work-detail. Hoping to find less taxing labor, he approached an older darkie who sat beneath a tree cleaning and polishing rifles.

"You need hep wid dat?" Franklin asked.

"Yes, sonny, clean de mud off'n dos rifles fur me," the elderly man ordered. He then motioned for Franklin to take a seat on the ground next to a pail of water. Franklin carefully washed the mud from the weapons and lay them in front of the old man who in turn polished them as he sang some old spirituals. Franklin found comfort in the songs and the man's deep, melodic voice. So carried away by the hymns, he didn't even notice that the more he dipped his hands in the water, the more the silver nitrate washed away. Franklin's temporary boss, however, was observant, and he suddenly stopped singing. "Sonny, I does believe yur turnin' white."

"Yes'um, my mammy was white so I always figerred that I'd turn white one day too," Franklin joked nervously.

The old black man gave a good-natured laugh, then grew serious. "You knowed what I tink? I do believe dat you sur is a spy for the uder side."

Unsure of what to say, Franklin's stomach knotted as a trickle of sweat rolled down the side of his face. Then the old man winked. "Relax, sonny, I assure you dat we be on de same side. If'n anyting gives ya way, it'll be dat white skin. My only intrest be helpin' Father Abraham and de Union cause. You see, I's a spy, too." He looked around to make sure no one was watching before unbuttoning his shirt. Franklin recoiled when he saw the gruesome scars that this man carried on his back.

"Cat-haulin'," he explained. "Dis be de work of de soudern man. He aint no broder to me. I'd go to my grave gladly only ta see da day dat de black man be free." He leaned in closer to Franklin. "Now do somting 'bout dat skin o' yours."

•••••

On his third day in the enemy's camp, Franklin realized what he really needed was information only the officers would have. In an effort to mingle among the camp's superiors, Franklin resorted to bribery. He offered a young water-boy a coin in exchange for his pail. Franklin then walked through camp, doling out water to the men—always careful to keep his hands dry. His status as a slave made him a nonentity to the Rebel soldiers as they discussed the upcoming battle as if he weren't there. He ascertained their numbers, from where they had come, as well as their plan to evacuate Yorktown. By day's end, Franklin returned the water bucket to its rightful owner and rejoined the black men, who were packing up goods.

"Where we be go'n?" Franklin asked one of the younger boys.

"We been ordered to take dis food to a post a few miles from here." The youngster's dark eyes seemed older than his years. "You comin'?"

"I gis I can go wid you an' help." Franklin shrugged.

Franklin followed the group as they walked to another Rebel post. One Confederate soldier working with the detail of Contraband singled out Franklin by spitting at his feet. "You there, darkie! Walk the line until someone comes to relieve you. A goddamned Yankee done killed our picket!"

Franklin obeyed without a word and remained at his assigned post until nightfall. Under a moonless sky, he looked around to be sure no one could see him and then ran from the picket line into the woods.

Just before dawn, Franklin reached the Union camp and slipped inside unnoticed. He went directly to his tent and removed his disguise—scrubbing the silver nitrate from his skin. He donned his uniform before reporting directly to General McClellan's tent. With traces of stain still lingering on his face and hands, Franklin stood at attention in front of Little Mac. He reported all that he had learned behind Confederate lines. He gave the general his drawings and notes on the enemy's positions. He even described the peddler/Rebel spy that he had encountered.

"Well done, young man." McClellan smiled, impressed by the intelligence Franklin had uncovered during his maiden mission.

"The Federal Government is grateful for the valuable information you have obtained. I can assure you that another assignment will be forthcoming, Private Thompson. For now, return to your post and carry on with your duties until you hear from us."

Chapter 13

An Admirable Rebel

In early May, 1862, following the Confederate retreat from Yorktown, Brigadier General Joseph 'Fighting Joe' Hooker faced the Confederates near Williamsburg. Hooker, hoping to ultimately capture Richmond, unsuccessfully attacked Fort Magruder—the thirty-foot high earthen fortification strategically located between Yorktown and Williamsburg. Confederate Major General James Longstreet fought hard launching counterattacks, which threatened to overtake the Union flank until Brigadier General Philip Kearny's division arrived to strengthen the Union position. With more than seventy thousand men wearing both blue and gray on the field, the Battle of Williamsburg, also known as the Battle of Fort Magruder, would prove to be a gruesome conflict.

Franklin's regiment was one of many in attendance on that rain-soaked battlefield saturated with mud and blood. It had been a long day with unrelenting cannonade echoing between the ranks. By late afternoon, the wounded lay fallen among the dead as far as the eye could see. The men, who were still breathing, moaned and begged for help from the medics, or pleaded with a merciful God to take them quickly. During a lull in the fighting, the exhausted medical team, including Franklin, searched for wounded men, placing them on stretchers and carrying them one by one from the field to a makeshift hospital tent.

As Franklin and another soldier laid one unconscious man on the ground underneath the canvas, he checked the man's right arm, which hung bloody and lifeless. Franklin gave the surgeon an imperceptible shake of his head knowing full well what was to come.

"At least this one isn't awake," the doctor sighed as he began to saw at the man's arm as if he were a butcher carving away unwanted fat and bone. "Makes it easier on all of us."

Once removed, he haphazardly tossed the useless limb onto a blood-stained pile of carnage. By now, Franklin was numb to the grisly sight. He shivered from exhaustion and the fact that he was soaked to the bone by the cold rain. His grimy clothes were caked with a crusty mud-blood mixture. There was no time to reflect upon the repulsive situation, and he forced himself to press on, returning to the battlefield and tending more wounded.

The sound of a musket ball soaring past made Franklin look up. Under the cloudy sky, he spotted Captain Morse speaking with Colonel Poe near the front line just as the ball struck his friend from Flint in the knee. He watched in disbelief as Morse fell to the ground, wrenched in pain. Franklin, along with three other soldiers, rushed to assist him and remove him from the field.

"Just carry me out of range of the guns and leave me!" Morse ordered as they placed him on the stretcher. "There are many others worse off than I am!"

"I'll not abandon you, sir!" Franklin insisted. "Even if you order me to. I will personally see you safely aboard the hospital transport vessel. Mrs. Morse would want that."

Against his orders, they placed Morse inside an ambulance wagon and Franklin climbed in to tend to his leg. The other three followed the ambulance on horseback as it made its way along the mud-soaked road to the hospital ship.

"There are other men who need a nurse more than I do, Frank," Morse tried again.

Franklin ignored his pleas as he dressed the wound. About five miles from the Williamsburg Landing where the *U.S.S. Commodore* waited, the ambulance jolted over a deep rut and lost a wheel.

Franklin and the other soldiers carefully removed Morse from the wagon and carried their captain via stretcher the rest of the way to the ship. Despite Morse's continued protests, Franklin remained by his side until he was hoisted safely aboard the *Commodore*.

"Where will you take him?" Franklin called up to the soldiers on deck.

"Back to Fort Monroe," one answered.

"Go on now, Frank." Morse waved. "There's nothing more you can do for me. I'll be fine. You need to take care of the men who really need you."

Franklin gave the captain a silent salute, grateful that the injury wasn't more serious.

The Battle of Williamsburg claimed almost three thousand Union casualties while the Confederates numbered over sixteen hundred. Even though the Rebels retreated, there were no clear-cut winners and one of the Civil War's bloodiest encounters was considered indecisive.

•••••

After several straight days of heavy rain, Franklin's troop was sent ahead to the Chickahominy River to repair bridges that had been destroyed by the Confederates in an effort to prevent Union forces from crossing. Franklin and his troop worked along the shore of the rain-swollen river, whose raging current overflowed its banks. Before his work was done, however, Franklin received new orders from the Secret Service.

Within days, Franklin perfected his latest disguise—an old, Irish peddler woman, complete with gray wig, white apron, and faded green bonnet. He studied this unfamiliar reflection in the mirror until he was satisfied that his newest cover might just be believable. "Rebels . . . meet Bridget O'Shea," he said to his image with confidence and a thick Irish accent. He then slipped Betsy's handkerchief in the pocket of his apron. After all, it had come from Ireland and might add to Bridget's authenticity.

After gathering a basketful of household items, Franklin strapped the pack on his back before mounting his horse and heading to the rough waters of the Chickahominy. An expert rider, Franklin spurred his horse into the white-foamed rapids without fear. Midway, however, the rough current became even stronger, causing his horse to panic. Realizing that the animal would never make it across, Franklin reluctantly slid from the saddle and sent him back to the shore from which they'd come. He watched as the horse struggled toward the bank, knowing that the creature would most likely return straight to camp.

Now on his own, he fought the turbulent current doing his best to reach the opposite shore. He had always been a strong swimmer, but the heavy basket secured to his back, was cumbersome and the waters rapidly swept him downstream. The current pulled him under more than once, but each time, he struggled back to the surface. Catching his breath, he fought hard against the tug of the violent waters until he finally managed to reach the opposite shore, where he collapsed, exhausted.

Franklin wasn't sure how much time had passed before he came to his senses and found himself deep in the middle of a murky swamp. He tried to gain his bearings, but couldn't due to the overcast sky and lack of sun. He was soaked through and the heavy load on his back made traversing the thick marshland difficult. In desperate need of rest, he clambered to the highest ground he could find and removed the pack from his back before slumping against a large tree. Unfortunately, the patchwork quilt and extra clothing he had brought were drenched and would provide no relief from the dampness. The night brought no comfort as he alternately shivered and sweated, racked by chills and high fever.

In the early hours of the morning, Franklin was startled from his sleep by thunderous cannon-fire and whistling shells, which penetrated the swamp along with the sunlight. He was too weak to stand so he scavenged through the food in his basket, but all had been ruined by the river. As day turned to night and then again to day, he lay helpless in the swamp, his body fighting fever, which at times led him to delirium. *He hadn't bargained on a severe attack of malaria or swamp fever as the men called it* and was ill-prepared to handle it. There was nothing to be done, but to let the ague run its course and hope for the best. *For three days, he battled unbearable pain and fever, before finding enough strength to drag* himself from his stupor.

Franklin slowly found his footing on shaky legs and stumbled through the swamp. Dry, yet still shivering, despite the dead summer heat, he remained disoriented until the cannon-fire recommenced. Letting the sound guide him, Franklin walked toward the battle, hoping to find help. Instead, he chanced upon a small white farmhouse with a smokeless chimney and assumed the place was deserted.

Franklin cautiously entered the house. As his eyes adjusted to the dim light, he discovered a Confederate soldier lying on the floor. The man looked to be about thirty. Tall and thin, he wore no jacket to signify his rank. His breathing was labored, but Franklin could see no visible wounds. He noted a plain gold ring on the stricken man's right hand—not a wedding ring, but perhaps a memento of happier times.

"Don't be alarmed, sir." Franklin donned his thick Irish accent. "I'm a harmless old lady. My name's Bridget O'Shea. Do ye have a name, soldier?"

"Allen Hall," the prone man whispered.

"Are ye ill, Allen Hall?"

"I came down with typhoid fever weeks ago, but was sent back to fight with General Stoneman at Cold Harbor before I had a chance to recover."

"How might I be of help to ye?" Franklin's compassion took over despite the Rebel uniform, and he was energized by the fact that someone needed him, even though he was most likely as sick as his newest patient.

"Water . . . food. I haven't eaten for days."

"Maybe whoever lived here left something in the kitchen. I'll have a look around."

Even though he was weak, Franklin built a fire and prepared a meal with the supplies he found in the pantry. He placed cornmeal and water along with some salt-pork in a pan over the fire, as well as a pot of water for tea. When all was ready, Franklin sat on the floor next to Hall and fed him with the same tenderness he would have shown his own men.

"Thank you for your kindness, ma'am." Hall smiled weakly. "You have taken such good care of me even though I can see you are plainly sick yourself."

"No worries for me, sir. I am quite all right, I am." Franklin maintained his Irish brogue noting the man's somber, hazel eyes and thick dark hair. He was handsome—even for a Rebel. *Sickness and disease somehow removed all prejudice and although he was the enemy, Franklin saw him only as a man in pain.*

Finally relaxed, the soldier fell into a sound sleep. Only then did Franklin tend to himself—eating, washing, touching up his disguise, and resting, but always remaining on guard in case his patient called for help. When Hall awoke, Franklin once again put aside his own needs to take care of him. He gently wiped the man's brow with a wet rag to cool his fever and held his hand so he wouldn't feel alone. As the day progressed and the man's color waned, Franklin realized the end was near. As many times as he had tended to dying men, he had never felt so disturbed by the fact that he was about to lose another patient. Something about this man intrigued him. "Tell me Allen, are you a Soldier of the Cross?"

"Yes, thank God. I have fought longer under the Lord than I have under Jeff Davis."

"How then can you, as a disciple of Christ, fight for such an inhumane institution like slavery?"

"Ah, Bridget, you have touched upon a point for which my own heart condemns me." Hall fixed his mournful eyes on Franklin. "Pray with me, please?"

"Of course, my dear." Franklin took his hand and caught up in the moment forgot to use his Irish brogue. "Oh Lord, have grace and give mercy to sustain this man in this trying hour and to bring about the triumph of truth and right. Give him strength and grant him peace for he knows he has sinned and wishes your forgiveness."

"Please, tell me who you really are." Hall looked directly into Franklin's eyes.

"That I cannot do, sir." Franklin ached to tell him the truth but knew that he mustn't.

"But I won't betray you, for I shall very soon be standing before God."

"My story is a long one, Allen, but I promise that if you become stronger, I will tell you everything."

"We both know that I will not be getting any stronger," Hall whispered with a smile. "But regardless of your name, I believe you are an angel sent by the Lord to ease my burden and comfort me in my final hour."

Franklin found himself overwhelmed with emotion and sorrow for this man who just a few days ago would have been his foe. Unexpected emotions like the ones he had felt upon James's death flooded over him, causing his eyes to fill with tears. He checked Hall's pulse and frowned.

"Am I dying?"

"Yes, my friend, I believe you are. Is your peace made with God?"

"My trust is with Christ thanks to you, but I do have one last request."

"If it's something I can do, Allen, I assure you, I will."

"If you ever pass through the Confederate camp between here and Richmond, look for Major Joseph McKee and give him the gold watch that is in my pocket. He will know what to do with it and please tell him I died happy and peacefully in a good woman's care."

"I give you my word, I shall find your major and personally deliver your watch."

Hall took the gold ring from his finger and placed it in Franklin's left hand. "Keep this ring to remember me by, Bridget. It's important to me that you don't forget our brief time together. I know I won't . . . wherever I am going." He seemed at peace and folded his hands together as if in prayer. He tried in vain to raise his head, and Franklin cradled him like a babe in arms rocking him back and forth. Within moments, he ceased to breathe, yet Franklin held Hall's body close and wept for all that had been lost before and during this terrible conflict.

After his tears were finally spent, Franklin gently closed Hall's eyes, folded his arms across his chest, and drew a blanket up to his chin before lying next to the body. The dim light flickered around the curve of Hall's jaw and a distinct peace settled over the room. This man's suffering was over, and Franklin imagined *that there were happy spirits hovering around his lifeless form.* Oddly enough, *he welcomed this brief respite away from the tumult of war, where he found unexpected tranquility in the* peaceful *presence of the angel of death,* if only for a little while.

In the morning, Franklin arose, cut a lock of Hall's hair and slipped it into his pocket. He took the gold watch from the dead man's pocket, as well as a small packet of letters. Franklin kissed Hall's forehead and then reverently covered his face with the blanket. Afterward, he packed his basket with additional house goods that he thought the Rebel soldiers might buy, as well as the remaining food from the kitchen.

Before leaving, Franklin adjusted his disguise and sprinkled pepper on Betsy's handkerchief, which he then put it in his pocket. Lastly, he donned a pair of green-rimmed glasses that he had found on a dresser in the main bedroom. Satisfied with the results, he said a final farewell to Hall before heading toward the Confederate camp.

As he neared the Rebel encampment, the picket on duty came into view. Franklin reached in his pocket for the pepper-laced cloth. Remembering Hall's ring, he removed it from his finger in case anyone should recognize it and then, as a peaceful gesture to the picket, he waved the handkerchief before rubbing it under his eyes causing them to water.

The Confederate picket turned out to be a friendly Englishman with an immense, jolly presence, a heavy British accent, and merry blue eyes. "And what might be your business, ma'am?"

"I'm here to sell my wares," replied Franklin in his best Irish accent, knowing that if anyone could detect a fraudulent brogue it would be an Englishman. "I've been walking for days without much to eat. Trying my best to avoid those damn Yankees, you know!"

"Ah, a foreigner like myself." The picket smiled broadly. "You may pass freely, my good woman. Just don't be staying here too long. One of our spies says the Yankees have nearly finished their bridges and intend to attack us within a day."

"You don't say!"

"That's right, dearie, but don't you worry. Jackson and Lee are ready for them. You see those masked batteries they prepared?" He pointed toward a brush heap by the roadside. "That will give those Yankees more trouble than they can handle if they come this way. You haven't seen any Yanks, have you?"

"No, sir, and I hope not to." Franklin took silent note of the batteries. "I want no trouble. My husband is sick, and I need to get home to him as soon as I can."

"I wish I was home with my good wife and children," the Picket sighed wistfully. "The Confederacy might go to hell for all I care. Englishmen have no business here."

"Nor do old Irish women." Franklin once again dabbed at his eyes with the handkerchief. "I only wish they were all home with their families. It's us women, mothers and wives, who are heartbroken over this unnatural war. Thank you, sir, for your kindness. I'll take care of my business and be on my way before long."

Franklin walked through the camp mostly unnoticed, listening to the soldiers as they discussed the impending attack on the Union Army. After one Rebel made a purchase, Franklin asked where he might find Major McKee.

"Normally, over there, ma'am." The soldier pointed to a modest field tent. "But the major has gone to set a trap for those devil Yankees. He should return soon."

With imminent danger in store for the Union Army, Franklin knew he must report back to his superiors quickly, but he was first bound by his word to locate

Major McKee and fulfill Allen Hall's final wishes. Most importantly, he knew he must find some real food. His bout of malaria and lack of nutrition had left him weak. Franklin spotted a shanty where a tall, thin Negro woman was cooking meat, and he approached her. "I'm so hungry. Is there any chance you might spare some food for a starving old lady?"

"Oh my, yes, honey. We got plenty o' meat an' bread, but we ain't got no salt."

"Never mind that, dearie. It could taste like an old shoe and I'd feel like I might be eating a king's feast right about now." Franklin smiled broadly as the woman handed him a generous plate.

The Negress looked pleased as she watched the old peddler woman devour the food. "Goodness, honey . . . 'pears you aint had a real meal in a coon's age."

•••••

Franklin used the afternoon to gather intelligence until he saw a tall, middle-aged man enter Major McKee's tent. Franklin followed him, but waited a few moments before entering. After taking a breath, he swept through the flaps with confidence, as if he were an aide reporting to his commanding officer.

"Might ye be the brave Major McKee, sir?" he asked with a deep, Irish curtsy.

"I'm afraid I'm pressed for time today, madam." The officer barely looked up, distracted by the map laid out on his camp desk. "What is it that you need and hurry up with it!"

"I have a message from Allen Hall."

"Allen?" Startled, McKee looked up, now giving the old peddler woman his full attention. "Where is he? Have you seen him?"

"That I have, sir, but I'm afraid I must deliver bad news. Your friend died of the fever last night in a farmhouse down the road."

"Good God, no!" McKee was visibly shaken.

"I'm afraid it is the honest truth, sir."

"Was he alone?"

"No, I was with him, and a fine man he was. I tried to give him comfort as best I could before the Lord called him home." Franklin reached into his apron pockets and handed over Hall's watch and letters. "He asked me to give you these."

At the sight of the gold watch, the Major covered his face with his hands and sobbed.

"It's all right, sir." Franklin patted McKee's shoulder while fighting back his own tears that seemed to spring forth without the aid of pepper. "I'm sure Allen would not want you to mourn like this."

"You're a good woman, my dear." The major tried to compose himself, but his breath came in short gasps. "And you shall be rewarded for your kindness. Can you show my men where the body is? There's a ten-dollar bill in it for your trouble."

"Yes, of course, sir, but I cannot take the money."

"But why would a poor peddler woman like you refuse payment?" McKee grew suspicious.

"Because the Lord would frown upon it," Franklin wailed in an effort to cover his mistake with dramatics. "Please forgive me, Major! It's not that I don't appreciate your generosity, but my conscience would never give me peace in this world or the next if I took money for carrying out that sweet boy's final wish. God rest his holy soul!"

"Very well, then." The major accepted this reasoning. "Wait here."

McKee left the tent, giving Franklin a brief opportunity to look around. *It was the first time he had ever experienced any pangs of guilt about spying on the enemy.* Nevertheless, his attention quickly focused on the map that the major had been studying. Franklin was surprised to find that it marked the exact locations of the Confederate traps that McKee's troops had set that very afternoon. He did his best to memorize the details. It was now more urgent than ever that he report back as soon as possible.

Just as Franklin was taking a final look around, McKee returned and summoned the peddler outside. "I have a detail of men who are prepared to follow you to the farmhouse and bring back Captain Hall's body."

"Sir, if I could please, might I trouble you for a horse?" Franklin knew he could travel faster that way. "I have been quite ill myself and do not feel as if I can walk that distance again."

The major didn't answer, but turned to his men. "Saddle a horse for your guide."

Franklin gave McKee a broad smile and a grateful curtsy.

As the group approached the little farmhouse, with Franklin leading atop his mount, the sergeant in charge spoke to their guide. "Madam, would you ride down the road a little way, and if you see or hear anything of the Yankees, come back as fast as you can to warn us?"

"Of course, sir." Franklin smiled, pleased with his stroke of good luck. "I just hope I don't run into any of those ruthless killers. I don't believe they would show mercy to an old woman like me." He turned his horse and continued riding slowly down the road until he was well out of sight.

Not seeing or hearing anything of the Yankees, Franklin thought it best to keep on in that direction until he did. It was like the colorful Zouave from New York, who after the battle of Bull Run, said he was ordered to retreat, but never ordered to halt so he kept on going until he was home. And Franklin was grateful for the trusty steed that the Major had given him. He decided then and there to call the animal Reb. Franklin rode hard through the night until he reached the swollen river, pushing Reb across. His new mount was amazingly strong and easily spanned the river's rough current without fear or hesitation.

Franklin rode straight into camp, not stopping until he reached the commanding officer's tent. Still dressed like O'Shea, he entered to find the one-armed General Philip Kearny writing at his desk. Remembering his disguise, Franklin quickly removed his wig and bonnet causing Kearny a moment of confusion.

"Private Thompson reporting from the Rebel camp, sir! I have first-hand intelligence regarding the Confederate Army."

The general stood in astonishment as Franklin described all that he had learned. He even sketched a detailed map of the entrapments built by the Rebels. Kearny must have been impressed because later that same day, Franklin was assigned to be his aide and carry out his every order—both on and off the battlefield.

•••••

The heavy rains continued flooding the area even more. The dousing prevented the battle from starting, since neither army could safely ford the river. The swamp turned into lakes, and the swollen river remained a raging torrent. *Had it not been for McClellan's faith in God's covenant with Noah, he would no doubt have contemplated building an ark in order to save himself and his army from destruction.*

Chapter 14

Aiding General Kearny

By May 31, 1862, the weather began to clear. That morning, Little Mac stayed in bed with the ague while the Army of the Potomac remained divided by the overflowing Chickahominy River. The Confederates planned to take full advantage of what they perceived as their enemies' reduced force. The nearby Battle of Hanover Courthouse had just been fought four days before, resulting in a Federal victory. Now, General McClellan wanted Father Abraham to send reinforcements so that he would be fully equipped to take the Confederate capital at Richmond, about fifteen miles away. President Lincoln, however, was growing rather impatient with McClellan's slow pace.

In the midst of the overwhelming state of things, the Confederates led by General Joseph E. Johnston, attacked McClellan's troops in the early afternoon, rousing Little Mac from his bed. They believed that the geographical split of the Union troops would ensure an easy victory in what would later be known as the Battle of Fair Oaks or the Battle of Seven Pines. For three hours, the Rebels relentlessly assaulted their foe along a wide battlefield that alternated between wooded areas, open fields, and wet marshes.

Franklin, in military uniform and reunited with Reb, was now acting as orderly to General Kearny amid bursting shells and airborne bullets. Realizing the gravity of the situation, the general pulled an envelope from his pocket and scrawled, "In the name of God bring your command to our relief, if you have to swim in order to get here . . . or we are lost."

He ordered Franklin to carry the note directly to General Grant as quickly as possible. Kearny watched Franklin gallop off, duly impressed once more by the young man's bravery. Rushing along mud-soaked roads that were nearly impassable due to the recent heavy rains, Reb's mouth was white with foam. Nevertheless, Franklin relentlessly spurred him into the fast-flowing river. Upon reaching the other side, he quickly located the Union forces, who were already approaching, to find General Grant in the lead. Franklin handed Grant the note. "From General Kearny, sir! It's urgent!"

Directly after reading Kearny's words, Grant shouted his orders. "Secure the Grapevine Bridge so that our troops can cross! Our boys on the other side need help now! There's no time to waste!" Immediately, engineers began to secure the swaying bridge as many anxious soldiers started across the turbulent river on foot. The weakened bridge tottered as supports were placed beneath it, but miraculously it held.

Amid all of the activity, Franklin was eager to return to the battle. "Pardon me, General Grant, but I'd like to be excused so I may let General Kearny know that you are sending reinforcements."

Without a word, General Grant nodded to the private, touched his hat, and then turned to study the precarious bridge. Deciding that entering the river was a safer bet, Franklin spurred Reb to ford the raging waters once again. As he reached the other side, he looked back to see the men somehow making it safely across the unsteady bridge. Riding hard, Franklin located General Kearny on the field, in the thick of battle under heavy gunfire and artillery. "Sir, General Grant, with his command, is on his way."

Armed with this good news, Kearny turned to his troops and, with his one arm, swung his hat in the air. "Reinforcements! Reinforcements!" he shouted along the line, energizing the exhausted troops with new hope.

"Push forward, men!" Kearny continued hollering as the Union soldiers took on the enemy with renewed strength and vigor. "Reinforcements are nearby! General Grant is coming and he's bringing his boys!"

During that celebratory moment, Maine's General Oliver Otis Howard was hit in the right arm by a Minie ball. Franklin saw him fall from his horse and requested Kearny's permission to tend the wounded officer. With Kearny's approval, Franklin rode to Howard's side, dismounted Reb, and tore away the sleeve from the general's arm. The injury was severe, and Franklin knew that the limb would mostly likely be amputated, but in the meantime, it was critical to stop the bleeding. As he stood to get bandages from his saddlebag, the unpredictable Reb turned and bit him hard on his upper left arm, leaving his torn flesh hanging. Instinctively, Franklin pulled away, but Reb wasn't through with him just yet. The horse then kicked him in the side, throwing him several feet. Now the medic was also badly wounded. His swollen arm was bleeding and his rib cage throbbed, leaving him unable to assist Howard any further.

"Leave him!" Kearny rode by, shouting to Franklin. "Get to the old sawmill at White Oak Swamp. Tell every able-bodied man there to grab their weapons and get back to the field immediately."

"But General Howard needs a surgeon, sir." Franklin swayed on shaky feet.

"I assure you that General Howard will be taken care of! Now go take care of yourself and be sure to send more men to the front or we will all need surgeons—or shrouds!"

Doubled over on Reb, Franklin rode toward the sawmill, still bleeding from his arm. There, he discovered many injured men who had crawled to safety from the battlefield. As he gave the available men their orders to head to the frontline, Franklin realized that there was no one left to care for the injured. After wrapping his own arm and making a sling for it, he set to work cleaning, examining, and dressing the other soldiers and their many wounds.

When he ran out of bandages, Franklin walked to a nearby house, hoping to obtain material. The owner, a small man with narrow black eyes, slammed and quickly locked the door in his face. Undaunted, he desperately approached a second house. This time, however, when a wiry old man answered, Franklin pulled his pistol from his belt with his undamaged hand. "Sir, I need anything that can be used for bandages . . . cotton sheets, pillowcases, even old clothes if you have any."

Shaking, the thin man tossed a questioning look to his round wife, who stood behind him in the doorway. "I believe I might find something suitable," she answered, then added, "If you are able to pay."

"I can do that, ma'am." Franklin nodded still holding his gun.

The woman disappeared momentarily and returned with an old sheet, four pillowcases, and a bolt of cotton cloth wrapped in a canvas sack. "This will cost you five dollars."

Franklin reached for the goods with his bad arm keeping the pistol steady. Even though it was light, the sack sent a sharp pain clear through to his shoulder, and he was forced to set the package down. Catching his breath, he slowly reached in his pocket and found only three dollars. "I think this will do today, ma'am," he handed over the money. "The Federal Government thanks you for your assistance and your generosity."

Franklin put away his pistol, picked up the sack, and turned back toward the sawmill, not realizing that all of the activity had caused his arm to bleed again. Feeling dizzy, he sat by the roadside in an effort to steady himself. As he tightly rebound his arm with some of the cotton material he had just garnered, Franklin spotted a Union chaplain riding toward him. Surely, this man of the cloth would help him get back to the sawmill so he could take proper care of his injury as well as the fallen men who languished there. His relief was short-lived, however. Instead of helping Franklin, the chaplain and his horse crossed to the far side of the road, totally ignoring the bloody Union soldier who was in obvious pain. Stunned by the slight, Franklin still gave him the benefit of the doubt. Maybe the chaplain was just in a hurry to assist at the sawmill himself where others needed him more.

Once he was able to stand, Franklin returned to the suffering men, but to his dismay, the chaplain was not there. It seemed, he had gone to a neighboring house, preferring a good meal over tending a good soul. Never mind that war was waging just outside or that Franklin and the other soldiers had not eaten in nearly twenty-four hours. Discouraged by the man's lack of Christian values and commitment to his cause, Franklin ripped bandages and bound wounds with renewed energy despite his own discomfort.

Darkness fell and the battle subsided for the night. Franklin watched the setting sun as it illuminated the crimson carnage dotted with blues and grays. The moans and cries of the wounded mingled with the sounds of nature. Frogs called out to one another with a croak while the eerie hooting of owls accompanied the departing souls to their eternal rest. Franklin wished, that like the woodland animals, he could lose himself to oblivion for just a moment, but that wasn't possible. He drew in a deep breath and then sought out that cavalier chaplain for so many soldiers in his care were dying and in need of God's comfort. As he stepped outside, his ears were greeted by a loud snore. There, on a bed of hay, sound asleep, lay the unsavory chaplain, oblivious to his surroundings. Franklin was so sickened by the sight of him and his lack of ethics it temporarily shook his faith in mankind. Instead of confronting the slacker, however, he walked away in disgust, leaving the man of God to his own Judgement Day when the good Lord would no doubt take him to task for such callous behavior.

It was nearly dawn when Franklin finally returned to camp. Weakened by his long ordeal, injuries, malaria, and lack of food, he collapsed before he could make it to his tent. His fellow soldiers picked him up and carried him to his cot, waking Damon Stewart from his sleep. "Frank, you are burning up." Stewart felt his friend's forehead. "I'll see if I can find a medic."

"I'm fine, I just need sleep," insisted Franklin as he swallowed quinine pills from his pack.

"You don't look so fine, my friend." Damon shook his head.

"Don't worry. I'll be better in the morning." *Franklin knew as well as his insistent comrade that he should check himself into a camp hospital for treatment, but that would mean revealing his secrets*, and that he was not willing to do.

•••••

After a few hours of sleep, a bite of hardtack, and a swig of coffee, Franklin went back to work. General Kearny ordered him to resume his medic duties, and so Franklin cared for the sick and wounded, despite the shivers and shakes that rattled his own body. The morning had brought with it the Sabbath, but that didn't stop the battle from recommencing. Hundreds of injured and dying men were dragged to the enormous 'hospital tree,' as it was called, at Fair Oaks. Under its protective umbrella, Union soldiers were laid side by side on the blood-soaked ground, each waiting their turn for amputations, drugs, or death. Some prayed, some wavered in and out of consciousness, while others begged for food and water. A few even managed a weak 'hurrah' when over the booming sounds of battle bells rang. "Men!" General Kearny called out in encouragement. "We are so close to Richmond we can hear the church bells."

Franklin took advantage of that triumphant moment to speak with the general. "Sir, the men are starving." He pointed to a small wooden structure near the front line, which was still intact. "May I have your permission to see if there's food in that farmhouse?"

"Are you sure you are strong enough to make the trip, son? That house is in the line of fire, and you don't look so well yourself."

"Yes, sir." Franklin nodded with confidence. "I believe I can."

"You continue to amaze me, lad," Kearny gave his approval. "I only wish the Union could claim more like you. Wait for a break in the fighting and then go. Bring whatever you can, but if you feel the risk is too dangerous, turn back. No one will fault you for it."

Franklin waited until late afternoon when both sides temporarily ceased fire. As medics rushed into action to help the wounded off the field and drag the dead away, he left the camp crawling on his side toward the shell-riddled house. He tried not to think about his weakened arm and battered ribs as he struggled to remain unseen by the enemy. When he finally reached the deserted house, he discovered the table set and a pantry full of food. The tenants, it seemed, had left in a hurry. He quickly pulled a large quilt from one of the beds, then filled it with ham, bacon, cornmeal, flour, and jars of canned fruits and vegetables, as well as cans of condensed milk from the pantry. But, just as he was folding up his loot to drag it back to camp, a musket ball whizzed past his head. The Rebels were coming.

Franklin had no choice but to hide the bundle and climb down into the cellar to hide himself. The Confederates searched the house, but found no Union soldiers. To ensure that no Yankees took cover within its walls, they set it on fire, intending to destroy it.

Still in the cellar, Franklin heard the trampling of enemy feet and muffled voices overhead. Although he couldn't make out their words, he knew what the Rebels had done when the smell of smoke reached his nose. He tried to quell his panic, knowing all he could do was wait. To show himself meant certain capture, but to stay hidden could mean certain death.

The minutes dragged on as Franklin listened, his eyes beginning to sting. Once he heard the Rebels leave, he emerged from the cellar only to be greeted by fire and smoke. With one hand covering his mouth and nose, he dropped to the floor and crawled across the room. He located the food-filled quilt and dragged it toward the door. Breathing was difficult and his sore bones ached, but he wasn't about to die inside the burning building when his men needed him most.

After he finally reached the doorway, he poked his head outside and gasped in the fresh air, relieved to find the Rebels gone. Franklin crept from the now blazing structure, back toward camp, pulling his heavy load behind him. He managed about twenty yards when he heard the hissing of burning timber grow louder and then an even louder thud. The ground beneath him trembled as the burned out house collapsed. Cinders and hot ashes rained down all around him. Franklin covered his head as best he could while making sure his precious loot did not catch fire.

When he reached the outskirts of camp, he stood up. It was important to Franklin that he walk inside. He didn't want the men to see him on all fours. The hearty welcome he received from the starving soldiers made him temporarily forget the excruciating pain it had cost him. He took pleasure in the way the wounded men raved over the canned goods and ham. Given the circumstances of war, they were indeed a delicacy.

•••••

That evening, a weary-looking Franklin and Reb stood at attention in front of General Kearny just outside the general's tent.

"Private Thompson, you have served as a valuable asset during this battle. I'd like to commend your brave service to the Union Army and the Federal Government. In appreciation, I offer you this sword, which was struck directly from the hand of a Rebel colonel this very afternoon."

"Thank you, General, I will treasure this weapon all the days of my life and remember the important work that was done here today." Franklin accepted the sword, then added, "Sir, it's an honor serving next to you, and I know your horse was a casualty of war today so I would like to offer you my horse. I call him Reb, since I acquired him from a Rebel major while I was working undercover, though I should warn you that he is a tad unruly and may not be meant for routine use in battle."

"Nonsense!" Kearny approached the animal, not heeding Franklin's warning. "I never met a horse I couldn't handle." The general patted Reb's back, then caressed his limbs as if it were the tamest creature in the world.

"He is a splendid horse, my boy." Kearny smiled broadly. "And worth three hundred dollars of any man's money. All he needs is a little kind treatment and he will be as gentle as a newborn lamb."

"Ahh, sir," Franklin tried, but before he could say more, Reb kicked the General in the backside, sending him sprawling upon the ground. Kearny gathered himself and stood, only to have the pony knock him to the ground once again.

"My boy." Kearny looked up at Franklin. "I believe this horse is tainted with Confederate blood and there may be little hope for him."

Chapter 15

A Hasty Retreat

The Battle of Fair Oaks lasted two long, bloody days. The battleground was painted red as both sides suffered severe losses—790 Union soldiers died with 3,594 wounded, while the Confederates totaled 980 killed and 4,749 injured. The scent of death hung in the air, drawing flies that buzzed around the battered men who clung to life and the inert bodies awaiting burial. Both sides deemed themselves victorious, since there were no definitive winners—only survivors whose memories would burn with that carnage every single day for the rest of their lives.

Confederate General Johnston was seriously injured at dusk that first night. He was briefly replaced by General G. W. Smith, but once all was said and done, the Rebel President, Jefferson Davis, appointed General Robert E. Lee as the man in charge of his troops. The Rebels retreated back to Richmond, and Little Mac chose not to charge the Rebel Capital. Instead, he sent daily dispatches to President Lincoln and Secretary of War Harry Stanton, requesting reinforcements.

Franklin took a one-week leave of absence, hoping to heal his badly bruised side and torn arm. During his respite, he visited various hospitals, first stopping at Williamsburg, where Nellie was stationed. Although her hand was still bandaged, *she was a most faithful nurse and had endeared herself to all the boys by her kindness and patience toward them*. Satisfied that she had kept her word, Franklin continued on to Yorktown where he was pleased to find many of the injured men he had treated on the field now recuperating—some eager to go home and others anxious to return to their troops. Lastly, he visited White House Landing, where Union Army supplies were kept. The pristine country village looked neat and peaceful, seemingly untouched by the butchery that surrounded it of late.

Feeling better and ready to return to camp, Franklin requested transportation for himself and his horse from Colonel Rufus Ingalls, the Union Army's Chief Quartermaster, who was also in charge of the train depot at White House Landing. Once aboard and on his way back to Fair Oaks station, Franklin settled into his seat for what he thought would be a restful ride. Things changed quickly, however, upon their approach to Tunstall's Station, not far down the tracks.

An oncoming train heading toward White House Landing whistled loudly, and sensing trouble, the engineer on the inbound train carrying Franklin quickly switched the locomotive off the track. The distressed oncoming train thundered past with its engineer frantically signaling for Franklin's train to follow.

Both trains returned to White House Landing, where troops had been ordered to protect the depot. It seemed that in an effort to cut off Union supplies, even temporarily, a group of Rebels led by General James Ewell Brown "JEB" Stuart had attacked Tunstall Station and the train that had raced away. Telegraph lines had been cut and even the tracks torn up. While damage was done to the depot and several men killed, only a few aboard the train were injured thanks to the quick-thinking engineer.

Franklin, always eager to help, went to work administering to the wounded. One of them wore a familiar-looking eyepatch and Franklin recognized the man as the peddler/spy he had seen not long ago in the Rebel camp near Yorktown. Once he knew the other men were cared for, Franklin reported the peddler to the provost marshal. A search of his person revealed proof that Franklin was indeed correct and the man was arrested for espionage.

•••••

After the Battle of Seven Pines, Confederate General Robert E. Lee used the next few weeks to reorganize his army and reassess their military situation. At 8:30 a.m., on the twenty-fifth of June, Little Mac decided to make his move in what would later be called the Battle of Oak Grove. This brief but fearsome fight marked the beginning of 'the Seven Days Battle.' It was a relentless encounter that kept the surgeons and nurses so busy they could not attend to all who needed them. By noon, General McClellan rode onto the field with orders to advance. By sunset, over one hundred Union and Confederate soldiers lay dead with almost nine hundred more wounded. The Federal Army claimed victory, but in reality, McClellan had advanced a mere six hundred feet.

The next day, it was Lee who attacked, believing that General Thomas J. 'Stonewall' Jackson was on his way from the Shenandoah Valley with Rebel reinforcements. Unknown to Lee, however, Jackson and his men were running late. This gave Federal troops the advantage and the Union Army fought back with everything they had, resulting in a terrible slaughter of the Confederates. Despite all that, McClellan began to withdraw his troops.

On June 27, 1862, the third of the Seven Days Battle began at Gaines's Mills when Lee went after the Union Army's right flank. Lasting just two days, it was the fiercest fight of all so far waged on the Virginia Peninsula. Between the North and the South, over two thousand were lost and almost ten thousand wounded. Ultimately, the Confederates succeeded in pushing the Union Army back over the Chickahominy River. Little Mac gave orders to burn the bridges and retreat to the James River. As far as the Rebels were concerned, they believed that Richmond was now safe from the enemy.

•••••

As the Union soldiers fell back, Franklin was sent to several nearby hospitals to inform the occupants and staff that the Army of the

Potomac was retreating to the James. All able-bodied patients, doctors, and nurses were ordered to find their way to the river. During his final hospital stop, Franklin recognized four patients— three very young lieutenants and a fair-haired captain. He relayed the orders to evacuate immediately.

"Will an ambulance come to carry wounded and sick soldiers like me?" the captain wanted to know.

"It is unfortunate, sir, but, no. The carriages are busy with those who can't move on their own accord."

"Surely you can't expect me to walk!" the captain snapped. "I have not been well for quite some time, so I believe that you are obligated to leave me your horse."

"Why should you get the horse?" one lieutenant grumbled.

"We are all wounded and in need of a ride," another complained.

"That's right," the third chimed in. "You are trying to pull rank on us, Captain, and we won't stand for it."

"My good men," Franklin spoke up with noticeable irritation in his voice. "With all due respect to each of you and your rank, I have little time for debate. I am expected to report back immediately to verify that this mission has been completed and obtain my next assignment. We are at war here, in case you have forgotten."

"Private, let me remind you that I am the superior officer here." The captain raised his voice. "And, as such, I believe that the Federal Government would agree that my importance to this army far surpasses yours and these three lieutenants combined. If you do not give me your horse so that I might safely ride to meet McClellan at the James, I shall report you, Private . . . Private . . . ?"

"Thompson, sir . . . Franklin Thompson from the Second Michigan Volunteer Infantry, Company F. Be certain you remember that when you relay the story, sir."

"Private! I demand that horse is mine! Now, I order you to dismount and hand it over to me immediately!"

Franklin hesitated for just a moment and then slipped off of the saddle. While the four men watched curiously, he pulled a small paper from his pocket and ripped it into quarters. He then wrote a number on each piece before folding them in half. "Now then," he glared at the Captain. "I will obey your orders and give up my horse, and face the consequences when I return to the Union camp without him."

"I knew you would see my point, son." The captain smiled, reaching for the reins as the three lieutenants groused under their breath.

"Not so fast." Franklin jerked the reins out of the captain's reach. "I've been thinking and I've come to the conclusion that my horse should not benefit just one of you, but all four."

"I don't know what you think you are doing here, Private Thompson," the captain began, but stopped short when Franklin thrust out the four slips of folded paper. "You will each pick one, and the number chosen will be the order in which you will ride," Franklin explained as he allowed the lieutenants to draw first, while the captain rolled his eyes in frustration.

Franklin handed the captain the remaining paper. The officer begrudgingly opened it to find the number 4. "It seems you must walk the first part of the journey, Captain." Franklin handed the reins to the lieutenant who had drawn number one.

"Nonsense!" The captain was now furious. "Do you think this is some sort of game?"

"No, Sir, I do not believe this is a game." Franklin could no longer contain his anger as he stepped within inches of the captain's face. "I have seen more death and carnage in the last year than most experienced surgeons see in a lifetime. I have seen thousands of men give up their comfort and privations for their fellow soldiers, Father Abraham, and this great nation for the cause of ensuring that all men might be free. No . . . there is nothing about this war that could be mistaken for a game! So no Captain . . . I will not cater to your selfish, individual willfulness when I have the ability to insure the safety of four valuable officers." The captain blinked, indignant but astonished at Franklin's outburst. He said nothing further as a calmer Franklin continued with instructions.

"Gentlemen, by giving you my horse I am running the risk of incurring my superior's displeasure, and I am exposing myself to the very danger from which

*I am assisting you to escape. That being said, I expect that you follow my sim-
ple rules. Don't play false with each other. Those who ride are not to go faster
than the others can walk, and you are to ride equal distances, unless otherwise
arranged among yourselves. You are to take care of my horse when you arrive
at your destination and see that it is returned to me. I trust these matters to your
honor, but if honor should forget to assert its rights, this case will be reported to
headquarters."*

The men left, one riding and three walking, including the captain who remained silent, but continued looking peevish.

With the sounds of cannonading growing ever louder, Franklin
needed a ride back to safety. To the east of the hospital, he spotted
a small, abandoned farmhouse and barn. A number of mules and
one young colt lazed in a nearby corral. With no one in sight and
the battle drawing closer, Franklin slipped into the barn, hoping to
find a saddle. All he found there, however, was an old black halter
that hung from a rusted nail on the back wall.

Taking the halter, Franklin stepped into the corral and cautiously approached the colt, but the animal proved skittish and
wild. Noticing that it seemed to shadow the mules, Franklin
herded them into the barn and the young horse followed. Once
inside, he cornered the colt and slipped the halter over its head.
It took several attempts to mount the untrained animal without a
saddle, but Franklin finally managed to climb on its back and tear
out of the barn astride the young colt.

The woods ahead were sparse, allowing him to see clearly, but
as he neared a thicket of brush, he heard the click of at least a
dozen rifles and a shower of Minie balls whizzed past him. For-
tunately, not one found its target, but the unexpected barrage not
only caught Franklin off guard, it frightened the colt so badly that
it plunged through the woods in the opposite direction. Franklin
clung to the colt's mane, but it was all he could do to hang on until
the panic-stricken animal slowed down once they reached an open
field.

In the distance, Franklin spotted a group of Union soldiers and
bounded toward them. When he came within a hundred yards of

the troops, one of the soldiers waved him off in another direction. That man was rewarded for his bravery by a hard butt in the head from a Rebel rifle. Realizing that these soldiers were actually prisoners guarded by a band of Confederates, Franklin jerked the colt away, once again fleeing a volley of Minie balls. Thankfully, this barrage proved as harmless as the first.

Nothing but the power of the Almighty could have shielded Franklin from such a storm of shot and shell, and brought him through unscathed. It was almost as much of a miracle as that of the three Hebrew children coming forth from the fiery furnace without even the smell of fire upon them.

●●●●●

McClellan soon wrote a dispatch to Secretary of State Stanton:

> *"I have lost this battle because my force was too small. I again repeat that I am not responsible for this. I could take Richmond, but I have not a man in reserve and shall be glad to cover my retreat, and save the material and personnel in order to save this army. I tell you plainly that I owe no thanks to you, or to any other persons in Washington, since you have done your best to sacrifice this army."*

But Little Mac's words and lack of action were not winning friends in Washington and he was not the only one wrestling with his demons. Although Franklin did not feel the least bit guilty about stealing that colt, his conscience did bother him when he thought about his treatment of the captain and lieutenants. According to the 'Good Book,' gambling was wrong and Franklin knew firsthand the trouble it could cause. Nonetheless, he had made the four men cast lots over riding his horse, feeling this was the fair thing to do under the circumstances. Now remorseful for his sin, he prayed for the Lord's forgiveness, but the shame of his actions kept him awake for several nights thereafter.

Chapter 16

Seven Days Battle

The Peninsula Campaign had started at Oak Grove on June 25, 1862, then moved on to Mechanicsville and Gaines's Mill, but it didn't stop there. Garnett's and Golding's Farm saw action followed by gruesome battles at Savage Station, Glendale, and White Oak Swamp. Over those six days, more than three thousand men were lost and another fifteen thousand wounded. The worst, however, was yet to come when the two armies once again clashed on the seventh day at Malvern Hill.

Malvern Hill rose above the north bank of the James River in Henrico County, Virginia about eighteen miles from the Confederate Capital of Richmond. Occupied by the Union troops, the elevated slope offered a sweeping view of the field below. During the night of June 30, many soldiers, including Franklin, retreated there to rejoin their regiments, leaving a great number of wounded men in the hands of the enemy. Though fast asleep on the ground, the artillery had already been arranged and the exhausted troops had positioned themselves in line for combat. On Poindexter Farm, near the battlefield, stood a white farmhouse, where some of the wounded were carried and where the Union Army set up their headquarters. Not anticipating an attack that day, Little Mac left no one in charge as he boarded the *U.S.S. Galena*, which was set to sail along the James toward Harrison's Landing.

Early on the afternoon of July 1, 1862, Confederate artillery fired the first shots. From the hill upon which the Union Army had positioned itself, Franklin was about to witness a staggering showdown. Eight batteries with thirty-seven guns were situated on the Union side against three Rebel batteries with sixteen guns. In the distance, the *U.S.S. Galena* along with two more gunboats, the *U.S.S. Jacob Bell* and the *U.S.S. Aroostook*, fired missiles onto the battlefield from their position on the James. Under Brigadier General John Fitz Porter, who stepped up to lead them, the Army of the Potomac not only occupied the hill, but also swept east to Harrison's Landing while additional Union troops, from as far as the eye could see, marched toward the battlefield.

Both armies wasted no time in elevating the battle to a fearsome level. By nine o'clock, the reflections of the flashes of fire from hundreds of guns upon the dense cloud of smoke hung suspended in the air, turning it into a pillar of fire. Vivid flashes of lightning and terrific peaks of thunder, mingled with the continuous blaze of musketry and sudden explosions of shell—all nearly drowned out by the deafening roar of cannon. The Union infantry lay in wait on the ground until the Rebel advance was within musket range and they sprang to their feet, driving the Rebels back with a mighty vengeance.

The battle raged most furiously hour after hour; the enemy advanced in massive columns, often without order, but with perfect recklessness; and the concentrated fire of the Union gunboats, batteries, and infantry mowed down the advancing host until the slain lay in heaps upon the field. In between the firing, Franklin, along with other medics, raced across the blood-soaked terrain, amid the growing chaos, to remove the wounded and stack the dead on the sidelines, one on top of the other, three and four deep. *At four o'clock that afternoon the firing ceased, and all supposed the battle was over; but it was only the calm before an even more terrible storm.*

That evening, the enemy unexpectedly attacked the left of the Union line and fiercely pushed forward. In a moment, the entire hill was one blaze of light as those terrible siege guns belched forth their murderous fire. Numerous Union batteries, with back up from the gunboats, sent the Southern enemy reeling back to shelter, leaving the ground covered with their dead and wounded. Then the Union soldiers dashed forward with their bayonets, shouting wildly and cheering as they captured prisoners, and drove the confused Rebels from the field.

By eight thirty that evening, the battle was over. Colonel William W. Averell of the Third Pennsylvania later described the scene:

> *"By this time, the level rays of the morning sun from our right were just penetrating the fog, and slowly lifting the clinging shreds and yellow masses. Our ears had been filled with agonizing cries from thousands before the fog was lifted, but now our eyes saw an appalling spectacle upon the slopes down to the woodlands half a mile away. Over five thousand dead and wounded men were on the ground, in every attitude of distress. A third of them were dead or dying, but enough were alive and moving to give to the field a singular crawling effect . . ."*

The Union medics worked as quickly as they could removing the wounded from the field. They even assisted fallen Rebels, since their own army had abandoned them. Due to the high number of casualties (314 killed and 1,875 wounded on the Union side; 869 killed and 4,241 wounded on the Confederate side), Franklin and the medics stopped using stretchers and, instead, dragged the dead away by their arms and legs, piling them in stacks along the side of the field. The horrific job of burying the maimed and bloated bodies was later left to the local citizenry if they chose to help.

The Confederates felt terrible casualties that day without gaining an inch of ground. It was a terrible slaughter . . . enough to make angels weep, to look down upon that field of carnage.

Despite the overall Union defeat during the Peninsula Campaign, the Battle of Malvern Hill was a pronounced victory for the North. As such, General Porter wanted to move on to Richmond, but Little Mac disagreed and ordered his troops back to Harrison's Landing, about nine miles to the southeast. As the troops marched in retreat that night, bridges were burned and trees felled to block the roads in order to keep the Confederates from following. The exhausted Union troops hardly felt like winners as they marched away from Richmond instead of toward it. Despite their many losses, they had gained no ground. And to make matters worse, it began to rain yet again, soaking the spent men to their very souls.

On the Fourth of July, 1862, General McClellan issued the following statement to his troops:

> "Soldiers of the Army of the Potomac: Your achievements of the last ten days have illustrated the valor and endurance of the American soldier. Attacked by superior forces and without hope of reinforcements, you have succeeded in changing your base of operations by a flank movement, always regarded as the most hazardous of military expedients. You have saved all your material, all your trains and all your guns, except a few lost in battle, taking in return guns and colors from the enemy. Upon your march, you have been assailed day after day, with desperate fury, by men of the same race and nation, skillfully massed and led. Under every disadvantage of number, and necessarily of position also, you have in every conflict beaten back your foes with enormous slaughter. Your conduct ranks you among the celebrated armies of history. No one will now question that each of you may always with pride say: 'I belong to the Army of the Potomac.' You have reached the new base, complete in organization and unimpaired in spirit. The enemy may at any moment attack you. We are prepared to meet them. I have personally established your lines. Let them come, and we will convert their repulse into a final defeat. Your government is strengthening you with the resources of a great people. On this our nation's birthday, we declare to our foes, who are enemies against the best interests of mankind, that this army shall enter the Capital of the so-called Confederacy; that our national constitution shall prevail, and that the Union, which can alone insure the internal peace and external security to each state,

'must and shall be preserved,' cost what it may in time, treasure, and blood."

•••••

As the weeks went by and an uneasy peace permeated the Virginia Peninsula, the men became restless. Little Mac continued requesting reinforcements from Washington and, at the same time, protested against retreating. *In August, however, orders to evacuate Harrison's Landing finally arrived. The troops were demoralized, for they had confidently expected to advance upon Richmond and avenge the blood of their fallen comrades, whose graves dotted so many hillsides on the peninsula.* Instead, they marched away.

Unknown to the men when they set out, their destination was some seventy miles east at Newport News, Virginia. Franklin's companions on that trek were the chaplain and Mrs. B., Dr. Bonine, and Nellie who had since arrived in Harrison's Landing to tend the sick and wounded. The five friends made the best of their difficult journey and at times, found it pleasant. The quartermaster even returned the horse that Franklin had loaned to the four surly officers during their retreat to the James. Franklin allowed Nellie the luxury of riding and marched alongside her. On the way, they visited the grave of James Vezey and Franklin *rejoiced that James had been taken away from all of this evil—the terrible marches, the horrible battles, and especially from the humiliating retreat.*

Unhappy with McClellan's choices, Father Abraham ordered a reorganization of his men. As a result, the Army of Virginia was formed under the leadership of General John Pope, who had orders to take Richmond. Little Mac's Army of the Potomac was left with fewer men, but was told to provide reinforcements to Pope nonetheless. McClellan believed the entire matter was a grave mistake and was reluctant to follow the plan. He did not think that Pope had the slightest chance of winning what would later be called The Second Battle of Bull Run.

•••••

Franklin's troop was sent on to Alexandria, where General Heintzelman assigned him to another spy mission—penetrate enemy
lines to determine where and how Confederate troops were assembled. Remembering how invisible he had seemed living among the
enemy, disguised as a contraband slave, he chose once more to
masquerade as a darkie. Franklin again colored his skin, but this
time donned women's clothes and an apron, adding a course black
wig and bonnet to become Bertha—a female cook.

Crossing over into the Confederate camp, Franklin, dressed as
Bertha, easily mingled with the other slaves in the kitchen area.
He helped the cook in charge—a black lady named Big Mama
MayBelle, who was as broad as she was tall. "Why you no escape
an' run to de Unions?" Franklin asked one of the middle-aged men
as he mixed the Johnnycake batter.

"Cuz I stay wid my famlee." The man who was assigned to brew
the morning coffee shrugged. "It be too har' ta all escape tageder."

"I got no famlee. Dey all kill by de soudern man," offered Franklin in Bertha's lilting voice.

"De soudern man, he kill many of us like we nothin' but dogs,"
Big Mama MayBelle sighed over a pot of boiling water.

Franklin nodded his agreement as he fried the johnnycakes in
bacon grease. He couldn't help but smile and think of old Jack
who would be sure to find fault with his cooking methods.

"What ya grinnin' 'bout, Bertha?" Big Mama MayBelle frowned
at her underling. "Is der somethin' funny in my kitchen?"

"Lawd, no." Franklin shook his head. "I was jus' thinkin' 'bout
my pappy. He sho' did love his johnnycakes when he could get
'em."

"Ya miss yo pappy?"

"I sho do and I miss my mammy, too!" Franklin turned his attention to the stove as two officers strolled by. With his back to them,
he listened closely as one spoke.

"The plan is to press the enemy back to their soil and take Washington once and for all."

"It needs to be done soon," the second officer replied.

"Just a few more days before the Union government is dissolved and the Confederacy will take charge. If he knows what's good for him, Mr. Lincoln will start packing his bags."

While the Rebel soldiers snickered, Franklin shivered at the thought of them raiding Washington, but before he could dwell on it further, Big Mama MayBelle ordered him to prepare the officers' table. As he laid out the dishes and utensils, he moved a gray coat that had been draped over a chair on the far side of the table. Papers fell from one of the pockets. Franklin had a feeling they might be important so he quickly scooped them up, hiding them in his wide apron before anyone noticed.

As the officers ate, he continued to wait on them, praying they would not realize that their documents were gone. Their conversation gave no more useful information as they mostly talked about their personal plans after the war. It sickened Franklin to hear them discuss their slaves like chattel and, in the same breath, refer to themselves as 'southern gentlemen.' The meal dragged on and the officers lingered over their coffee longer than they should have, or so it seemed to Franklin who had to keep their cups full. When they finally left and he had finished clearing the breakfast dishes, Franklin slipped away, heading back to the Union lines on foot.

As he neared an old wooden farmhouse, shots rang out forcing him to seek shelter there. Once inside the empty house, Franklin took cover in the cellar as the fighting drew closer. Soon, the house was caught in a hellacious crossfire, causing it to shake and literally collapse, leaving Franklin buried in the rubble. Dust filled his lungs, but he didn't dare come out until the battle finally moved on. When all was quiet, Franklin dug his way out, scraping his hands on the debris as he pushed aside bricks, glass, and broken bits of stone.

That night, Franklin, now in his Union uniform, handed over the documents directly to General Heintzelman, who seemed confused by the younger man's darkened skin.

"I infiltrated the enemy's camp dressed as a contraband, sir," Franklin explained. "While I was there, I was able to acquire these regimental instructions detailing how and when the Rebels plan to capture Washington."

Heintzelman studied the documents with great interest. "This information is invaluable and will surely assist the Union Army in their efforts to win this war. Fine work, Private Thompson! Fine work! You have done an outstanding job today, and the Army of the Potomac will be forever in your debt!"

•••••

While Pope and his men waged war, Franklin paid three more visits to the Rebels within a period of ten days, always disguised as Bertha. Each time, he came away with vital information. *While the battle raged, he divided his time between the Confederates and the Federals.* His final trip past enemy lines occurred on August 31, 1862—one day after the Union suffered a bitter loss at the Second Battle of Bull Run and the night before the fateful Battle of Chantilly.

On September 1, 1862, Confederate General Robert E. Lee ordered General Stonewall Jackson and his troops to attack the retreating Union Army near Ox Hill in Fairfax County, Virginia. Heavy fighting took place that afternoon in the midst of a raging tempest with thunder and lightning adding to the already booming sounds of war. Visibility was poor, allowing Franklin, still dressed as Bertha, to escape the Confederates just as General Kearny inadvertently rode across enemy lines. Realizing his mistake, the general quickly turned his horse around, but it was too late. A hail of Confederate bullets took him out, and he dropped dead from his horse. Franklin watched in horror as the Rebel soldiers cheered with joy over Kearny's lifeless body. It was a coup for the South. The one-armed General, Philip Kearny, was a much-feared and respected leader. When General Lee returned the body, he even included a note of sympathy.

Franklin not only grieved for the Union's loss of a great general, but for the man he had come to know and respect. He sorely wished that he had taken that bullet instead. He would have willingly died to save such an extraordinary hero.

• • • • •

After the Battle of Chantilly, the Union Army continued their retreat toward Washington. Within the week, Robert E. Lee turned his attention toward Maryland, hoping to invade the North and open a supply-line for his troops. Father Abraham disbanded the Army of Virginia and hesitantly put McClellan back in charge, partly because of the general's impressive organizational skills. The president's decision caused some controversy in Washington, but he remained firm in his choice. Several skirmishes ensued, but little else occurred until the two armies met at Sharpsburg, Maryland on September 17, 1862—a day of carnage later referred to as the Battle of Antietam.

Despite being outnumbered almost two to one, the Confederates fought hard. The fighting resulted in the largest loss of life in a twenty-four-hour period that America had ever seen with over two thousand Union dead and more than fifteen hundred Confederates lost. Thousands upon thousands more were wounded on each side. Men fell one upon the other often times with the dead sprawled atop the wounded. Soldiers with missing or mangled arms, legs, and heads lay in pools of their own blood. The men began calling the road along which the battle was fought, 'Bloody Lane,' as they stepped over their fallen comrades.

At night, both Rebels and Yankees cared for their wounded and buried their dead with the help of locals. Franklin was once again among the medics who tended the injured and dragged the dead from the field. *He had witnessed such horrific scenes before, but he wondered how it was possible for one person to watch so much death . . . so much suffering and still maintain his sanity.*

In passing among the wounded, Franklin was drawn to the gentle face of one young soldier who lay by the side of the field suffering from a serious neck wound. Franklin knew from experience that there was nothing to be done as the blood rushed out matting the combatant's fair hair. The small, trembling hand beckoned Franklin closer. *"Can I trust you with a secret?"*

"Of course, you can."

"I am not what I seem; I am a female and as my final wish I ask that you bury me with your own hands, so that none may know the truth after I'm gone."

"I assure you, my girl, that you will be buried with the honor you deserve and your true identity will be kept in confidence, but have you no family to notify?"

"I had only a brother, but he was killed earlier today as I stood next to him. Took a bullet in his head. I knew he was dead, but I closed his eyes so he wouldn't see me cry."

"Did you enlist together?"

"Yes, we had to." Her voice was fading. "After our parents died, we vowed to always stay together, but now he is gone and I am still here."

"Are you afraid to be alone, my dear?"

"Oh, no." She gave the slightest smile. "I will join him on the other side soon. It wouldn't be right to keep my brother waiting, but I couldn't go until I was sure someone would help me."

"You can rest easy." Franklin nodded. "For I have a secret, too. Maybe someone will be as kind to me should my own death occur on the battlefield." The young soldier smiled, understanding what Franklin was saying, and she momentarily relaxed, trusting that her secret would be safe.

As Franklin held her hand, the girl began to shake and choke. Franklin gently lifted her to a sitting position, watching helplessly as the blood flowed from her open mouth. Knowing there was nothing else he could do, he held her there until she slumped into a lifeless corpse.

That night Franklin carried the woman's remains to an isolated area where he carefully buried her body with only a blanket for a shroud. He then took a moment and prayed for her soul.

•••••

By the time Franklin returned to camp that night, lights were out and all but the sentry were asleep. He had missed the evening meal and went directly to the mess tent, hoping to find some leftovers. Still preoccupied with the fate of the young soldier he had just buried, he rounded up a few cold johnnycakes and several pieces of bacon. Once he finished, he stood and turned only to find Randolf Meade, a soldier from his regiment, blocking his way.

"Are you looking for something, soldier?" Franklin, caught off-guard by Meade's stealth, felt uneasy. When the man didn't answer right away, Franklin grew wary as he watched Meade slowly and methodically light a cigarette. When Meade still didn't speak, Franklin tried to rush past him.

"Hold on there." Meade bumped him hard with his shoulder. "You asked if I was looking for something. Well, I am and I do believe that you have exactly what I want, Franklin. Or, is it . . . Emma?"

Shocked to hear his real name, Franklin blinked, uncertain what to say.

"I overheard you talking to Major Butler's wife a while back." Meade took a long drag on his cigarette. "And I know you have a secret, but what I don't know is how far you are willing to go to keep that secret."

"What do you mean? What is it you want?"

"Well, now, I've been giving this a lot of serious thought," Meade sneered before sucking another smoke. "How's about a little of what you were giving Private Vezey?"

"Private Vezey is dead." Franklin took a breath. "And I don't know what you're talking about."

"But I think you know precisely what I'm talking about, Miss Emma." Meade came closer. "A little lovemaking could keep things between us—real friendly-like."

Meade threw his cigarette down, then roughly jerked Emma against him and kissed her forcefully on the mouth. She pulled away and slapped him, hard.

"Now, Emma," he threatened with a smile. "If you're not interested in being friends, then I'll be forced to let our superiors know just who you are." His face hardened. "Then see how long you'll be a soldier in this army."

"If that's what you feel you need to do private, then I guess I can't stop you."

"Emma, you'll find I'm a reasonable man. Take a little time to consider my offer. And when we meet again, maybe you'll come around to my way of thinking." Meade lit another cigarette. "You know I'd much rather feel your charms than have you removed from duty."

"You'll not be touching me again . . . do you understand?"

"It's all up to you, Emma." Meade shrugged and walked away.

Franklin took deep breaths, trying to regain his composure, as hard reality set in. This could very well be the end of his military life.

But, the next day brought heavy fighting, giving both Franklin and Meade more immediate things to worry about. *The Battle of Antietam was the first major conflict fought on Federal lands.* It all ended with Lee's retreat, but Little Mac refused to go after him, still citing his need of more troops. Washington was incensed by the general's decision, and although the battle was in reality a draw, the Union claimed victory to pave the way for Lincoln's Emancipation Proclamation.

Chapter 17

A Rebel Sympathizer

After the bloodbath at Antietam, the Army of the Potomac took some time to regroup. They needed food, clothing, and more men in order to recover their heavy losses. With each passing day, life in the Union camp quickly became routine. Every morning the soldiers were awakened at sunrise by drummers, after which an official roll call ensured that all were present and accounted for. Once breakfast was eaten, patients were examined by the medics and surgeons. A formal changing of the guard then took place and military drills were completed. After lunch, there was more of the same and at 5:00 p.m. sharp, a dress parade ensued, followed by dinner. Another roll call was held before 9:00 p.m. and then it was 'lights out' for the camp.

Franklin had neither seen nor talked to Randolf Meade since Antietam. He hoped that Meade's absence meant his threats were no longer an issue. Maybe the man had come to his senses. With no imminent battles to fight, Franklin continued his duties as mail carrier and medic, during which time, he also attended the many funerals of those fallen soldiers who would never again return home.

During this reprieve from battle, Franklin traveled to Harper's Ferry, Virginia. There, he visited the courtroom where the treason trial of abolitionist John Brown had been held. Through his deadly raid in Harper's Ferry in October, 1859, Brown intended to start an armed slave revolt. His violent methods, however, were interpreted by the courts as an act of treason against the State of Virginia. Brown was convicted and hanged, but much to the regret of the South, as well as many Virginians, he became a hero and martyr to Northern sympathizers. For the Union troops, Brown remained a champion and Franklin was pleased to find that the activist's memory still inspired those who fought against slavery.

President Lincoln was anxious for McClellan to move his troops, but as usual, Little Mac dragged his feet, causing great concern among the politicians in Washington. Finally, at the end of October, 1862 some of the men, including Franklin's regiment, marched southward. The soldiers were now rested and in much better spirits, but on November 5, 1862, Father Abraham abruptly relieved McClellan of his duties, leaving his loyal men stunned. It had become apparent to the president that McClellan's strategy of outmaneuvering the enemy was not working. This was a civil war fought by ordinary citizens and the conflict would only end when one side annihilated the other.

Two days later, Little Mac was replaced by the mutton-chopped Major General Ambrose Everett Burnside. He reluctantly accepted the position after learning that General "Fighting Joe" Hooker (a man Burnside disliked) would be considered if he refused.

McClellan wrote to his wife:

> ". . . I feel I have done all that can be asked . . . I feel some little pride in having, with a beaten and demoralized army, defeated Lee so utterly. . . . Well, one of these days history will I trust do me justice."

While a disappointed Franklin commiserated with his comrades about the dismissal of their beloved leader, Ambrose wasted no time in moving his troops along the Rappahannock River toward Fredericksburg, Virginia about sixty miles north of Richmond, which was his ultimate goal. Ambrose had ordered several bridges to be built across the river for his men to cross, but plans were delayed for weeks because the materials didn't arrive when scheduled. Bored with killing time, instead of Rebels, the Union soldiers stood at the narrow portion of the river and threw stones across the water at Southern soldiers who were also waiting for action. The opposing sides were often close enough to carry on a conversation with each other. Even Brigadier General Orlando Metcalf Poe, who had recently been promoted from colonel, noted in a letter to his wife, Eleanor, that the Rebels personally asked him if he "was in the habit of eating Rebels fried or stewed, for breakfast, declaring their readiness to undergo either culinary process for my pleasure."

As cold winter weather set in, supplies arrived and the Union Army finally began to erect six wooden spans over the Rappahannock. They were met with Rebel gunfire that killed or wounded two out of three men, but nonetheless, their work continued. Once the pontoon bridges were finished, the troops crossed the river to take the city of Fredericksburg in yet another bloody battle.

During this campaign, Franklin shed his medic responsibilities to assume the role of orderly to General Poe. Poe had taken a liking to Franklin after the young soldier had brought him some tasty fruit and doughnuts. Franklin remained with the general throughout the fighting and only left Poe's side when ordered to carry messages to other officers amid the gunfire and cannonading.

Franklin's bravery during that violent time, however, was also noted by many who saw him mounted upon his horse for hours without pause. He watched in horror as one assault after another added broken men to the ever-growing heap of mangled bodies. As much as he ached to help them, he knew that his primary duty was to Poe and he considered it an honor to personally serve the general.

Unknown to Franklin, Randolf Meade was also lurking. He carefully watched Frankllin's every move and took a keen interest in Franklin's special status with the general. The green dragon of jealousy reared its ugly head as Meade bided his time, determined to wait for just the right moment to turn Emma in.

On December 14, the night before the carnage finally ended, the heavens created an unusual sight when the colorful Northern Lights, or Aurora Borealis, appeared in the skies, casting their eerie glow over the bloody landscape. Franklin gazed upward in wonder and pulled the collar of his coat around his face while bitter winds blew over the lifeless and wounded who lay helpless on the frozen ground. The Battle of Fredericksburg resulted in Union losses totaling 1,284 dead and 9,600 wounded while the South claimed 608 killed and 4,116 injured. As the Confederates declared yet another victory and the Union forces retreated, a devastated Father Abraham wrote: "If there is a worse place then hell, I am in it."

In the weeks that followed, the Army of the Potomac once again settled into their various camps, trying to make the best of the long winter days and the frosty temperatures that embraced them with the dark of night. Dealing with the severe weather did little to improve morale. To further their dour spirits, Little Mac was not reinstated to lead them as they had hoped. Instead, Lincoln replaced Burnside with General Hooker, who had been very vocal with his criticisms about the mishandling of Fredericksburg. He also openly stated that a dictator might be just what the country needed. Lincoln, well aware of Hooker's views, told him with no uncertainty, "What I now ask of you is military success and I will risk the dictatorship."

It was during this shuffling of leaders that Randolf Meade made his move. He appeared at General Poe's tent late one afternoon. After casting a threatening glance toward Franklin, who worked nearby, Meade strode inside. Franklin steeled himself for the worst, but it never came. Instead, a dejected Meade returned from his audience with the general unable, or unwilling, to speak. He slunk away and, from that day on, kept his distance from Franklin. Meade wasted little time, however, in joining the ranks of other soldiers who whispered that Poe and his aide were unusually close.

Years later, it came to light that some individuals, including Mrs. Poe, wondered whether the general had known the truth about his charge all along. It was even speculated that the two may have shared a romance. Maybe upon learning that Franklin was indeed a woman, Poe chose to protect the soldier that he so admired, rather than reveal her secret. In any case, Franklin remained on good terms with the general.

•••••

In March of 1863, Franklin was sent along with the Ninth Corps to Louisville, Kentucky under the command of Colonel William Humphrey who had recently been promoted from captain. At the time, Kentucky was considered a 'border state' and housed both Rebels and Yankees. Louisville was located in the northern part of the state and served as a transportation hub for the Union Army. The city also contained a supply center, a hospital, and a military prison where captured Confederate soldiers, as well as Union deserters, were taken. Union leaders had also siezed a large house one block down from the penitentiary and converted it into a female military prison where a number of Secesh women were detained. Most of these southern women were charged with 'harboring guerillas', 'smuggling', or 'aiding the enemy.' They had to be removed from the general population in an effort to protect the Union. In addition, the area was a hotbed for escaped slaves who had established a contraband camp nearby. Franklin had only been in Louisville a short time when the Secret Service tapped him for a new spy mission.

This time, he chose to take butternut-colored clothes from a Rebel prisoner and assume a southern drawl. Using the name Robins, he pretended to be a civilian Rebel sympathizer and made his way by train to Lebanon, Kentucky, about seventy miles southeast of Louisville. Lebanon had seen its share of skirmishes and both the Union and the Confederacy alternately controlled the local railroad depot, each side hoping to use it for their own purposes.

Shortly after Franklin arrived, he traveled door-to-door, asking for eggs, butter, and other goods to be used for the Rebel cause. He made sure to engage each resident in lively conversation while they prepared their donation. His congeniality often caused the citizenry to loosen their lips and unwittingly confide useful information that he could take back to his superiors. Upon approaching one large, two-story brick home, Franklin unexpectedly encountered a Confederate wedding party. A group of well-heeled, Rebel soldiers stood in the front yard—each man enjoying a glass of brandy and a fat cigar. "Afternoon, men," Franklin greeted the soldiers with a broad smile. "How's the war progressing? Are we beating those damned Yankees back to where they came from?"

"Who wants to know?" a handsome blonde-haired man wearing a full-dress Captain's uniform demanded.

"John Robins, sir." Franklin extended his hand to the man whose thick, yellow mustache seemed to have a sneer all its own.

"Captain Logan." The soldier accepted the handshake. "What's your business here, Robins?"

"I'm just a poor old Kentucky boy trying to help the Rebel Army by obtaining butter, eggs, and whatever else I can scrounge up, for our soldiers, Captain." Franklin gestured to the festivities attempting to change the subject. "Looks like someone just got married here."

"Yes indeed, son, today is a day of celebration. It was my good fortune to marry a beautiful widow who shares our belief in slavery."

"Your brother's widow." One solder with missing teeth gave a drunken laugh.

"My brother died at Antietam." Logan shrugged. "Took a bullet as he stood next to me. He'd been married only three months, and as he lay dying, he asked me to look after his new wife."

"You were looking after her before Tommy died." A dark-haired man swigged his brandy with a giggle.

"I am a man of my word." Logan scowled and pulled himself up to his full height. "And it's best none of you forgets that."

"Congratulations, sir." Franklin tried to break the tension. "I'm sure you have a mighty fine bride."

"And, on most days, I have a mighty fine troop." Logan glared at his men who grew quiet. He then sized up Robins. "You seem like a healthy enough specimen. Instead of collecting food, why don't you join the company? Serve a real purpose in this war."

"I don't know, sir." Franklin hesitated. "I don't think my ma would like it if I up and left her."

"Look here, boy." Logan frowned. "You can either be a man and enlist for a bounty or refuse and be conscripted for nothing."

"If it's all the same to you, sir, I will bide my time until I'm conscripted."

"Well, you won't have long to wait. From this moment on, consider yourself a soldier of the Confederacy and subject to military discipline, Private Robins."

The other men congratulated Franklin with hardy pats on the back and words of welcome. For the moment, there was no good way out so Franklin went along with the charade. Besides, this unexpected turn of events might just present the perfect opportunity to garner information about the enemy. How better to learn about the inner workings of the Confederate army than from within?

"Do you have orders for me, sir?" Franklin asked meekly.

"We'll be leaving first thing in the morning after I spend the night with my wife . . . So for now, soldier, I order you to join the party." Logan took Franklin's arm good-naturedly. "Have a drink and come inside to admire my new bride . . . from a distance, of course."

"That I can do." Franklin grinned despite the feeling of dread growing in his gut.

Music and dancing continued through the night as Franklin mingled among the many guests and soldiers. They talked of war and shared a deep hatred of the Yankees that Franklin found disturbing. It seemed to him that these Southern men had somehow forgotten that after everything was said and done, in spite of their differences, they were all Americans. Even the auburn-haired bride seemed equally tainted. She looked much too young to be a widow and certainly her mourning had been short-lived. Franklin disliked the woman almost as much as he disliked her groom, but he offered his congratulations to her anyway.

In the morning, a tired Captain Logan met up with his men. His blue eyes were ringed with red and his blond hair unkempt. "The Yankees might make a dash upon us at any moment," Logan advised from atop his mount. "Saddle up and prepare a horse for Robins."

The captain rode over to Franklin. "You will soon thank me for the interest I have taken in you," he smirked. "And you will come to appreciate the gentle persuasions I used to stir up your patriotism and remind you of your duty to your country."

Franklin said nothing, but mounted up, watching as Logan turned to lead his men out. Along the roadside, Franklin's horse was spooked by a snake, and it took some time to bring him right again. Just as the horse calmed down, a reconnoitering party of Federal Calvary advanced on the Rebel troop, with Infantry bringing up the rear. Almost instantly, the soldiers found themselves in hand-to-hand combat, taking both sides by surprise.

During the melee, Franklin, unnoticed by his Southern companions, quickly rode across to the Federal side. A Union acquaintance immediately recognized Franklin and waved him in. Franklin, with pistol in hand, opened fire at the Confederate soldiers he had partied with the night before. When Logan saw his new recruit fighting on the opposing side, the enraged officer charged straight for him and Franklin found himself face-to-face with the newly-wed Rebel captain. Without thinking, and in self-defense, Franklin discharged his pistol directly into Logan's face.

The Confederates watched in disbelief as their captain went down at the hand of the very man they thought to be their comrade. Every Rebel then turned on Franklin with sabers drawn. Seeing this, the Union soldiers rushed between him and the enemy, warding off blows with their own sabers and driving the Rebels back. Without Logan to lead them, the Confederates fled, abandoning their dead and wounded, including their beloved captain.

Franklin dismounted and knelt over Logan—his handsome face now disfigured with part of his nose and much of his upper lip shot away. "As you said earlier, I do appreciate the interest you have taken in me, Captain. However, I did not need you to stir up my patriotism to my country or to the Federal Government." He stood up but returned to one knee with an angry afterthought. "And please give my condolences to your loving bride. I only hope for your sake that she finds you equally captivating now that the curve of your mustache is ruined."

As Franklin stood to take his leave, he realized that several of his own men were mortally wounded. His nursing instincts took over, and he rushed to the side of the nearest bloody soldier. Franklin took in a sharp breath as he recognized Randolf Meade. The man had taken a bayonet in the chest during the scuffle. Meade's fear-filled eyes met Franklin's who knew immediately that there was no hope for his former nemesis.

"F-forgive me," Meade choked. "P-please."

"It's more important that God forgive you, Mr. Meade," Franklin whispered. "I will ask Him to grant you mercy."

"Why w-would you be so k-kind to me . . . after what I did to you?"

"Because we are all God's children, Mr. Meade, and if I have learned anything out here in the trenches, it's that war makes men do things they normally wouldn't."

"I-I am truly sorry." Meade struggled to speak as blood bubbled from his lips.

"It's all right." Franklin nodded. "I forgive you and I know that God will take you home." Relieved, Meade closed his eyes before drawing his final breath.

●●●●●

"Thompson, I commend you for your coolness throughout this entire affair," *Colonel Humphrey told Franklin later that day. "But I cannot, in good con-* *scious, allow you to spy near Lebanon again or go directly behind enemy lines.*

You would most likely meet with those same Rebels who saw you desert their ranks and you would be hung up as a traitor in the nearest tree."

"To be perfectly honest, sir," responded Franklin. *"I have no particular fancy for such an elevated position, nor having my name handed down to posterity among those who paid for their crimes upon the gallows. I shall be happy to turn my attention to more quiet and less dangerous duties."*

"I'm glad you agree, son, but the truth is that you are still a Union soldier and a Federal spy. Your work is not done as long as there is a war to win, but for your own safety, we are sending you back to Louisville as a civilian," Humphrey continued. "All you need to do there is mingle with the secessionists and see what plans they might have. We hear there is a dry goods store in the downtown section where someone appears to be leaking information to the enemy. You might garner good information from the soldiers and spies who frequent that store."

It took Franklin just a few days to prepare for his journey to Louisville. He arrived there wearing plain clothes and using the name Tom Smith as a nod to his brother. On his first day in town, he visited Dodd's Dry-Goods Store and applied for a job. He claimed to be a Canadian who barely knew the difference between the Confederacy and the Union. As luck would have it, the merchant's clerk was leaving to join the Confederate Army so Franklin was hired on the spot. Recalling his past experience at Annie's millinery shop, he soon grew familiar with the store's routine as he stocked merchandise, folded fabric, and waited on customers. His efforts impressed the proprietor, who worked with him daily behind the counter totaling numbers in his books and ordering new inventory. Franklin soon became one of Mr. Dodd's most trusted and valued employees.

"Smith, you do a fine job here, but I do have one complaint." Dodd, who often referred to the Union soldiers as 'those damned Yankees,' frowned.

"What's that, sir?" Franklin was careful to don his old Canadian accent.

"You have got to stop calling those Yankees Confederates!"

"But you know I'm from Canada and I find your local politics confusing. In fact, I hardly know which side is Confederate and which is Union."

"I know that, but you need to understand that those Yankees want to abolish our way of life and change the way we've been doing business for decades! Why they'd kill us all if they had the chance. Just ask our customers." Dodd leaned in closer to Franklin. "Especially the ones that might actually be Confederate spies."

"You mean there are real spies working right here?" Franklin spoke like an awe-struck tourist.

"Now, I'm not naming names, but I can tell you this." Dodd looked around making sure the place was empty. "There is a Union man who comes here regularly. He has taken an oath to the Federal Government, but he's really a Rebel spy."

"I've never seen a real spy before," Franklin gasped in delight. "You must point him out to me next time he's here."

"I'll do better than that . . . I'll introduce you to him!"

While waiting to meet this mysterious stranger, Franklin threw caution to the wind and traveled to both the Union and Confederate camps selling provisions and novelties. Each time he returned to the store, having sold out his inventory, he thanked the angels for watching over him especially when visiting the Rebels.

One afternoon, three Union Soldiers entered the store, talking freely among themselves about an upcoming battle. Dodd gave Franklin a subtle nod toward one of the men who spoke the loudest about those 'damned Rebels.' Franklin noted a distinctive scar above the man's left eye as he approached the counter to pay for tobacco and newspapers. Dodd accepted his money with a smile. "So, Anderson, how have you been since I last saw you?"

"Been busy killing Rebels, Winston." Anderson winked. "How about you?"

"Just taking care of business as usual. Have you met Tom Smith yet?" Dodd gestured toward Franklin. "He's my new clerk and does a fine job, too . . . for a Canadian, that is."

"You don't say!" Anderson grinned and held out his hand. "If Dodd says you're a good man, Tom, then I'm glad to meet your acquaintance."

Franklin knew better than to rush into a dangerous situation so he was careful to bide his time, earning the trust and interest of Dodd, as well as Anderson—all while feigning special concern for the Confederate cause. He even went so far as asking Dodd how one might cross Union lines and become a Confederate partisan. In turn, Dodd arranged for Anderson to guide Franklin into Rebel territory.

The day before the planned expedition, Franklin visited the Union camp under the pretense of delivering supplies. While he was there, he met with Colonel Orlando Moore, the Provost Marshal, and explained in detail the situation with Anderson. The two men formed a plan. Franklin suggested that Moore stop by the store the following afternoon in case he had any last-minute details he might need to pass along. When the Provost Marshall arrived at Dodd's the next day, Franklin slipped him a note, which contained both his exact time of departure and the route he and Anderson planned to take to the Union camp.

Franklin and Anderson set out around nine that evening. Anderson, convinced of Franklin's dedication to the South, bragged of his many exploits in the Confederate Secret Service. He even revealed the identity of two other spies who currently remained in the Federal camp. As they made their way in the darkness, a troop of Union cavalry suddenly descended upon them, capturing both men as prisoners. Upon searching Anderson, the Union soldiers found documents that provided definitive proof that this man, who wore a Federal uniform, was indeed a spy for the South. Franklin's cover was kept, as they pretended to also arrest and imprison him once back in Louisville.

When the spy was taken away the next morning, Franklin met with the Provost Marshall in an effort to help locate and arrest the other two spies. Unfortunately, one man had gotten wind of the events and managed to elude capture, but the other one was not so lucky and was apprehended two days later.

Despite his satisfaction with the results of his mission, Franklin knew that staying in Louisville meant certain death, so he joined his troops as they headed south toward Vicksburg, Mississippi. There they were to link up with General Grant's army. But, ill and weary, Private Franklin Thompson would not make it any farther than Lebanon, Kentucky. The Battle of Vicksburg was to be fought without him.

•••••

Franklin's long battle with malaria began to best him. The chills, fever, and excruciating pain that racked his body were compounded by the physical and mental strains he had endured during the past two years. Franklin returned to camp at Lebanon, clearly unable to make the march to Mississippi. After suffering for several days, with no relief, despite the steady stream of quinine pills he swallowed, Franklin's health took a turn for the worse. His fellow soldiers urged him to seek medical care at the hospital, but Franklin refused. There was no way he would reveal his true identity to the Army medics.

Instead, Franklin submitted a formal request for an approved leave of absence. This would allow him to check into a remote hospital for treatment. *Ironically, however, his success in retrieving intelligence for the Federal government had worked against him.* His superiors found Franklin much too valuable to grant him a leave and denied his request.

Franklin remained in his tent for days, barely able to sit up. Several of his friends, including Lafayette Bostwick and Richard Halsted, cared for him and continued to encourage him to see the surgeon or check into a hospital. Eventually, he agreed. The surgeon on duty gave him a superficial exam before ordering him directly to the military hospital. Unwilling to reveal himself and fearing that without medical attention, he would die, Franklin left the Union Army in the wee hours of April 19, 1863 after tucking Betsy's handkerchief inside his sleeve.

Barely able to stay in the saddle, Franklin rode north until he reached the small town of Oberlin, Ohio, where there was little military presence. He requested a room at Widow Wattles Boarding House and then asked for the nearest physician. The petite proprietress promptly took him in, and then concerned for her boarder and not wanting bad publicity to circulate about her rooming house, Mrs. Wattles called on her friend and neighbor, Doctor William Bunce. As the good-hearted physician tended the nearly unconscious soldier, Bunce learned first-hand that Franklin was indeed a she, but he never betrayed her.

Days passed as Emma, delirious with fever, hallucinated about days gone by. She relived the past in bits and pieces from her life on the farm with her vicious father; to the gentle touch of her loving mother; to the banter of her sisters; to the sadness of her epileptic brother. She dreamed of James and their brief time together. Over and over again she watched him die from the bullet that was meant for her.

During her darkest hours, when her fever was dangerously high, Bunce thought he might well lose her. It was then that she had nightmares of the violence and endless bloodshed that she'd witnessed on the battlefield. Dismembered arms and legs danced around her head, making her scream out loud in her delirium. Finally, her fever broke and she awoke, imagining her mother's hand on her brow. Then reality set in with a jolt. She sat up in bed and wept as she had never wept before.

All of her soldierly qualities fled and she was once again a poor, cowardly, nervous, whining woman, who could do nothing but cry hour after hour until her head felt like a fountain of tears and her heart one great burden of sorrow.

PART 3

Seeking Justice

(1863–1898)

Chapter 18

A Brush with the Angel of Death

"Mother! Mother! Mother!" Emma, clutching the red hand-kerchief, awoke with a scream.

"It's all right, my girl." Dr. Bunce leaned over his patient and gently wiped her face with a damp cloth. "You're safe here and you're back among the living, I'm happy to see."

"Who are you?" Emma asked in a weak voice as her eyes focused on the man who spoke so kindly.

"Doctor Bill Bunce at your service." The salt-and-pepper-haired man winked. "Mrs. Wattles called me last week after she put you to bed. I've been caring for you ever since. As a matter of fact, I thought I might lose you there for a while, but you are much improved now, ma'am."

Startled by the realization that Bunce was aware of her true sex, Emma tried to sit up, but found herself too weak. "What do you know about me?" She choked out the words as one tear skimmed along her right cheek.

I know you are a woman in soldier's clothing." Dr. Bunce took her hand in his. "But I am not here to judge you . . . only to help you. I don't see much swamp fever in this neck of the woods, but I have treated the occasional patient when I worked on the east coast. Yours is by far the worst case I've handled. Your liver is enlarged and you'll have to take good care of yourself from now on as I am afraid there is no cure, but you probably already know that. Would you mind telling me how you came by this terrible disease?"

"I served in the Great Dismal Swamp back in Virginia a couple of years ago when the war first started." Emma relaxed a little. "I've been treating myself with quinine pills ever since. I couldn't risk revealing my real identity so I was never really treated by a doctor. Now that I'm here, and you know the truth, can I trust you to keep my secret?"

"Of course. What kind of doctor would I be if you couldn't trust me? But after all we've been through, I would like to know one thing."

"What's that?"

"It would be nice to know your real name."

"My name is Emma. Emma Edmondson. And this handkerchief belonged to my mother. Somehow, it keeps me close to her," she sighed, relieved to finally confide in someone. "Tell me, does Mrs. Wattles know?"

"She only knows that you are a very sick Union soldier named Franklin Thompson, but I certainly hope you aren't planning to return to that life. You are in no condition to fight a war."

"I have to get back to my troop," Emma insisted as her guilt got the better of her. "I should never have left in the first place."

"I'm sorry, Emma." Dr. Bunce shook his head. "I admire your dedication, but you can't go. You're not strong enough. My God, girl, you almost died. At the very least, take a few days to regain your strength."

"Tomorrow," Emma insisted. "I must go back tomorrow."

The next morning, a weak Emma put on her Union uniform, paid Mrs. Wattles what was owed, and slowly walked behind the boardinghouse to the stable where her horse was housed.

"I'll need my horse as fast as you can saddle her." Franklin handed the stable boy a few dollars.

"Yes, sir! Right away, sir!" the boy whooped at the money. He couldn't have been more than seven or eight years old, and his resemblance to Mrs. Wattles let Emma know that this child was most likely the lady's son. He returned a few moments later, leading Franklin's horse all saddled up and ready to ride. "Will you be coming back soon, sir?"

"I have to rejoin my troop." The weary soldier shook his head as he mounted the horse. "Can you tell me where I might find the nearest recruitment office?"

"Down the road next to the bank." The boy pointed westward, a hint of regret in his voice. "I wish I could fight in the war like you."

"You can do your part right here, young man." Franklin slowly walked his horse toward the stable door. "By taking care of your mother and helping soldiers like me get well."

Franklin squinted in the bright sunlight as he left the stable and rode several doors down toward the recruitment office. He painfully dismounted and walked inside, pausing a moment so his eyes could adjust to the dimmer light. A bearded recruiting officer looked up from the corner desk. "Can I help you, soldier?"

"No, sir." Franklin shook his head. "I've been ill and I just want to check on the Union muster rolls to see if there is any news about my troop."

The officer pointed toward the back wall where several long documents were tacked up. Franklin quickly scanned the latest postings, hoping to determine exactly where his troop might be. Instead, he found the name 'Franklin Thompson' and written next to it the word 'Deserter.' Franklin gasped as his stomach clenched in sick disbelief. How could this be? He had sacrificed everything for the Army of the Potomac and now he was a wanted man due to circumstances he had no control over! He took a few deep breaths and gave a sideways glance toward the officer at the desk who thankfully paid him no further attention. Franklin then pulled his hat low to cover his face before walking outside where even the fresh spring air now seemed stifling.

Not only had he been deemed a deserter by the Confederate Rebels, but his own company and country had deemed him a deserter as well, leaving him no choice but to make Franklin Thompson, the Civil War Hero, disappear without a trace, forever.

He rode back to the stable where the young lad seemed surprised to see him again. "Something's come up and I have to take a trip," Franklin told the boy as he handed over the reins and several more dollars. "Can I trust you to care for my horse until I return?"

"Yes, sir! Of course, sir! I'll take real good care of her, sir. I'll brush her and feed her and walk her as if she were my own."

"Her name's White Lightning." Franklin removed the saddlebags and gave the animal one last caress. "And I trust you to keep your word."

"Yes, sir! I will, sir!"

Franklin then headed toward the train depot. He had business to tend to and that business was best done in a large city where no one would notice if a man quietly transformed into a woman. Burdened by disease and a heavy heart, he bought a one-way rail ticket to Pittsburgh, thanking God he'd been given the good sense to save most of his pay.

•••••

With more than one thousand factories and about fifty thousand residents, Pittsburgh, Pennsylvania was a large industrial city that churned out steel and munitions for the Union cause. It was dangerous work, as the explosion at the Alleghany Arsenal proved. The deadly blast had occurred about six months prior to Franklin's arrival, killing seventy-eight workers—mostly young women and children. The city had since buried their dead and resumed production, but the memory of that awful day still lingered as citizens scurried from place to place against a backdrop of factory noise. In their haste, no one noticed a lone Yankee soldier who stepped from a train carrying two saddlebags one fine spring day in 1863.

Franklin had rested on the train and was feeling much better, but not quite up to his normal level of strength. The journey had also given him some time to formulate a plan for the future, which started at a women's clothing store located in downtown Pittsburgh not far from the train depot. There, Franklin explained to the clerk that he needed to buy his twin sister some clothes starting with undergarments. With the sales assistant's help, he bought not only foundation wear, but also a calico dress, shoes, stockings, and riding pants. He then ducked into a nearby carriage house where Franklin Thompson disappeared and Sarah Emma Edmonds took his place. Back outside, she felt like a foreigner in her own skin, but fell into step with the locals—none of whom gave her a second look. She took her time as she adjusted to her new persona, as well as her new shoes.

Emma spent an entire month in Pittsburgh where she rented a room at a respectable boardinghouse and recuperated. She pretty much kept to herself as she readjusted to womanhood, learning how to once again be comfortable in a skirt. For Emma, becoming a lady was more difficult than fighting the war. She kept abreast of the civil strife by reading all of the available newspapers and visiting the local recruitment office. She even spoke to returning veterans who were not always willing to share their stories with a lady. All the while, her heart ached for her troop and she sorely missed the comradery that the Army had provided, but there was no going back and Emma knew it.

Feeling stronger and more confident with her reclaimed identity, Emma eventually returned to Oberlin, Ohio. She checked back into Mrs. Wattle's Boarding House, never once rousing the suspicions of the proprietress or any of her regular patrons. After settling in her room, Emma went to the stables to check on her horse. There she found that same young lad raking up a large pile of hay.

"Excuse me, boy," she began. "I'm looking for a horse left here by a Union soldier named Frank Thompson."

"That was over a month ago." The boy looked up from his chores.

"She's still here, I hope." Emma bit her lip. "I gave Frank twenty dollars for that old nag. White Lightning, he called her. Said he didn't need her anymore and sold her off to me."

"Yes, ma'am, White Lightning is still here. I been taking real good care of her."

"I'd like to see her."

"She's in the fourth stall on the left." He pointed.

She wasn't prepared for the enthusiastic nuzzles White Lightning offered. Emma had fooled everyone except that horse.

She also reacquainted herself with one more friend—Dr. Bunce. The physician was pleased to see her looking so well and continued to care for her during her long convalescence. In return, she sometimes helped him with his patients when she was up to it, but the entire time Emma remained in Oberlin, she was troubled by the war. The ferocious Battle of Gettysburg had especially left her longing for the men she'd left behind. She wasn't yet well enough to take on full-time nursing duties as a civilian, but she felt there must be something she could do to help the soldiers.

During her recovery, Emma decided to write a book detailing her wartime adventures. This was an activity that would not be physically taxing, but before she penned the first word, she decided that every penny she earned from her memoirs would go to aid her fellow soldiers. And so she settled in at Mrs. Wattle's Boarding House for the next several months and wrote, *Nurse and Spy, Or, Unsexed, The Female Soldier*. The words poured out quickly, as her pen completed page after page. She described the horrors of war, her spy missions, and life in an Army camp. She talked of generals and bunkmates—of heroes and scoundrels. She told stories of both bravery and cowardice with a soulful perception that only an eyewitness could have.

Writing proved quite therapeutic for Emma, and when she was done she mailed her manuscript directly to her old employer, Mr. Hulbert in Hartford, Connecticut. Finding the text compelling and unlike any other contemporary release, Hulbert, Williams and Company (the publisher's current name) agreed to issue the book. So, in early 1864, while the war still raged, Emma's memoir became a bestseller with more than 175,000 copies sold. Emma had given the publisher express instructions that all proceeds must go to the Sanitary and Christian Commissions and other Soldier's Aid Societies. The money was to benefit sick and wounded soldiers of the Army of the Potomac to whom the book was dedicated. In addition, commissions were also given to disabled soldiers and widows who sold the book by subscription. Emma herself made no monetary gain whatsoever from her painstaking penmanship.

•••••

During the months she spent writing, Emma had not so much as given a cup of water to the sufferers of the war—something of which she was quite ashamed. She mentioned her guilty feelings to Dr. Bunce one afternoon as she unpacked a new shipment of Bitters in his office.

"Emma, you have always been too hard on yourself." Dr. Bunce smiled.

"But so many men need help—help that I can give them."

"I would hate to see you go," the doctor sighed, then brightened as a new thought struck him. "Why don't you stay right here and enroll in Oberlin College? They have an outstanding nursing program, and I can put in a good word for you."

"I appreciate that . . . Really I do, but right now, there is a war being waged and taking time to go to school when I could be in the field . . . well, it just doesn't seem right."

"I understand how you feel." Dr. Bunce nodded. "But someday this war will be over and when it is, earning your formal credentials might not be such a bad idea. Just don't forget about my offer, Emma."

"I promise, I won't." She placed the last bottle on the shelf. "And maybe when the time is right, I will come back and take you up on it."

Even though her health was still not the best, she traveled to St. Louis, Missouri where she found work as a laundress at Marine General Hospital. The medical facility, located near the Mississippi

River, was opened in 1855 primarily for seamen who needed medical attention. At the time of the Civil War, it was converted to a military hospital where many sick and wounded soldiers were treated. During the war years, the medical staff there cared for almost five thousand men. Oftentimes, the soldiers were left to lay on the hospital's lawn because there was no room for them inside the building.

When she wasn't washing soiled bed linen or hanging wet towels, Emma visited the patients. She felt at home among the men and gladly listened to their war stories. She penned letters for those who could not write, and read books aloud to those who could not read. Back in her element, Emma decided to resume nursing, but she preferred to use her skills closer to the battle lines.

By the fall of 1864, after General William Tecumseh Sherman's zealous capture of Atlanta, Emma traveled back to the east coast. There she returned to nursing duty as a female civilian working in various military hospitals from Clarksburg to Harper's Ferry. She aided thousands of sick and wounded men who arrived after General Philip H. Sheridan's victorious, yet bloody, campaign in the Shenandoah Valley. Although she recognized some of the men she met, both patients and medics, she was unable to identify herself as Franklin Thompson, due to the desertion charges attached to her old identity. Still, some soldiers looked twice at the slender young girl as if trying to recall just where they had met her before. Others claimed that her eyes seemed familiar. Emma laughed them all away, claiming that their lengthy absence from home was causing their confusion. Deep in her heart, however, she longed to be honest.

She met one such medic while working in Harper's Ferry at St. Peter's Roman Catholic Church, which was being used as a military hospital in the war-torn city. Emma found the young man, who looked no more than twenty, standing with papers in hand at the church door—unsure whether to enter. She immediately recognized him as Nurse Calvin Johnson, a medic she had served with early in the war. Johnson had given up his own freedom to remain with his patients during the evacuation to Harper's Landing, when all were taken prisoner by the Rebels. The boy appeared quite thin and haggard since she'd last seen him. He was in dire need of a haircut and his clothes hung loosely from his gaunt frame.

"Would you like to come inside?" she asked kindly. "Are you needing some treatment?"

"No, ma'am, I'll not be needing help." Johnson handed Emma his orders. "I'm Nurse Johnson and I've been assigned to work here."

"You look awfully thin soldier." Emma glanced at the paperwork, pleased to have such a fine man on staff. "Are you sure you're up to working? It seems as if you could use some medical attention yourself."

"No, ma'am, I'm fine." Johnson smiled for the first time. "I was just released from a POW camp with some of my patients down on the Virginia peninsula. There's nothing wrong with me that a good night's sleep won't fix."

"Then you're a lucky man." Emma stepped aside to let him in.

"Very lucky." Johnson closed the door behind him. "But not all of us were so fortunate."

"How bad was it, living as a POW, I mean?" Emma asked.

"Oh, it wasn't so bad for me. Just not a lot of food or comforts. But for the men . . ." He choked on the words. "Well, I lost about half of the thirty to dysentery, typhoid, and swamp fever. I had no quinine pills or any other type of medication to offer them. I felt so helpless as they died one by one under my watch."

"You did what you could." Emma put her hand on his. "And you were a brave man to stay with your men. Very brave."

"Do I know you?" A flicker of recognition momentarily lit up his blue eyes.

"Does the name Emma Edmonds sound familiar?" She grinned.

"No, ma'am, it doesn't."

"Then I suppose we've never met before." She pulled him along behind her. "Now, let's get you fed. We need to fatten you up before we put you to work."

"Yes, ma'am." Johnson followed Emma to the kitchen.

Chapter 19

The War Is Won

While living and working in Harper's Ferry, Emma became acquainted with a gentleman of English heritage, who also hailed from New Brunswick, Canada. Linus Henry Seely was born on April 15, 1832 in the city of St. John near the Bay of Fundy about one hundred miles east of Magaguadavic, where Emma was raised. The warmth in his blue eyes and polished manner drew Emma in. Always dignified and reserved, he was very different from most other men she knew. A builder by trade, Linus had moved to the United States hoping to find work in the war-torn areas of the country.

When he had time, Linus volunteered at St. Peter's where he helped with the patients. There, under Emma's watchful eye, he emptied bedpans, changed bandages, and sometimes mopped the floor. He never once complained that a job was too dirty or beneath him. He just carried on, and his kind demeanor won over many of the patients who looked forward to seeing him. He had one peculiar habit, however. Linus always insisted on having his afternoon tea.

If he was at St. Peter's late enough in the day, he often persuaded Emma to join him. She grew to like the brew, but it was Linus's company that she enjoyed the most. During those brief breaks, they exchanged stories about growing up in New Brunswick. Emma even felt comfortable enough to tell him about her difficult years with Isaac and how she had run away to avoid an undesirable husband. In turn, Linus spoke of his brief marriage to Hannah Jones, a local girl he had met in school.

"A fine girl, my Hannah was," he sighed one afternoon as they sat together in the churchyard each cradling a cup of warm tea. "We were married in '61, and the next year our daughter, Lizzie, was born. She was a beautiful child with a perfect round face. Had her mother's eyes, you know, but she only lasted three days before the good Lord called her home. My Hannah was never the same after that. She cried a lot and said that Lizzie needed her. I watched my wife just waste away and a few months later, I buried her next to the baby."

"How awful for you." Emma was touched by his story.

"That's really why I left St. John." He sipped his tea. "I needed a fresh start."

"I know all about fresh starts." Emma ran her finger over the rim of her cup as if she were about to make a momentous decision. "Can you keep a secret, Linus?"

"I've been known to harbor the darkest of dark tales." He grinned at her. "Do you have a dark side, Emma?"

"I'm afraid it's worse than that." She looked down. "You may not invite me to tea again once you hear about it."

"Nonsense." Linus gently rested his hand on hers. "I'm afraid I've fallen in love with you and there's nothing you could ever say or do that will change my mind about that."

Emma took a deep breath and confessed everything to Linus, from the moment she left Salisbury dressed as a man named Franklin Thompson, to the day she was labeled a deserter for leaving her troop. She described her spy missions, her adventures as a mail carrier, and her grisly work as a field medic. She even told him about James. Relieved to finally talk to someone, she dabbed at her eyes as she finished her story and then sat back, bracing herself for Linus's reaction.

"Is that everything?" His blank look gave her no indication as to what he might be thinking.

"Yes, Linus."

"Good!" He winked. "Because I was worried you were going to say that you disliked my tea."

Throughout 1864 and the first part of 1865, the war continued sending wounded and maimed soldiers to St Peter's. After winning reelection, Father Abraham was once again inaugurated as President of the United States, while Linus courted Emma the old-fashioned way—buggy rides, long walks, and many evenings under the stars. Most afternoons they shared their ritual pot of tea. There was passion between them, but for Emma, their relationship had a calming effect. She found a welcome respite in his arms that renewed her strength and spirits. Better yet, Linus never tried to change or control her. He simply encouraged her to be herself. Most importantly, he never judged her. Instead, he admired her mettle.

"Whatever you do, I want you to be happy, Emma," he'd tell her. "And if you'll let me, I'll tag along for the ride."

•••••

On the evening of April 9, 1865, Emma was at St. Peter's taking inventory of their medical supplies. As she sat at a table near the door of the church counting bandages, a young printer's devil rushed in. "It's over! The war is over!" the curly-haired boy whooped with excitement. "General Lee surrendered this afternoon at Appomattox Court House! We won! We won! We whipped those Rebels, but good!"

"Are you sure, boy?" Emma asked, afraid at first to believe the news.

"Yes, ma'am! We just got word at the newspaper, and Mr. Gandy sent me out to tell everyone. The whole story will be in the morning paper! The Union Army has claimed victory!"

Emma slumped in her chair as the welcome news sunk in. The men began shouting, and those who could danced around the church, unable to contain their excitement. The bells at St. Peter's rang loud and steady, almost drowning out the enthusiastic sounds of the cheering men. Overcome with emotion, Emma sunk to her knees and cried. "Thank God! All of this bloodshed has come to an end and we are once again one nation under God!"

Blanketed in emotion, Emma was vaguely aware of two strong arms lifting her back to her feet. Her senses returned when she focused on Linus's blue eyes. Impulsively, he gave her a celebratory kiss, and she kissed him back, making the memorable moment even better. Linus then lifted her from the ground and twirled her around, making Emma laugh as if all of her cares had vanished.

But the nation's joy was short-lived when the unthinkable happened just four days later. On the evening of April 14, 1865, while attending a play at the Ford Theater in Washington DC, Father Abraham was gunned down by the actor John Wilkes Booth. The President of the United States died the next morning. That same printer's devil arrived at St. Peter's with the horrific news. The shocked soldiers, some still bedridden, openly wept. On top of their weakened conditions, this disastrous turn of events was just too much to bear—the man they called father and friend had been taken from them.

"Oh, this just can't be true!" Emma cried to Linus, who had rushed to St. Peter's after he heard about the assassination.

"And they haven't even caught the killer." Linus shook his head.

"But Father Abraham worked so hard for peace and to keep this country united." Emma shrugged in bewilderment. "And now that peace has been attained, he's gone."

"It's a terrible thing." Linus brushed the hair from her face.

"What happens now?" Emma asked.

"The country rebuilds under President Johnson—it's what Father Abraham would have wanted."

"But what happens to us? Where do we go? What do we do? I can hardly remember a time when there wasn't a battle to fight or men to care for."

"I think you need a good rest, my girl." Linus pulled her close. "Maybe a trip home would do you a world of good."

"What about you?"

"New Brunswick is my home, too. I say we go together."

•••••

Both Emma and Linus had work to finish before they could leave Harper's Ferry. She stayed until the last patient left St. Peter's and the building once again took on its original role as a house of worship. At the same time, Linus completed a rebuilding project that restored a local hotel, which had been heavily damaged during the war. The couple left Virginia together in the late fall of 1865—a few months after President Johnson declared that the war was officially over. They first stopped in St. John's where Emma met Linus's family. He was especially close to his brother, Manley, a single man who was looking for work at the time. Linus suggested that Manley join them in their trip to Magaguadavic. After that, they would go on to Fredericton where, perhaps, they might both seek employment with a construction crew there.

After several weeks near the Bay of Fundy, the three set off for Magaguadavic. There, Emma found both joy and sadness. Elated to finally be reunited with her beloved mother, Emma felt a tug of regret for being gone so long. Betsy, now gray and frail, wept profusely at the sight of her youngest daughter. Isaac, on the other hand, refused to see Emma. Still bitter over her sudden departure, he stayed with a neighbor as long as she was there. Old Earl Harris had long since died when one of his very own mules had given him a solid kick to the head as he tried beating the animal during a drunken rage. Emma thanked God that she had escaped that purgatory, fearing that she may have well suffered the same fate as the mule. In fact, she could easily envision herself delivering the blow to old Earl's head, saving that indignant mule the trouble.

Emma's sisters were all married with babes of their own when she arrived, accompanied by Linus and Manley. In fact, Francis had just recently given birth to a girl that she named Emma in honor of her little sister. When Emma held her namesake for the very first time, an unexpected pang of longing rippled through her. Maybe, one day in the not-too-distant future, she would settle down and have children of her own. She certainly didn't wish to end up alone like her brother, Thomas. He never married, but despite his poor health, remained on the farm helping his mother and father as best he could. Easygoing and full of tall tales, "Uncle Tom" was a favorite among his nieces and nephews. He entertained them with fanciful stories about imaginary people and magical places.

Emma's heart stirred with old feelings of protectiveness as she sat alone with Thomas in the kitchen one evening, surprising him with a cup of tea.

"Since when did you start drinking tea, Emma?" Tom watched as his sister poured.

"Since I met Linus." She smiled. "He says that tea has a calming effect on a person and I tend to agree with him."

"I like Linus." Tom nodded. "He seems to bring out the best in you."

"I like him, too, Tom, but what about you?" She cradled her cup. "You know I still worry about you."

"No need." He tapped his spoon on the saucer.

"Is there someone special?"

"No." He shook his head. "Everyone here knows I have fits and spells, so no real lady will have me."

"Are you happy, Tom?"

"I'm content." He shrugged. "Between our sisters, there are lots of babies to love and the seizures are not so frequent now."

"What about Father? How does he treat you?"

"He's mellowed some with age." Tom smiled. "And it helps that I'm bigger than him now."

"Have you ever thought about leaving Magaguadavic?"

"No, Emma. Good or bad, this is home and what I know. I never had that adventurous spirit that you do. I believe Fanny Campbell had something to do with that."

"She did indeed." Emma sipped her brew. "And some days I thank her, but there are other days I curse her."

"That's pretty much how I feel about Father." He grinned.

•••••

After several weeks in Magaguadavic, Linus, Manley, and Emma traveled on to Fredericton—about forty miles east. Bisected by the St. John River, Fredericton was originally a French colony, but after the Revolutionary War in the United States, the British claimed it. They named it 'Frederick's Town' after Prince Frederick Augustus, the son of England's King George III. In 1785, the small city became the capital of New Brunswick due to its central location within the province and its name was shortened to Fredericton.

Once in the capital city, Linus found construction work along with his brother, and Emma tried her hand, once again, in the millinery business. She soon discovered, however, that her heart was no longer in hat-making. She felt there was more important work to be done. Emma had kept in touch with Dr. Bunce through written correspondence, and he continued to encourage her to study nursing and earn her credentials. In early 1867, she and Linus made a momentous decision to return to Oberlin, Ohio so that Emma might enroll in school.

Dr. Bunce was delighted to see his good friend again and paid her to work for him on a part-time basis while she attended Oberlin's nursing program. The university suited her well as it was the country's first college to allow Negros in its classrooms. The school opened in 1833, and two years later admitted its first black student. In 1844, George B. Vashon was the first Negro to graduate from Oberlin. He went on to become a lawyer, and in addition to being one of Howard University's founding professors, he was also the first black man accepted into New York's Bar. Now that the war was over, Oberlin continued to encourage Negros to attain their higher education.

Linus and Manley easily found carpentry work as the town was booming with opportunity during postwar reconstruction. Linus continued courting Emma, and whenever possible they shared their daily tea. As spring emerged with all of its greenery and flowers stretching skyward in their beds, the young couple took Sunday tea at a park near Lake Erie.

"Emma, you know how I feel about you," Linus spoke once he settled on the old blue and white checked blanket they had laid out on the grass. "And I think I've proven that I support whatever you choose to do."

"And I appreciate it more than you know, Linus." She smiled as only a content woman can. "I love you for letting me live my life instead of trying to control it."

"I don't want to control you." Linus took her hand. "But ever since I saw the look on your face when you held your little niece and namesake back in Magaguadavic, I've been wanting to marry you. What do you say, my love? Will you honor me by being my wife . . . as equal partners, of course?"

"Oh, Linus!" Emma kissed him on the lips. "An equal partnership would be magnificent!"

"Is that a yes?" Linus winked.

"No, my darling." She grinned. "It's a certainty!"

Their engagement was short—only a few scant weeks—and with her sisters in attendance, Emma, making sure to tuck that worn red handkerchief in the sleeve of her bridal gown, became Mrs. Linus Seely on April 27, 1867. The couple was wed at the elegant Weddell House in Cleveland, Ohio originally known as the Astor House of the Lakes. The regal brick hotel boasted two hundred rooms, lavish décor, and had welcomed many distinguished guests throughout the years, including President Abraham Lincoln, General Philip Sheridan, and opera singer Jenny Lind. Reverend A. J. Merchant, a local Methodist minister, performed the simple ceremony.

●●●●●

The first thing Emma did as a new bride was add an *e* to their surname making it 'Seelye.' What she didn't do was finish her formal education. From the time they were first wed, the Seelyes rarely stayed in one place long enough to establish roots. They, along with Manley, lived in Kansas City, Missouri for a while, but soon moved on to Charlevoix, Michigan where Emma's first child, Linus Jr., was born on April 14, 1869. While living in northern Michigan, Manley soon met and married a young girl who ran the one-room schoolhouse near their home. Two years later, when Emma and her family relocated to Evanston, Illinois, Manley and his bride remained in Michigan.

On June 21, 1871, Emma delivered another boy, they named Homer. The frail baby, however, died within the day, leaving devastated parents to bury his doll-like body inside a miniature pine coffin. They both grieved their unthinkable loss, but soon their attention focused on Linus Jr., who grew ill with a serious fever and cough.

The doctors in Evanston tried all of their tricks from tonics to ice baths. They held hope as some days the boy's health saw improvement, but over time, it became apparent that they could do nothing more to help him recover. Out of desperation, Emma and Linus took their only living child to Oberlin, Ohio where their old friend Dr. Bunce still practiced. The good doctor examined the little lad and with a heavy heart met Emma and Linus in his parlor.

"Your son is very sick." He took Emma's hand. "It would take a miracle to save him. You must prepare yourselves for the worst."

"I . . . I can't do that," Emma gasped just above a whisper. "I brought my boy here so you could help him. Why can't you make him better?"

"I wish to God I could, Emma, but the pneumonia has claimed his little lungs. It's just a matter of time before he takes his last breath. You must pray for strength."

"But I haven't any," she screamed. "I just buried a newborn and now you are telling me that I must bury my first son, too?"

Dr. Bunce looked toward Linus whose face had gone white as he quietly tried to absorb the overwhelming news.

"My darling," Linus spoke quietly as he drew his wife in what he hoped was a comforting embrace. "We must pray that our little

Linus doesn't suffer and we must accept what God has in store for us."

"I can't accept it!" she cried. "How can you accept it? This will be the third child you have lost and yet you sit here talking about what God has in store for us? Where is God now?"

"Emma, we are Christians, and as such, we have seen the worst that mankind has to offer and yet we have also witnessed the unbreakable spirit that has given new life to broken men. Like them, we are not faithless, and it is that faith that will see us through this valley of darkness."

Linus's faith was unshakeable as his helpless son went in and out of consciousness. The child sometimes cried for his mother and took solace in her arms. Emma rarely left his side, and when she did, it was just for a moment. Sleep was out of the question. She had to fit a lifetime of mothering in the short time he had left. She rocked him, sang to him, and stroked his long curls. She memorized the shape of his nose, the line of his lips, and the arch of his brow. Unable to care for herself, she relied on Linus's quiet strength to pull them through the worst of it when the boy died ten days later.

•••••

Perhaps because the area was familiar, the now childless couple decided to remain in Oberlin. Emma once again worked for Dr. Bunce while Linus appropriated a job building cabinets. Slowly, their life took on a normal pace, but Emma longed for another child. In early 1874, she found herself expecting for the third time. Terrified of losing yet another baby, she prayed for a healthy child—even if that meant losing her own life in the process. On August 12, 1874, with the help of Dr. Bunce, Emma delivered a little girl, Alice Louise. She was perfect with a full head of dark hair and apple cheeks that turned an even brighter red when she cried. Smitten by his new daughter, Linus especially loved her little bow lips and the way her tiny fists curled around his finger.

There was but one dark moment brought by Dr. Bunce soon after Alice's birth when he came to check on Emma and the baby. All was well with Alice, but Emma's strength was slow in returning.

"You know, my girl." Dr. Bunce took a deep breath as he watched Emma dress her baby after his examination. "This pregnancy and delivery have taken a toll on you and you are not as young as you once were."

"I don't need a doctor to tell me that." She smiled.

"But you do need a doctor to tell you some facts." His expression remained serious. "And I would be remiss if I kept them from you."

"Is Alice all right?" The little color she had drained from Emma's face.

"Rest assured, baby Alice is fine. It's you I am concerned with, Emma. You are not physically strong enough to have any more children. I am afraid that you would probably not survive another pregnancy."

"I'm just a little tired," she insisted. "You know that new mothers don't get much rest."

"It's more than that, Emma." His voice grew stern. "Your body has been weakened by the ague you've suffered from all these years. Now, it has been through three deliveries, and I can assure you, that it will not tolerate a fourth."

"I didn't want to hear it, but to be perfectly honest"—Emma picked up the baby and kissed the top of her head—"I know how I feel. My strength is not what it once was and this confinement was harder than the others. I knew in my heart right after Alice was born that she might be my last. I've even told Linus that I'm afraid to try again."

"I know you want more children, but try to enjoy this one. Alice needs a mother, and Linus would be lost without you. Concentrate on the family you have and be grateful for them."

"I intend to do just that, but I can assure you that Alice will not be an only child," Emma insisted. "When the time is right, I will talk to Linus about adoption. He will agree to it, I'm sure."

Emma was right. Linus not only agreed to adoption, but suggested they take in two boys in memory of the sons they lost.
So before Alice's first birthday, they brought home three-year-old
George Frederick and then an infant named Charles Finney. Emma
relished her busy household and enthusiastically cared for all of
her children. Although she missed her own two boys, the little
ones needed her and filled her days with joy. Linus loved them
all, but doted on Alice who seemed to share his genteel ways. The
Seelyes, now a family of five, thrived in Oberlin, until Emma read
about an orphanage for colored children in Louisiana.

•••••

A small ad in the local paper caught Emma's attention in 1875. The
Freedman's Society in Louisiana had established an orphanage for
the young children of Negro Union soldiers. Many of these inno-
cents had been living in the streets of New Orleans with no one to
care for them. A good number simply died from starvation along
the roadside. In an effort to improve this dire situation, the society
had set up an Orphans Home on an abandoned sugar plantation in
St. Mary's Parish for these neglected colored children. They were
now looking for a married couple to run the place. The thought
of these poor, disadvantaged youngsters struck Emma's heart, and
so the Seelyes' nomadic lifestyle continued when they moved to
Lateche, St. Mary's Parish, Louisiana where they stayed for the
next three years.

Emma was in her element caring for the children, learning their
names, and getting to know them as individuals, while Linus kept
up the grounds and the building. The Seelyes even had their own
two-story home nearby, but Emma spent most of her waking hours
with the children. Her own youngsters were sometimes jealous
of the love she lavished on her charges. She had to remind Alice,
Charles, and George (now called Frederick) that they had been
blessed with two good parents while these underprivileged and forgotten children had been cast aside through no fault of their own.

Emma was content to stay at the orphanage forever, but the damp Louisiana air finally got the best of her. Weakened by her recurring malaria, she grew frail and, for weeks at a time, suffered through bouts of ague. The disease haunted her for the remaining days of her life, causing serious damage to her organs and overall health. Worried for his wife's well-being, Linus convinced a reluctant Emma that it was in her best interest to move away from the stifling humidity.

During the fall of 1880, Linus found work in the dryer climate of California, Missouri—about 150 miles west of St. Louis. With a population close to 1,000, California's busy main street claimed several stores, pharmacies, and a bank. Upon their arrival, the Seelyes rented a room in a boardinghouse near the downtown section. Emma went straight to bed, as fever and chills had gotten the best of her during the move. In addition to looking for work, Linus took care of the children while his wife recovered. Just when Emma began feeling better and Linus started a new construction job, however, all three children came down with the measles.

Eventually, Frederick and Charles improved as their symptoms subsided and their appetites returned. But little Alice Louise was not as robust as her brothers. The six-year-old had little energy and slept through most days. Linus brought in a doctor who prescribed an elixir, but Alice remained weak. By Christmas Eve, he and Emma knew that they would bury yet another child. Six-year-old Alice Louise died on Christmas Day in 1880, leaving Emma bereft and the normally strong Linus inconsolable. As she watched her daughter's coffin settle into the cold December ground, Emma cried into Betsy's thinning handkerchief, and couldn't help but think that perhaps death had followed her from the battlefield.

•••••

The Seelyes' stay in Missouri was short. Too many bad memories enveloped them there. By 1881, the family moved to Fort Scott, Kansas. It was not only one of the largest cities in the state, but also one of the biggest on the western frontier. Linus and Emma may have picked Fort Scott because that same year Kansas had prohibited alcohol—the first state to do so. Being good Christians, the Seelyes wanted to ensure that their boys grew up around other good Christians. Tea, however, was not outlawed, which kept Linus's afternoon ritual in good standing with the locals.

Emma settled in at Fort Scott, determined to create a home for her sons. She liked the community, the school, the church, and for the first time in a very long while, she made friends. Although the war had been over for sixteen years, Emma's recurring malaria and the curse of death her family endured kept the memories of battle alive in her mind. She thought about the memoir she had written when the war was still in its bloodiest days. Emma had never been happy with the work she had penned, since back then she refused to identify herself, as well as many others she wrote about. In fact, she had often used only initials or fictional names to maintain privacy.

Things were different now and the truth weighed upon her. It was time to set her story straight, so she decided to write a new book and an honest one—this time chronicling her dalliance into the world of masculinity. The world that in her youth she had hoped would bring her exhilarating adventure, had instead overwhelmed her with death and suffering. For the first time, she wrote truthfully *about the war and the costs to all of those who were touched by it. She told of the horrors and the tragedy of the human spirit that allowed it to happen in the first place.*

One sunny autumn afternoon while Linus was preparing tea, Emma sat at her writing desk. From her top drawer, she pulled the gold ring that Captain Allen Hall had given her so long ago. She gently fingered it as she thought back on the night she spent next to the body of a Rebel that she had come to admire and quite possibly love. Linus caught her in her reverie as he entered the room carrying a tray of tea.

"It seems my memory has served me too well, Linus." Emma put down the ring. "All I've written about is death. I certainly can't imagine that anyone will wish to read about that."

"Nonsense, Emma." Linus poured her a warm cup. "Your story is fascinating. It will be a best-seller just like your first book. And this time you need to keep some of the royalties for yourself."

"It would help buy the groceries." Emma grinned. "I swear those boys will eat us out of house and home before they are grown."

"We'll manage," Linus sighed as he pulled a chair next to hers. "We always do."

"I've been thinking, Linus," Emma began, but hesitated.

"Not always a good thing." He poured the tea.

"Wouldn't it help us out if I could collect the government pension due me? I was a soldier for the Federal Government, after all."

"And an honorable one at that." Linus squeezed her shoulder.

"Franklin Thompson was honorable," she said more to herself than to her husband. "I just wish there were a way to clear his name before I die."

"Why don't you do it then?"

"I wouldn't know where to begin."

"Maybe you should start with some of the men you served with."

"But they will never believe that I was Franklin Thompson," Emma sighed.

"My dear wife, I've been married to you long enough to know that if you put your mind to it, you could make a believer out of General Lee!"

Chapter 20

Revealing Her True Identity

The early 1880s brought its own set of troubles. The American Indian Wars were waging in full force out West. The nation suffered the violent loss of yet another president, James A. Garfield, who also succumbed to an assassin's bullet. And, news of a bloody gunfight in Tombstone, Arizona, at some obscure location called the O.K. Corral, traveled fast across the nation. The thirty-second shootout between lawmen and brothers, Virgil, Morgan and Wyatt Earp, as well as the Georgia-born dentist Doc Holliday, effectively ended their long-simmering feud with cowboys, Tom and Frank McLaury, Billy Claiborne, along with Billy and Ike Clanton. The clash would go down in history as the most famous gunfight in the American West.

It wasn't all bad news, however. Former Civil War nurse Clara Barton founded the Red Cross, and Thomas Edison dabbled with innovative ways to use electricity, while Alexander Graham Bell experimented with an improved method of long-distance communication.

For the Seelyes, their move to Fort Scott, Kansas brought stability to their family—something they had been lacking. For the first time in their married life, the Seelyes stayed in one place for more than a year or two. Happy to call Fort Scott home, they raised their sons and were relieved that their nomadic existence had finally come to an end. In between her motherly duties, her periodic writing, and her household chores, Emma thought about her past long and hard. She also took in a shepherd dog that she called Jack. The black and white pup had followed her home one afternoon after she had gone to the butcher. "It must have been the stew meat I bought," she liked to say because Jack rarely left her side—even when the boys tried to entice him outside to play.

As Emma went about her daily chores, she remained haunted by her desertion charges and the loss of her soldier's pension. For many months, she discussed her anxieties with Linus who, as always, encouraged her to follow her heart. As a parent, however, she worried that revealing her past deceptions would negatively impact her sons. What would they think of their mother once they learned she had masqueraded as a man? But she knew that she wasn't getting any younger or healthier. Something had to be done before it was too late.

Emma felt it was only right that Uncle Sam grant a pension to *one female soldier who had actually served two years, or nearly so, of faithful, hard service, when he had pensioned so many males who never so much as smelt powder on the battlefield.* She convinced herself that the Federal Government owed her that much, but she knew that she couldn't collect her pension on her own. She would need help from her fellow veterans. It was Linus who suggested they both take the train to Flint, Michigan, where Franklin Thompson's military journey had started. Linus also called upon Uncle Manley who came to stay with Frederick, Charles, and Jack.

In the early spring of 1883, Emma and Linus stepped off a train at the depot in Flint, Michigan. The sun shone brightly, despite the winter chill that still lingered in the air. The city was different than Emma remembered—it was larger and noisier. After taking their luggage to a local inn, Emma was anxious to find her old bunkmate and friend, Damon Stewart. She asked the clerk who stood guard at the hotel's front desk if The Old Scotch Store was still open and to her delight, it was. Her husband offered to accompany her, but she wanted to meet Stewart alone. Linus opted for a cup of tea while he waited for his wife to return.

Emma set off on foot, wearing a dark print dress and a small black hat with thick veiling that covered her face. She looked around as she walked, hoping to see someone or something familiar, but the people and places she passed were unknown to her. Several blocks down, she stopped in front of The Old Scotch Store feeling more and more like a stranger in the town that she had once called home. The building was the same, but it had a fresh coat of paint. The windows, now much larger, housed eye-catching displays of various household goods along with the latest fashions. It looked nothing like the plain structure that Emma had once visited. She peeked in the large window and saw several customers and a very young clerk—none of whom she recognized. Emma took a deep breath and went inside.

"I'm looking for Damon Stewart." She approached the worker who had his back to her. "Do you know where I can find him?"

"In the back office." The boy, who was in the midst of repairing a glass case, pointed over his shoulder without so much as looking up.

Emma took another deep breath and walked through the open doorway. An older-looking Stewart wearing spectacles and a black shirt sat behind a large wooden desk, studying a ledger—a pen in his right hand. "Can I help you, ma'am?" He stood up as soon as he saw her.

"Damon?" She lifted her veil. "I was hoping you'd remember me."

"You look so familiar." He gazed directly at her.

"Do you remember your old bunkmate, Franklin Thompson?"

"That's it!" He grinned. "You look like Frank! Are you his mother? His sister? Where is he? Is he all right?"

"I am neither his mother nor his sister." Emma smiled. "Franklin Thompson is standing right in front of you—none the worse for wear."

"But you're a woman?" Stewart gasped in disbelief.

"I believe you used to call me 'your little woman' when we served together during the war."

"I . . . I never meant it to offend you." He fell back into his chair, removed his spectacles, and nervously cleaned them with his shirt-tail before repositioning them on his nose.

"I was never offended." Emma reached for his hand with a grin. "And now you understand why I never had to shave."

"And why your boots were so small!"

A stunned Stewart offered her a seat while she offered an explanation of who she really was and why she came to call on him after all these years.

"We have to get the men together!" Stewart couldn't hide his excitement. "Morse and McCreery and all the others! They won't believe it till they see for themselves! And you must meet my wife, Frances. I'm afraid she won't believe it either! We all wondered what happened to you, Frank! I . . . I mean Emma. We were all afraid that damned ague went and killed you."

"It's left me weaker than I'd like." She smiled. "But it hasn't done me in . . . at least not yet."

That evening, Emma and Linus were welcomed to the Stewart home for dinner where they met not only Frances, but the six Stewart children. Emma and Damon reminisced about the hardship of war and the way it made men out of young soldiers—at least most young soldiers. Damon suggested calling a meeting that weekend at his home. He contacted all of the men who remained in the area. He didn't tell them the reason for the gathering, but he personally assured each and every one that they were in for a big surprise that they wouldn't want to miss. His cryptic invitation was more than enough to rouse their curiosity and guarantee their presence.

•••••

As Emma readied herself to meet her fellow veterans that Sunday afternoon, she examined her image in the mirror. Two decades had passed since she'd served in the Union Army and her looks had changed. Not only was she twenty years older, but the burdens she carried—both physical and emotional—had left her frame gaunt and her face worn. She appeared matronly, yet still attractive for her age. She couldn't help but wonder if her old friends would recognize her and more importantly if they would be willing to accept her, let alone help her. Just because Damon Stewart had no hard feelings didn't mean the rest of them would forgive her as easily.

When Emma and Linus arrived at the Stewart home that Sunday afternoon, the parlor was filled with familiar faces. She immediately recognized Bill McCreery, as well as Captain Morse and his wife, Mary. She was even more pleased to see the chaplain and Kate Butler, along with other members of the Second Michigan Infantry, Company F—all anxiously awaiting Damon's mysterious guest. Although he had told them that they would be meeting one of their mates, he hadn't disclosed who it was. Catching sight of the Seelyes, most of the men assumed that Linus had served with them in the Second. An older Morse, his hairline receding, stepped forward and extended his hand to Linus. "My apologies for having a bad memory, sir. Please remind me which battles we fought in together."

Linus smiled with amusement as he shook Morse's hand. "We never served together, sir. Your comrade-in-arms was my wife, Emma, here. But, I believe you knew her as Franklin Thompson."

Morse, in unison with the others, let out a loud gasp.

Emma stepped from her husband's side and took Morse's hand. "It's good to see you well, Captain."

"No one has called me that in a very long time." Morse studied her face closely. "You sure do resemble Frank, but how is that possible? The Frank I knew was most definitely a man."

The other men, too, gathered around Emma. They seemed quite curious and more than a little skeptical until the Butlers spoke out. "I'll be damned." The chaplain smiled. "If it isn't our little woman!"

"You were the finest nurse we had in Company F." Kate embraced her. "You worked harder than many of our surgeons and

I thoroughly appreciated having another lady to talk to when we were in the trenches. I truly missed you when you disappeared." Keeping one arm around Emma, Kate turned to the astonished men. "I can attest to the fact that Emma here is most certainly the soldier you all knew as Franklin Thompson."

"I can second that." Chaplain Butler nodded. "What my wife says is true."

Emma turned to McCreery. "Bill, remember that last sermon Willie preached the night before Bull Run? We were all so touched by his words and then we lost him the very next day."

"I remember." McCreery nodded. "He even sang a hymn afterward."

"And he had the voice of an angel," Emma recalled with a sigh. "I'm sure he is still singing the sweetest hymns in heaven."

"How could I not know the truth?" A gray-haired Mary Morse shook her head. "All the time you spent at my house and I never knew."

"Oh, Mary, there was so much to worry about back then." Emma smiled. "And you hated all that war talk. You always tried to get me to side with you during our meetings in your parlor."

"And now I believe I owe you a debt of thanks." Mary took her hand. "You took care of my William after he was shot on the battlefield. You saw to it that he made it home to me."

"And as I recollect it"—Emma grinned—"your William didn't want my help that day, but I told him that I couldn't face Mrs. Morse if I let something bad happen to him."

"Emma . . . strange calling you that." Morse heaved a sigh. "I still think of you as Frank, but either way it is only due to your determination and persistence that I still have my leg. I want to formally thank you for disobeying my orders to leave me there on the field."

"I can't say it was my pleasure," Emma addressed Captain Morse with a grin. "But there was no way I could have left your side until I knew you were safe."

"Knowing now that you are a woman, I finally understand your compassion . . . and your stubbornness." He chuckled.

Emma then spoke to all of the veterans. "I promise you, I am that young boy you believed to be Franklin Thompson. I nursed those of you who were sick or wounded and carried your mail. I am sorry I deceived you, but it was my honor to have fought beside such brave and dedicated brothers while serving this great nation. You must understand that I could never have been a soldier of the Army of the Potomac if anyone thought for one minute that I was a woman . . . So you see I had to keep my secret . . . until now."

Emma then noticed General Orlando Poe and his wife, Eleanor, inching closer in an effort to get a better look at her. Poe even put on his spectacles just to be sure. "I do believe that this woman is telling the truth. Eleanor and I would recognize him, uh her, anywhere."

Eleanor cast a glaring look at her husband, which Emma duly noted, but chose to ignore for the moment.

"Thank you, General." Emma gave a little bow. "It's good to see you and Eleanor again."

Despite Eleanor's polite smile, Emma sensed an underlying animosity. Could she possibly think that Emma had an eye on the general? But then, some women did have jealous natures and just couldn't help themselves. For the moment, Emma dismissed it as nonsense. There were only two men that Emma really loved—one she had buried beneath that pear tree in Virginia and the other she had married.

"Now that I look back," the general interrupted Emma's fleeting thoughts. "I am not surprised to discover that you are a woman. I should have known—especially after Randolf Meade's visit. I refused to hear him out that day, but when I think about it, you always did seem too delicate to be in harm's way even though your actions painted quite a different picture."

"I must say, Emma." Colonel Frederick Schneider came forward. "That as Franklin Thompson you were the most devoted and bravest soldier I have ever had the honor to know."

Their lively conversation continued filling the parlor with memories as they reminisced, sharing war stories and mourning their lost comrades. They even found some good times to laugh about—like when Jack stole the chickens.

Just before the day turned into evening, Damon requested everyone's attention. "Firstly, I want to thank each and every one of you for accepting my invitation this afternoon. I must admit that I was as surprised and taken aback as you were when this little lady confessed to me that she was in fact our very own Frank Thompson. And I am sure that nearly every man here will remember our comrade with fondness and respect for all she did. I asked you all here today not just to meet Emma and clear the air, but to enlist your support for something that is long overdue. Emma Seelye must clear the name of Franklin Thompson from an unjust desertion charge and obtain her soldier's pension that she so rightly deserves. In order to do this, she needs affidavits attesting to her identity and activity during the two years she served with us." Damon gestured for Emma to join him. "Please . . . Emma, I believe you have something that you would like to say."

While Linus looked on with a proud smile, Emma took her place next to Damon. "I'm afraid I owe you all an explanation." She took a breath before continuing. "As most of you know, I suffer from malaria. Something I caught in the Great Dismal Swamp during the war. I experienced recurring attacks that continue to this day. There is no cure and each bout of fever and chills leaves me a little weaker. On the morning of April 19, 1863, I knew I would die if I did not get appropriate medical attention. The quinine pills I'd been taking were no longer effective. I'd requested a leave, but my superiors refused to grant me time off. I could not risk revealing my true identity by checking into a military hospital, so I did the only thing I could—I left the Union Army and rode to Oberlin, Ohio where I sought treatment as a female civilian. I almost died there, but the Good Lord wasn't quite done with me. He and a fine doctor nursed me back to health. Now I beg your help in exonerating me from the desertion charges and in obtaining my monthly twelve-dollar military pension. If you would be so kind as to submit written statements to the Military Department of the Michigan Adjutant General's office by way of your Congressman attesting to my service in the Union Army under the name of Franklin Thompson, I would forever be in your debt."

The men unanimously and without hesitation agreed to help.

Chapter 21

Clearing Her Name

Emma had gone to Flint in order to clear her name along with her military record. While the men rallied around her, the last thing she expected was Eleanor Poe's disparaging slur to her reputation. Perhaps it had been Mrs. Poe's displeasure in discovering that the aide who had spent so much time alone with her husband, both in camp and on excursions and missions, had in fact been a woman—an attractive one at that. Or, perhaps it had been Mary Morse or Frances Stewart—two women she had trusted—who started these rumors, which could damage Emma's reputation as a moral woman.

Whatever the source, Emma was hurt quite deeply and started to question her own actions and deceptions perpetrated during the war. So distracted by the slight, she stopped going to church even though Linus and the boys dutifully attended the Methodist service each week. Still pulled in the direction of her Christian roots, however, Emma did hold prayer meetings in the parlor of her own home, which were not only well attended by the locals, but secretly pleasing to Linus. Maybe it was her dishonesty with her friends and comrades that made her feel unworthy to enter a holy place, or possibly, all that she had witnessed during and after the war, shook her belief in a traditional God, as well as her once solid faith.

Unlike the womenfolk, her trusted comrades-in-arms did not let her down. Quartermaster William B. McCreery, Colonel Frederick Schneider, James H. Brown, Colonel Sylvester Larned, Captain Damon Stewart, Captain William R. Morse, William Shakespeare, William Turner, Sumner Howard, Milton S. Benjamin, and General Poe were among the men who wrote individual affidavits to their Congressman, Byron M. Cutcheon of Michigan's Ninth Congressional District. They all testified that Sarah Emma Seelye was indeed one and the same person as their regiment mate, Franklin Thompson. Each one confirmed her upstanding character and loyal commitment to service while in the Union army.

• • • • •

Captain Damon Stewart wrote: ". . . Private Franklin Thompson . . . bore a good reputation, always behaved as a person of good moral character and a consistent Christian, and was always ready for duty . . ."

• • • • •

Colonel Frederick Schneider, James H. Brown, and Colonel Sylvester Larned joined together to attest that: ". . . In view of her many ministrations of tenderness and mercy, thousands of soldiers who were the recipients of her timely attention and nursing must remember her with the most filial regard. She is now the same true, loyal woman that she was in those eventful, stormy days of 1861 to 1865, when the country was passing the agonizing throes of civil war. . . ."

• • • • •

Captain William R. Morse confirmed: ". . . Franklin Thompson . . . by her uniform faithfulness, bravery, and efficiency, and by her pure morals and Christian character, won the respect, admiration, and confidence of both officers and men in said company and regiment. . . ."

•••••

Emma penned her own letter, telling her story: "I felt called to go and do what I could for the defense of the right . . . I went with no other ambition than to nurse the sick and care for the wounded . . . I had inherited from my mother a rare gift of nursing, and when not too weary or exhausted, there was a magnetic power in my hands to soothe the delirium. . . ."

•••••

Unfortunately, Emma did not elaborate on her work as a Union spy. Instead, she simply wrote: "I make no statement of any secret services. In my mind, there is almost as much odium attached to the word 'spy' as there is to the word 'deserter.' There is so much mean deception necessarily practiced by a spy that I much prefer everyone should believe that I never was beyond the enemy's lines rather than fasten upon me by oath a thing that I despise so much. It may do in war time, but it is not pleasant to think upon in time of peace. . . ."

•••••

In his historical sketch entitled 'Michigan in the War,' John Robertson, a Civil War veteran and Adjutant General of Michigan Volunteers, did address Emma's role in the Secret Service: ". . . She succeeded in concealing her sex most admirably serving in various campaigns and battles of the regiment as a soldier; often employed as a spy, going within the enemy's lines, sometimes absent for weeks, and is said to have furnished much valuable information. . . ."

•••••

In addition, Emma's doctor in Fort Scott, Thomas Barnett, wrote: "This may certify that I have examined Mrs. S. Emma E. Seelye and find her suffering from symptoms pointing to disease of the heart which may be the sequence of inflammatory rheumatism. She also has disease of the liver, the viscera is enlarged so as to be felt below the ribs, the skin and cornea have a yellow tinge; there is enlargement of the spleen, and symptoms of disease of the kidney."

•••••

On March 18, 1884, two appeals were presented to the First Session of the 48th Congress on Emma's behalf: H.R. 5334 to remove the desertion charges and H.R. 5335, to grant her a soldier's pension.

With the help of former Michigan governor Edward B. Winans, now a Congressman from Michigan's Sixth District, who presented bill H.R. 5335, Emma was given her pension. United States President Chester A. Arthur signed the bill authorizing payment on July 7, 1884:

> "Be it enacted by the Senate and House of Representatives of the United States of America in Congress assembled; that the Secretary of the Interior is hereby authorized and directed to place on the pension roll the name of Sarah E.E. Seelye, alias Franklin Thompson, who was a late private in Company F, Second Regiment of Michigan Infantry Volunteers at the rate of $12 per month."

The following statements were also part of the official record:

> "Truth is often stranger than fiction and now comes the sequel. Sarah Emma Edmonds (sic), now Sarah E. Seelye, alias Franklin Thompson, is now asking this Congress to grant her relief by way of a pension on account of failing health which she avers had its incurrence and is the sequence of the days and nights she spent in the swamps of the Chickahominy in the days she spent soldiering.

*"That Franklin Thompson and Mrs. Sarah E. E. Seelye,
are one and the same person is established by abundance of
proof, and beyond a doubt, she submits a statement, under oath,
setting forth her history from the time, and also the testimony of
ten credible witnesses, men of intelligence, holding places of high
honor and trust, who positively swear that she is the identical
Franklin Thompson who enlisted in Company F, Second Michigan Infantry, May 25, 1861. Her history from the time she left
the camp at Lebanon to the close of the war is mainly interesting
and pertinent to this report, as showing that though by the rules
of war a deserter, yet her course and conduct after shows the
same zeal in the service of her country in her proper character as
actuated her when she first dedicated herself to the cause which
she felt to be the highest and noblest that can actuate a man or
woman . . ."*

H.R. 5334, addressing the desertion charges, was another matter. This bill was presented by Byron M. Cutcheon and required
additional investigation from the Committee on Military Affairs.
It took another two years, the tireless efforts of Congressman
Cutcheon, and yet another president to pass what is now referred
to as H.R. 1172.

•••••

In the meantime, word of Emma's remarkable tale had spread
throughout Michigan's former Second Infantry. A reunion of the
surviving veterans was planned in Flint, Michigan during the fall of
1884. Emma was invited by her comrades to attend, and they even
offered to pay her way. Hesitant at first to make the long journey
alone, Linus encouraged her.

"They all want to see you, my girl." He winked. "I believe you
are legendary!"

"Look at me," Emma sighed. "I am hardly a legend. A tired, old
woman, maybe, but certainly not a legend."

"There are those who would disagree." Linus smiled. "I think you should go."

"What about the boys? And Jack?"

"I believe I am perfectly capable of taking care of two boys and a dog while you are gone."

"But I'd feel better if you went with me. Maybe Manley could come and stay here with Frederick and Charles. Jack likes him well enough."

"Nonsense!" Linus insisted. "No one in Michigan wants to see me, Emma. It's you that they are clamoring to meet and with good reason. If I weren't already married to you, I'd be curious myself. Go see the boys you loved so much and let them know you haven't forgotten them. Besides, I believe you owe them a debt of thanks."

And with that the matter was closed.

•••••

It was a warm fall day in Flint, Michigan. The scent of apples wafted in the air if the wind blew just right. Approximately ninety members of the Grand Army of the Republic, or GAR, gathered together on the grounds of the old 'Casino' where a special program ensued. Speeches were given by General Poe, William Shakespeare, and William R. Morse, and the local glee club sang accompanied by Professor Gardner's Flint Band—a home-grown favorite. But the afternoon's highlight came when Colonel Sylvester Larned convinced Emma to speak. As she took the stage, her simple words were brief, but met with resounding approval. "My dear comrades, my heart is so full, I cannot say what I would to you. Tears are in my eyes, but I shall never, never forget your love and kindness to Frank Thompson. All that I can say is that I am deeply grateful, and may God bless you."

In the meantime, work continued on clearing Emma's name of the desertion charges. Investigations were completed, testimonials were given, and character references were documented, but Emma believed that a letter written on her behalf by General Poe helped her cause the most. The general stated, "I would be perfectly willing to go upon the stand and swear that the soldier known as 'Frank Thompson,' of the Second Regiment Michigan Volunteer Infantry, and the woman now known as Mrs. S. E. E. Seelye are one and the same person. There is not the shadow of a doubt about it, and I know that my wife, as well as many officers of the regiment, would give the same testimony."

Eleanor Poe's true feelings on the matter, however, remain unknown.

Finally on July 7, 1886, President Grover Cleveland signed H.R. 1172 ordering that ". . . the charge of desertion borne against the name Franklin Thompson, alias S. E. E. Seelye, late a private in Company F, Second Michigan Infantry, be, and the same is hereby removed."

The bill further stated:

> "That the proper accounting officers of the government are hereby directed to liquidate and settle the amount of back pay, bounty and allowances due to said Franklin Thompson, alias S.E.E. Seelye, at the date of his (her) alleged desertion; and thereupon the proper disbursing officers are authorized and directed to pay to said Franklin Thompson, alias S.E.E. Seelye, the amount of back pay, bounty and allowances so ascertained to be due, the same as if no charge of desertion ever existed against the said Franklin Thompson, alias S.E.E. Seelye."

In addition, the report filed also noted:

> "From all this mass of testimony it is established beyond a doubt that 'Frank Thompson,' private, of Company F, Second Michigan Infantry and Mrs. S. E. E. Seelye are one and the same; that she served honestly and faithfully for two years as a private soldier in the ranks, in the hospital, as mail carrier, and as orderly to General O.M. Poe; that during her term of service

she bore an unblemished character as a soldier, and for prompt-
ness and cheerfulness in the discharge of every duty . . .

" . . . This bill removes the charge of desertion, and gives Mrs.
Seelye her back pay and bounty, if any, which may be due her.

"A pension of $12 per month was granted her by the last
Congress. . . .

"As the general law makes no provision for such an anoma-
lous case, the committee recommend that the bill do pass."

On March 29, 1887, a certificate of honorable discharge was officially given to Emma by the Adjunct General's office.

Emma finally achieved what she had set out to accomplish so
long ago, and she once wrote: "Of all the blessings of my life, my
kind husband Linus, my two sons, the one thing that had eluded
me was the ability to clear my name for duty to my adopted country. Having the accusation of deserter removed from my record all
but made my life complete, that I had finally been recognized by
the government for which I risked my life and still suffer the physical ailments, which I acquired in such a service."

• • • • •

Emma's philanthropic nature continued to drive her, and with her
newly expected funds, she and Linus purchased property in Fort
Scott, Kansas. They called it Seelye Hill. It was here that they
intended to build a Soldiers Home and Hospital. When completed,
the attractive two-story white frame building housed several spa-
cious rooms including a kitchen, dining room, and four large bedrooms. Its sizable porch overlooked the picturesque countryside
nearby. Upon completion of the house, however, Emma had still
not collected even a part of the promised pension. She soon saw
firsthand how slowly the wheels of government turned, so slowly
in fact, that the Seelyes were forced to move into the home themselves just to ensure they could keep it.

It wasn't until April 2, 1889 and after many inquiries that Emma finally received her long-overdue bonus and back pension. Emma's pay, however, was only half of what she had hoped. She received just over one hundred dollars in total and her dreams of turning the grand white house into a home for soldiers were dashed. Instead, the Seelyes had to rent out the rooms in order to make ends meet. For Emma, this was a problem. She detested housework and only did the minimum required. She much preferred chopping wood to cooking and cleaning.

Not one to socialize, Emma kept to herself, continuing work on her new memoir. She also remained dedicated to various veterans' groups. Besides Linus and the children, her favorite companion was still her shepherd dog, Jack, who liked to sit at her feet while she wrote, or patrol the area while Emma tended her garden. Always neat, she rarely spent a lot of time on her looks—contrary to the handsome Linus, who never went to church without with his dapper top hat and swallowtail coat. Emma still hadn't grown to like dresses and continued wearing trousers more often than not. On occasion, when she did don a skirt, she refused to put on ladies' shoes. Instead, she always slipped on men's boots. The neighbors thought her a bit odd and eccentric, but pretty much harmless. For the most part, they paid her little attention until the *Fort Scott Tribune Monitor*, a local newspaper, printed her unusual story.

As a result of the press, Emma became an unwilling celebrity in town—especially to the neighboring children. They were in awe of the spy who lived on the hill. Her reclusiveness only served to intrigue them more and elevate her reputation to that of an enigma. In their little minds, the image of a woman dressed as a man fascinated the children so much that they took great delight in spying on her.

It wasn't unusual to find some daring little boy or girl willing to sneak up on Emma as she worked in the garden or shopped in town. Sometimes the youngsters even scared themselves silly by getting as close to her as they could. A simple frown from their mysterious neighbor often sent them home screaming in terror.

For the most part, Emma took it all in stride, as parents, who were just as curious, tried to assure their offspring that spies were not necessarily bad. They explained how many lives were saved for the Union side due to the covert work of undercover agents like Emma. Eventually, instead of an oddity, the woman on Seelye Hill became a hometown hero.

Chapter 22

Honoring a Secret War Hero

With the desertion charges now cleared and regular pension checks arriving to help support them, the Seelyes remained settled in Fort Scott, Kansas. Linus and his sons, now in their teens, still attended church while Emma continued conducting prayer services in her parlor. Frederick worked with his father in the construction business, and Charles, who preferred planting and sowing over mortar and brick, found odd jobs at nearby farmsteads.

Around 1890, Otway Cutler Sterling and his wife, Margaret, moved into a home not far from Seelye Hill. Originally from Virginia, the couple had five children—Addie, George, Mary, Otway Jr., and Lucy, their youngest. Lucy was an attractive child with long brown hair and eyes to match. She sometimes attended Emma's prayer services with her father.

It was there, at Emma's home, at the young age of fourteen, that Lucy first met Frederick, who was three years her senior. His thick auburn hair and penetrating gray eyes caught her attention, and she knew immediately that her future would be entwined with his. As much as Lucy was smitten with Frederick, she was also fascinated by his mother. She sometimes visited with Emma and helped her with mundane chores such as ironing and dusting. An unusual friendship of sorts evolved between the youngster and the ex-Civil War soldier and before long, Emma thought of Lucy as a daughter.

Otway Sterling was not as fond of Emma's son. He felt that Lucy was much too young to commit herself to one man, but as often happens, the daughter soon got her way. On January 15, 1891, George Frederick Seelye married Lucy Letitia Sterling at Fort Scott's Holiness Church and the newlyweds moved into the Seelye home. It was a good arrangement. From the beginning, Lucy called Emma "Mother Seelye" and happily agreed to take over the household duties so Emma could work outside. When attacks of malaria chased Emma to bed, it was Lucy who cared for her making sure Emma was at the very least comfortable. Even Jack liked to curl up near Lucy's feet at the end of the day.

Lucy also took an interest in Emma's memoirs and helped her complete them—rewriting the entire manuscript by hand. For Lucy, this was a labor of love. She was intrigued by her mother-in-law's story and felt that it should be documented for historical purposes, as well as for the family. Emma insisted on paying her daughter-in-law for her hard work, but Lucy wasn't interested in the money. She quietly put her earnings aside and later used it to buy Emma new clothes.

Linus, too, adored his new daughter-in-law. He even gave her a jade hairpin edged in gold that once belonged to his first wife. Perhaps, Lucy unwittingly gave Emma and Linus a glimpse of what their own little Alice might have been like had she lived. No matter the reason, the bond between them only deepened when Lucy's family left Fort Scott for a job in the newly formed city of La Porte, Texas.

In 1892, Lucy presented the Seelyes with a grandson, Harry Ernest. A new baby breathed even more life into their household. Emma and Linus became doting grandparents to the lad, but unfortunately, the fiscal climate of the country was not as sunny as their family life. In a prelude of what was to come the following year, construction slowed down and there was no longer enough work in Fort Scott to support both Linus and his son. Frederick took note of his father-in-law's move and with a heavy heart made the decision to follow the Sterlings to La Porte, taking Lucy and

Harry with him. At the same time, Charles also chose to leave Seelye Hill and join the army. The Seelye home became a depressing
place that a lonely Emma grew to dislike.

"I'm lonesome, Linus," Emma told her husband late one night as
they sat on the porch listening to the gulls cry.

"I know you are, my girl," he sighed, taking her hand. "The
house seems so empty now, but at least we still have each other."

"Are you ever sorry you married me?" she asked softly.

"My beautiful Emma." Linus raised her hand to his lips. "I may
regret many things, but marrying you has never been one of them.
My life would have been as dull as I am without you."

"But I feel that I've caused you a great deal of trouble."

"The 'trouble' you speak of"—Linus pulled her closer—"is what
made my life so interesting. How many men do you know can
claim that their wife is a genuine war hero?"

"None, I suppose." She smiled.

"My point exactly." He brushed her cheek. "And I look forward
to whatever is next as long as we're together."

•••••

What came next was more unpleasant business. Due to the finan-
cial panic of 1893 that gripped the country, hundreds of banks
closed, including two in Fort Scott. Businesses shut down throughout the country and unemployment rose to an unacceptable level.
Linus's construction company was one of the casualties, which was
a mixed blessing for Emma. She and her husband both agreed that
it made good sense for them to join Frederick, Lucy, and Harry in
La Porte where properties were still being developed.

La Porte, Texas was a fairly new community established by real
estate developers in 1892. Located near the San Jacinto Bay, it was
the site of the Battle of San Jacinto, which effectively ended the
Texas Revolution in 1836. As bathhouses, piers, and hotels were
built along the water, La Porte was on its way to becoming a popu-

lar tourist destination for people living in Houston, which was less than thirty miles away.

The Seelyes purchased a farm not far from La Porte. On the property stood a two-story home with an oversize front porch that faced the bay. The house was large, and to Emma's delight, she found herself once again living with her son, Frederick, beloved daughter-in-law, Lucy, and cherished grandson, Harry. Having the family with her again made Emma quite happy, but it wasn't long after the move a concerned Lucy noticed how rapidly Emma's health declined. It was more than her recurring malaria. Her hair was grayer, her step was slower, and the woman who once had so much energy seemed sluggish. A minimal chore like dusting drained most of her strength. Even Emma's eyes had lost their spark.

Emma spent most of her time sitting on the long porch with her grandson just watching the bay. On her good days, she took Harry and Jack for a walk along the shore. More often, she would rock the boy and let him sleep away the afternoon snug in her arms while she listened to the noisy birds, surveyed the ever-changing tide, and eyed the many boats that sailed by.

Their idyllic life came to an end when Frederick decided to move his family to a farm in Deepwater, Texas, about ten miles west. Lucy was pregnant again, and perhaps Frederick believed his growing brood would be too much for his elderly parents to handle. Whatever his reasoning, Emma was saddened by the absence of her treasured daughter-in-law and grandson. She couldn't keep up with the household chores by herself, and an aging Linus found it difficult to run the farm alone. The Seelyes thought it best to sell their property and move within the city limits of La Porte.

● ● ● ● ●

In La Porte, Linus built a smaller home with two rooms downstairs and two rooms upstairs. He also joined Otway Sterling in the construction business—an occupation that suited him much more than farming. The Seelyes faced a difficult winter in 1895, which brought freezing temperatures and snow measuring more than two feet. As blinding blizzards blew across the area, that winter went down as one of the worst in Texas history.

But the cold air eventually turned warmer and the Seelye family once again welcomed a new addition. Lucy delivered a baby girl, Blanche Caroline, early that summer, which prompted a visit from Emma and Linus. Emma was overjoyed to meet her new grand-daughter and once again play with Harry who smothered her with hugs and kisses. He couldn't wait to show his grandparents the new kittens and chicks that claimed their residence on the farm. Fred-erick's family seemed happy and that was good enough for Emma, but their visit was much too short for her liking. After promising to write soon, she and Linus once again returned to La Porte.

Upon coming home, Emma found it necessary to do some shopping at Buck's, the local dry-goods store. That afternoon, she stood at the register talking with the owner, Daniel Buck, as was her usual custom.

"We just got back from Deepwater yesterday." She laid her pur-chases on the counter. "Now, it's time to stock up."

"How's Fred and his family doing over there?" Buck pulled a pencil from behind his ear.

"They're all good," Emma sighed. "But I miss them so and I'm afraid the new baby will grow up without knowing us."

Oh, now, Emma, Deepwater's not that far away." Buck began to jot down a list of prices.

"It is when you're an old lady who finds it hard to travel, but at least it's not as far as the army took Charles."

"Have you heard from Charles lately? Do you know where he is?"

"The last letter he wrote was postmarked from Michigan."

A gray-haired gentleman, also shopping in the store, looked up from a colorful display of hair bows as soon as he heard the word 'Michigan.'

"Excuse me, ma'am." The man came closer. "I couldn't help but hear you mention that great state of Michigan. I lived there once . . . not far from Flint. Have you ever heard of it?"

"Isaac?" Emma's mouth fell open as she instantly recognized him. "Isaac Hagler? Is that you?"

"Why y-y-yes," he stammered. "I thought you looked familiar, but . . . do I know you?" He seemed confused as Emma extended her hand.

"You would only know me as Private Franklin Thompson, but I go by Emma Seelye now."

The shocked look on Hagler's wrinkled face made Emma chuckle. "I realize it's difficult to believe that this frail woman you are looking at now could possibly be the soldier nurse who dressed your wound when you were shot at Bull Run." She looked him over carefully and then pointed to his left side just below the ribs. "I believe I stitched you up right about there."

Disbelief quickly turned to surprise, then to delight. With a hearty laugh, he pumped her hand enthusiastically. "I'll be damned! How is this possible, Frank, er I mean, Emma?"

"It's a long story, Isaac." Emma smiled, never failing to enjoy the shock when someone finally realized that she once was a young military medic named Franklin. "Why don't you come to my house for dinner tomorrow tonight? It will give us a chance to talk and you can meet my husband, Linus. And if you have a missus, be sure to bring her along, too."

"There's no missus anymore." Hagler shook his head. "My Ella died of the consumption about six months ago so I moved to Houston where my daughter lives."

"What brings you to La Porte?"

"I wanted to spend some time by the bay. Everyone in Houston raves about it and I must say they are right. It's really lovely here and the hotel is one of Texas's finest, but I never thought I'd run into a fellow veteran here."

"So you'll have dinner with us then?"

"I would be honored to be your guest, Emma. No man I know could hold a candle to your bravery, but first maybe you could help me choose a hair bow for my daughter. I promised to bring her a souvenir."

•••••

The next evening Linus, Emma, and Isaac sat at the Seelye kitchen table reminiscing about the war as if no time had passed since those days of blood and glory. "I do remember the night before the first battle of Bull Run when Colonel Roberts asked Jack if he stole those chickens for our last supper."

"The colonel was so angry." Emma smiled at the memory. "I had to help Jack out."

"But I saw you pay for those damned chickens!" Hagler bellowed in delight. "And I'll never know how you managed to keep a straight face while Jack swore he brought those chickens with him all the way from Washington!"

Emma laughed with him. "Good ole Jack . . . he had a big heart. He just wanted to take care of his boys."

"That was the last decent meal we had before all hell broke loose," Isaac recalled, shaking his head.

Emma nodded in agreement. "It was a terrible day—that first battle. I'll never forget the bloodshed or the losses we all suffered. And to think, it was just the beginning."

"My wife wrote about all of that in her book, *Nurse and Spy*," Linus offered. "Maybe you read it?"

"I did read it!" Hagler's jaw dropped in amazement. "But I had no idea you were the author, Emma. And might I add that I enjoyed every page! What you did to benefit the soldiers is truly commendable. But I shouldn't be surprised. You always were looking out for everyone else."

"The Lord knows I tried," Emma sighed.

"Sometimes, you disappeared for days." Hagler thought for a moment before he spoke further. "And I remember seeing you with darkened skin. Now, it all makes sense. You were in the Secret Service! And here I thought you were just trying to keep from being seen at night when you delivered the mail."

"Emma has an amazing story," bragged Linus.

"It sure is a lot to take in," Hagler agreed. "And if I hadn't been there to see it with my own eyes, I would find it hard to believe."

"Well, I'm proud to say that the Federal Government finally recognized my wife's service in the war."

"As well they should." Hagler paused once again. "You know, Emma . . . you should join the Grand Army of the Republic. I'm a member and I believe you should be, too."

"Have you forgotten that no woman has ever been allowed into the GAR?"

"Let me remind you Emma, that no woman is like you . . . and now your honorable discharge certainly makes you eligible for enrollment."

"I don't know, Isaac. It seems impossible."

"Your whole story seems impossible, but it's true. Let me bring you an application."

"But I'd need a sponsor."

"And it would be my honor to sponsor you. After all, I owe you for all of your fine stitching."

●●●●●

The Grand Army of the Republic, or GAR as it was better known, was a fraternal organization formed for honorably discharged military veterans who served as Union soldiers during the Civil War. The group was founded in 1866 by Dr. Benjamin F. Stephenson—a Union veteran himself. Membership had peaked in 1890 with almost five hundred thousand men. By the time Isaac Hagler submitted Emma's application for membership to the George B. McClellan GAR Post No. 9 in Houston, Texas, the group had less members nationally, as the old soldiers had begun dying off.

Emma was interviewed by local GAR officers and her military record vetted by a team of investigators. The final step to acceptance was a vote held by the veterans. Members decided in their standard way by using black and white balls. Each man dropped one ball into the mouth of a model wooden cannon that served as a voting-box. A white ball meant a yes vote, while a black ball countered with a nay. In Emma's case, when the balls were tallied, there was not a single black one cast.

In the early spring of 1897, Emma and Linus, along with Frederick and his family, took the train to Houston where Emma would become the first and only woman ever inducted into the GAR. On April 22, 1897, the sun shone brightly over the red, white, and blue decorations that adorned the small park where GAR members of the George B. McClellan Post, dressed in their military finest, met for their twelfth annual encampment. This was an historic day for the group as a brass band entertained with patriotic music. The guests assembled, mingled, and then took their seats under a large banner that read: "Grand Army of the Republic". The GAR's Past National Commander-in-Chief A.G. Weissert spoke first:

> *"Every now and then a woman has appeared who has claimed membership in the Grand Army of the Republic and then proceeded to work the old boys or the community for transportation, cash or board; but they have always proved to be frauds. You know our order says only such as have an honorable discharge from the army or navy can be received into membership. Sarah Emma Edmonds Seelye has such a discharge. The Commander of the Post, of which she desires to become a member submitted the papers to me. I have found the discharge regular in all respects."*

Weissert then motioned toward Emma, who wore a crisp, new uniform, given to her by Isaac Hagler. She stepped up to the podium to enthusiastic applause from her fellow veterans. Weissert then ceremoniously placed the cross-shaped GAR medal around her neck and handed her an official certificate. "Emma Seelye . . . you have been inducted into the George B. McClellan Post of the Houston, Texas Grand Army of the Republic Post Number 9."

The applause and cheers reverberated throughout the park as tears of joy threatened to spill from Emma's eyes as she dabbed at them with her now tattered crimson cloth. This was a moment she never dared dreamed would become a reality. Weissert called for silence and then invited Emma to speak. Hesitant at first, her words touched the souls of everyone present that jubilant spring day:

> "I am not naturally born of these United States, but I am an adopted daughter of this great country. As a young person, I found it necessary to disguise myself as a man and put distance between me and my natural kin. This situation led me from Canada to Flint, Michigan where a group of brave men, who called themselves the Flint Union Greys, took me in as their own. I did not intend to become a soldier, but when Father Abraham sent out his call for help at the commencement of that deadly Civil War, it was only natural to follow in the footsteps of my newfound country and my newfound friends. Men of honor, the Flint Union Greys became Company F in the Second Michigan Volunteer Infantry. It was my privilege to be among them.
>
> "My comrades and I witnessed the many horrors of battle, the unsightly ravages of disease and the mind-numbing suffering of those who gave so much more than I ever did. Loss of limbs. Loss of eyesight. Loss of life. Fields colored crimson with blood. Bodies floating in the rivers making the water unfit to drink. The screams. The cries. All of this was in a day's work. If we had stopped long enough to think about it, we would have gone mad. But there was no time. Looking back, I know that even the mightiest of angels would have faltered at the sights and sounds we endured.
>
> "But no war is pretty. No battles pleasurable. We witnessed the worst humanity has to offer, but also the best. The unbreakable spirits. The unparalleled bravery. The small kindnesses that

only men at war afford each other. Despite the strife we faced, we just did the best we could during those difficult days. When the war ended, those that could returned to their normal lives. I was not so fortunate. I had to learn to live once again as a woman.

"It took quite some time and a long letter-writing campaign by my comrades-in-arms, but I was finally given my Army pension. Sometime after that and with more letters written on my behalf, I was cleared of my desertion charges and given an honorable discharge. I thought that there could be no better feeling than to collect what was owed me and clear my name. But I was wrong. To once again be counted among these Civil War heroes and recognized with this medal is an honor beyond all honors.

"None of us were there for the glory or the undertaking of adventure, but we shared a patriotic spirit along with a sense of what is right to ensure that America remains the land of the free and the home of the brave. During a time of great national despair, I served this country as a Union soldier to the best of my ability . . . something I could not have done in a dress."

Epilogue

In the early hours of Monday morning, September 5, 1898, Jack, whose fur was now more white than black, lay at the foot of Emma's bed, as was his custom. The old dog watched closely while Linus kissed his wife good-bye before leaving for work. "Lucy will be here in a bit and Jack will keep you company until she gets here." He squeezed Emma's hand. "Is there anything you need?"

"I have everything I could ever want." Emma smiled weakly, clutching at what remained of Betsy's handkerchief. "But do you think you could help me walk through the garden tonight? I really miss the fresh flowers and seeing the vegetables grow."

"Of course, my girl." Linus caressed her face.

"Thank you, Linus. You are always so good to me. I'm just sorry I am such a burden."

Linus kissed her forehead again. "Get some rest. I'm sure Lucy will have wonderful stories to tell you about the children." He patted Jack on the head. "Take care of Emma, old boy. Don't let her roam too far."

One hour later as Lucy approached her mother-in-law's house, she heard the mournful howl of a dog. Quickening her step, Lucy rushed to the bedroom where she found the dog curled up next to Emma's lifeless body. The dark hand of death that she had so easily avoided during that horrific war had finally come to claim her. She was only fifty-six.

Emma was buried in Houston's German Cemetery later renamed the Washington Cemetery in a GAR lot, Section G, Grave 26. Upon her grave is a simple limestone marker that bears the name 'Emma E. Seelye' and the unpretentious words 'Army Nurse.' To this day, she remains the only woman ever so honored.

Authors' Final Note: In 1992, Sarah Emma Edmonds Seelye was inducted into the Michigan Women's Hall of Fame. There, she joined the ranks of such great ladies as civil rights activist Rosa Parks, abolitionist Sojourner Truth, and former First Lady Betty Ford. So honored by her adopted state, her inclusion here ensures that Emma's legacy and remarkable story lives on to inspire future generations.

Appendix A

Whatever Happened To . . .

Linus Seelye

After his wife's death, Linus Seelye remained in Texas near his son's family. He made several attempts to publish Emma's revised memoir, but the manuscript was eventually lost. Sometime after 1910, Linus returned to Canada. He and Lucy routinely exchanged letters. He enjoyed writing to her about his good health, describing in detail his hearty appetite, excellent hearing, and overall perfect physical condition. He also continued his ritual of afternoon tea. His final trip to the United States occurred in 1912 when he attended the wedding of his eldest grandson, Harry. The following year, he was interviewed by a journalist from a Canadian magazine that ran a story about the exploits of Franklin Thompson. Always proud of his wife, he described her as ". . . deeply religious, fearless in all situations and . . . never happier than when she was doing some good for another; she spent but little money on herself, but gave away nearly all she earned for the benefit of the sick and poor. . . ." Linus died of pneumonia on January 15, 1918 at the age of 85 and is buried at Cedar Hill Cemetery in Saint-John, New Brunswick, Canada.

•••••

The Other Seelyes

Frederick and Lucy Seelye remained stateside and had five children: Harry Ernest (1892-1980), Blanche Caroline (1895-1984), Frederick Leroy (1900-1958), Leona Letitia (1903-1967), and Alice Louise (1911-1980) who was named after Frederick's deceased sister. The couple lived in Texas until 1903 when doctors advised Lucy that the climate was having an adverse impact on her health. They returned to Fort Scott, Kansas, and Linus joined them for a time before moving back to Canada. When the 1925 Kansas State Census was taken, Lucy listed herself as a widow still living in Fort Scott. She died there in 1964 at the age of eighty-eight and is buried, along with all of her children, in Fort Scott's Evergreen Cemetery.

It is believed that after Charles Finney Seelye enlisted in the army, he fought in the Spanish American War (1898) as well as the Philippine-American War (1899-1902), also known as the Philippine Insurrection, but very little information has come to light about him after his life in the military.

•••••

Damon Stewart

Damon Stewart returned to Flint, Michigan after the Civil War, but lost two brothers during the conflict: William who was killed at Resaca, Georgia in what is often referred to as the 'botched' Battle of Resaca; and Richard who died at Jonesboro, Georgia in the Battle of Jonesboro, which is considered the final battle of the Atlanta Campaign. Stewart married Frances McQuigg in 1867, and the couple had six children: Hobart, Mabel, Lucy, William, Bertha, and Frances. When the railroad came through the area in 1871, Davison Station opened and Stewart was appointed as its first postmaster; he also served as a town alderman. Stewart inherited the family farm and eventually gave up the dry-goods business in order to work the land. In his youth, he was a staunch Republican, but as he grew older, he became a temperance advocate and joined the Prohibitionists. He and his wife were originally Presbyterians, but later became members of the Congregational Church. Stewart was active in the Sunday Schools of both churches. A well-respected member of the Flint community, he died in 1905 from liver disease at the age of seventy-one and is buried in Flint's historic Glenwood Cemetery.

•••••

William Barker McCreery

Bill McCreery was wounded six times during the Civil War. He was also taken prisoner at Chickamauga and sent to the notorious Libby Prison where he and a group of military men made a daring escape by digging a tunnel to freedom. After his service, McCreery returned to Flint, Michigan and married Ada Fenton with whom he had four children: Fenton, Adelaide, Howard, and Katherine. A successful merchant with diverse interests, McCreery was a founder of Citizens National Bank and a director of the Chicago and Northeastern Railway. In addition, he was one of the original directors of Flint waterworks. The well-respected war veteran was elected mayor of the city of Flint in 1865 and in that capacity served two one-year terms. McCreery also held the position of the US Collector of Internal Revenue representing Michigan's eastern district and then served as Michigan State Treasurer for several years. After his wife's death in 1884, McCreery wed Genevieve Decker with whom he had no children. In 1890 under the administration of US President Benjamin Harrison, McCreery was appointed the United States Consul of Valparaiso, Chile, where he and his family resided for three years. He died at his home in Flint, Michigan in 1896 at the age of sixty and is buried at Flint's Glenwood Cemetery.

•••••

Orlando M. Poe

In the decade before the war began, a young Orlando Metcalf Poe graduated from West Point with an engineering background. He was then sent to Detroit and became part of the Great Lakes Survey—a project designed to improve navigation of these major, yet dangerous waterways. After the war, Poe was designated Engineer Secretary of the Lighthouse Board. Next, he was promoted to Chief Army Engineer of the Upper Lakes Lighthouse District. In this capacity, he was responsible for maintaining multiple lighthouses that stood in Eastern Michigan, as well as those that were located in the state's Upper Peninsula. Poe also produced an annual report that recommended sites where new lighthouses were needed and then oversaw the construction of those that were approved. In 1884, Poe became superintendent of iron and harbor works for the entire Great Lakes area. As such, he designed and managed the building of a new lock in Sault Ste. Marie, Michigan. Christened the Poe Lock, it was the largest shipping lock of its kind in the world measuring eight hundred feet long and one hundred feet wide. After suffering a serious fall while inspecting the locks, he died from an infection on October 2, 1893 at his home in Detroit at the age of sixty-three. Poe was buried with full military honors at Arlington National Cemetery in Virginia.

•••••

William R. Morse

Captain Morse was mustered out of the Union Army on August 22, 1863. He resigned in order to accept a position in the Veterans Reserve Corps—a newly formed military organization. The group was considered part of the Union Army and included disabled soldiers who could perform simple chores, and in turn, freed up the stronger men for battle. Morse eventually returned to Flint, Michigan, where his wife, Mary Hoyt Young, and young son, Willie, remained. In the 1870 United States Census, Morse listed his occupation as a 'hardware dealer.' Always active in military affairs, he helped establish a patriotic group called the 'Flint Union Blues' in 1872 in an effort to maintain a military presence in Flint. Members wore dark blue uniforms trimmed in white and carried muskets. Always admired for his leadership abilities, Morse was elected the company's first captain. He was also active in Flint politics serving as an alderman in 1874 and 1875. Morse was a widower (Mary died in 1893) when he passed away on March 9, 1899. Like his comrades, he was interred at Flint's Glenwood Cemetery. The Morses' graves are simply marked as 'Father' and 'Mother' Morse.

• • • • •

George B. McClellan

When the Civil War ended, Little Mac, his wife, Ellen, and four-year-old daughter, Mary, traveled to Europe where they stayed for three years. His son, George B. McClellan, Jr. was born in Dresden, Kingdom of Saxony in 1865. Upon their return, McClellan briefly considered running for United States President, but eventually declined any bid for the office. In 1870, McClellan was appointed Chief Engineer of the New York City Department of Docks; two years later he also took on the responsibility of president of the Atlantic and Great Western Railroad. From 1873-1875, the McClellans once again traveled to Europe. In 1877, he was nominated and elected Governor of the State of New Jersey (1878-1881). He campaigned for the presidential election of Grover Cleveland, hoping to be given the position of Secretary of War (now known as Secretary of State) in Cleveland's cabinet. Much to Little Mac's disappointment, the job was given to Thomas F. Bayard, a prominent Democrat from Delaware. For the remaining years of his life, Little Mac traveled and penned his memoirs, *McClellan's Own Story*, which was published posthumously in 1887. He died suddenly of a heart attack in Orange, New Jersey at the age of fifty-eight. Little Mac is buried in Trenton, New Jersey's Riverview Cemetery. Upon his death, the *New York Evening Post* reported: "Probably no soldier who did so little fighting has ever had his qualities as a commander so minutely, and we may add, so fiercely discussed." And the debate continues to this day.

•••••

Dr. William H. Bunce

Dr. Bunce was considered one of the leading surgeons in the northern area of Ohio and known for his gentle bedside manner. Many patients considered him their friend, as well as their doctor. During the Civil War, he served as a surgeon with the rank of major. In 1882, he took up the temperance fight and declared himself a good Christian who did not believe in drinking. He was quick to come to the defense of the local pharmacist, however, when that man decided to carry alcohol for medicinal purposes requiring a physician's prescription. The town was in an uproar, proclaiming that the druggist 'might' turn his business into a 'whiskey shop' just to make money. Dr. Bunce admonished the local citizens: ". . . Then you should hang him for fear he will kill somebody . . ." The good doctor died in his Oberlin home on February 13, 1892 at the age of sixty-one. Dr. Bunce is buried at Westwood Cemetery in Oberlin. He was survived by his wife, Ellen, and their three children—two daughters and a son who followed in his father's footsteps to become a physician.

Appendix B

Letters to Congress

The following letters were taken directly from the "Reports of Committees of the House of Representatives for the First Session of the Forty-Ninth Congress 1885-1886, Volume III, Report No. 929" and were submitted to the Committee on Military Affairs accompanied by bill H.R. 1172, which ultimately awarded Emma her pension and back pay:

Damon Stewart, being by me duly sworn, deposes and says that he is a resident of the city of Flint, county of Genesee, and State of Michigan, and that he was enlisted a private in Company F, Second Regiment Michigan Infantry Volunteers, at Flint, Mich., on or about the 18th day of April, A.D. 1861; and that he was subsequently promoted to corporal and sergeant of said company respectively. And deponent further states that S. Emma E. Seelye is the identical person who enlisted under the name of Franklin Thompson, as a private in said Company F, Second Regiment, Michigan Infantry Volunteers at Detroit, Mich., on or about the last day of May, A.D. 1861. And deponent further says that the said deponent remained with said company and regiment until May 5, 1861, when he was wounded and left said company and regiment. And the deponent further says that, during said time from on or about April 18, 1861 until May 5, 1862, when the said deponent was with said company and regiment, said Franklin Thompson (S. Emma E. Seelye) remained with said company and regiment, and performed cheerfully and fully and at all times any duty which was assigned her, and this deponent further says that so far he can remember, said duty consisted chiefly of either acting as nurse or carrying mail. And deponent further says that during all of said time said Franklin Thompson (S. Emma E. Seelye) bore a good reputation, always behaved as a person of good moral character and a consistent Christian, and was always ready for duty. And deponent further says that he makes this statement from personal knowledge, having known said Franklin Thompson as aforesaid. And the deponent further says that on or about the 5th day of August, A.D. 1862, he was mustered in as first lieutenant and adjutant of the Twenty-third Michigan Infantry Volunteers, by Lieut. Col. J. R. Smith, U.S.A., at Detroit, Mich., and was mustered in as captain of Company K in said regiment on September 1, 1862, and further saith not.

DAMON STEWART
Late Captain Company K,
Twenty-third Regiment Michigan Infantry Volunteers

Subscribed and sworn to before me this 8th day of March, A.D. 1882. Deponent is the person he represents himself to be, and a credible person.

JOHN J. CARTER
Clerk of the Circuit Court, Genesee County, Michigan

•••••

Flint, Mich., March 31, 1882

This is to certify that in the month of May, 1861, I enlisted in Company F, Second Regiment Michigan Volunteer Infantry, and that during the same month one Franklin Thompson enlisted as a private soldier in the same company. He proceeded with the company to Washington and was present at the first battle of Bull Run and in the several engagements on the Peninsula, Virginia. He was for some time regimental mail carrier, and was especially attentive to the sick in hospital. A few days since I met this same Frank Thompson (whom I immediately recognized) in the person of Mrs. S. Emma E. Seelye, now a resident of Kansas.

WILLIAM B. McCREERY
Late Colonel Twenty-first Michigan Volunteer Infantry

● ● ● ● ●

State of Michigan, County of Genesee:

I, William R. Morse, late captain of Company F, Second Regiment Michigan Infantry Volunteers being duly sworn do testify that, on the 25th day of May 1861, S. Emma E. Seelye enlisted as a private in Company F, Second Regiment Michigan Infantry Volunteers, under the name of Franklin Thompson and was supposed to be a boy; was mustered into the United States service at Fort Wayne, Detroit, Mich., by Lieut. Col. I.R. Smith, U.S.A., and faithfully performed the various duties which were assigned her, viz, in the ranks as a soldier. In camp and field hospitals as attendant on sick and wounded soldiers and as regimental and brigade mail-carrier and postmaster.

And I do further certify that S. Emma E. Seelye, by her uniform faithfulness, bravery and efficiency, and by her pure morals and Christian character, won the respect, admiration and confidence of both officers and men in said company and regiment.

I make this statement from personal knowledge, having known that Franklin Thompson remained with the regiment and performed these services as aforesaid, from the time of enlistment up to _____, and I know that S. Emma Seelye is the identical Franklin Thompson as aforesaid.

WILLIAM R. MORSE

State of Missouri, County of Pettis, ss:

Subscribed and sworn to before me, clerk of the county court in and for the aforesaid county of Pettis, this 15th day of April, 1882.

H.Y. FIELD, *Clerk*
By T. FRINTCHUM, *D.C.*

•••••

State of Michigan, County of Genesee:

Milton S. Benjamin, being by me duly sworn, deposes and says that he is a resident of the city of Flint, county of Genesee and State of Michigan, and that he enlisted as a private in Company F, Second Regiment Michigan Infantry Volunteers at Flint, Mich., on or about the 20th day of April, A..D. 1861. And deponent further says that S. Emma E. Seelye is the identical person who enlisted, under the name of Franklin Thompson, as a private in said Company F, Second Regiment Michigan Infantry Volunteers at Detroit Mich., on or about the 1st day of May, A.D. 1861; and deponent further says that he, said deponent, remained with said company and regiment until the 3rd day of June, 1864, when he was wounded and sent to the hospital, and never returned to said company and regiment; and deponent further says that during all of said time, from on or about May 5, 1861, until June 1, 1863, he said deponent, was with said company and regiment, and said Franklin Thompson (S. Emma E. Seelye) remained with said company and regiment and performed cheerfully and fully and at all times any and all duty which was assigned her, and deponent further says that during all of said time said Franklin Thompson (S. Emma E. Seelye) bore a good reputation and always behaved as a person of good moral character and was always ready for duty, and deponent further says that he makes this statement from personal knowledge, having known said Franklin Thompson, as aforesaid, and that he knows that said S. Emma E. Seelye is the identical Franklin Thompson as aforesaid.

MILTON S. BENJAMIN

Late Private Company F, Second Regiment Michigan Infantry Volunteers

Subscribed and sworn to before me this 8th day of March A. 1882; deponent is the person he represents himself to be, and a credible person.

JOHN J. CARTON

Clerk of the Circuit Court, Genesee County, Michigan

•••••

State of Michigan, County of Kalamazoo, ss:

William Shakespeare, of Kalamazoo, Kalamazoo County and State of Michigan being first duly sworn deposes and says he was a member of Company K, Second Michigan Infantry, from its organization in the spring of 1861 until June 1864, and that he was well acquainted with Frank Thompson, of Company F, of the same regiment from its organization, and that he knew Frank Thompson was a strong, healthy, and robust soldier, ever willing and ready for duty. This deponent further says he never knew of said Frank Thompson being sick, except in the spring of 1863, when he (she) had chills.

And this deponent further says that he is now the quartermaster general of the State of Michigan, and that he has no interest, either directly or indirectly, in any claim of said Frank Thompson pending against the United States Government.

WILLIAM SHAKESPEARE

Subscribed and sworn to before me this 30th day of January, A.D. 1884

T. HEDDINGS
Clerk Circuit Court

•••••

Flint, Mich., March 22, 1882

To who it may concern:

At the request of the friends and Army comrades of "Frank Thompson" (Mrs. S. Emma E. Seelye) I make the following statement:

I was a member of Company F, Second Regiment of Michigan Infantry Volunteers. Frank Thompson enlisted as a private soldier, at Detroit, about May, 1861, and served faithfully in that capacity until he (or, as we have since ascertained, she) developed a peculiar talent as a nurse. More than one member of the company can attest the care kindness, and self-sacrificing devotion of "Frank" to the sick soldiers of the regiment. I left the regiment in July, 1861, and saw nor heard nothing of or from "Frank Thompson" until the present month, when Capt Damon Stewart introduced us to a lady whom I recognized as "Frank Thompson," our former Army companion although now introduced as Mrs. S. Emma E. Seelye. Frank's "manly bearing," soldierly qualities, kindness and devotion to the sick deserve to be recognized in a liberal and substantial manner.

SUMNER HOWARD
Ex United States District Attorney of Utah

•••••

State of Michigan, County of Kalamazoo, ss:

William Turner, being by me duly sworn, deposes and says that he is a resident of the city of Flint, county of Genesee, and State of Michigan, and that he enlisted as a first lieutenant in Company F, Second Regiment Michigan Infantry Volunteers at Flint, Mich., on or about the 18th day of April, A.D. 1861. And deponent further says that S. Emma E. Seelye is the identical person who enlisted as a private in said Company F, Second Regiment Michigan Infantry Volunteers, under the name of Franklin Thompson, at Detroit, Mich. on or about the 1st day of May, A.D. 1861. And deponent further says that he, said deponent, remained with said company and regiment until on or about July 1, 1862, when he resigned and came home, leaving said company and regiment. And deponent further says that during said time, from on or about April 18, 1862, until on or about July 1, 1862, when he, said deponent, was with said company and regiment, said Franklin Thompson (S. Emma E. Seelye) remained with said company and regiment, and performed cheerfully and fully, and at all times, any duty which was assigned her. And deponent further says that during all of said time said Franklin Thompson (S. Emma E. Seelye) bore a good reputation, behaved as a person of good moral character, and was always ready for duty. And deponent further says that he makes this statement from personal knowledge, having known said Franklin Thompson as aforesaid and that he knows that said S. Emma E. Seelye is the identical Franklin Thompson, as aforesaid.

WILLIAM TURNER

First Lieutenant Company F, Second Michigan Volunteers

Subscribed and sworn to before me this 8th day of March A. 1882; deponent is the person he represents himself to be, and a credible person.

JOHN J. CARTON

Clerk of the Circuit Court, Genesee County, Michigan

•••••

To the Honorable Senate and House of Representatives of the United States of America in Congress Assembled:

We, the undersigned, officers and privates of the late Second Regiment of Michigan Volunteer Infantry, represent that on or about the 25th day of May A.D. 1861, and at the city of Flint, in the State of Michigan, one S.E. Edmonds, a female, was enrolled in Company F of said regiment under the name of Frank Thompson for the term of three years, and that the said S.E. Edmonds, alias Frank Thompson, served faithfully as a good and loyal soldier for nearly two years and until her health became greatly impaired by reason of said arduous service. At this juncture she felt impelled to ask for leave of absence to recruit her health, which being disallowed, she left the Army and resumed the habiliments of her own sex. She then prepared for the press a book, entitled the *Nurse and Spy*, published by Hulbert, Williams & Co., Hartford, Conn., and devoted the proceeds of its sale to the aid of the sick and wounded soldiers of the Union Army. Her labors upon her book being completed, she again continued her work of public benefaction, this time under the auspices of the Christian and Sanitary Commissions. In this work she appeared in the attire of her sex, and gave to the cause that unflagging interest and persistent toil and self-sacrifice that only a noble, patriotic woman can give.

In view of her many ministrations of tenderness and mercy, thousands of soldiers who were the recipients of her timely attention and nursing must remember her with the most filial regard.

She is now the same true, loyal woman that she was in those eventful, stormy days of 1861 to 1865, when the country was passing the agonizing throes of civil war. And whereas her health has been permanently impaired by reason of exposure in her arduous public service of her country, and whereas she has never received any bounty or back pay, and cannot receive the same until the pending charge of desertion is legally removed, we pray your honorable body to give her the amnesty which will make her eligible to receive the favors at your hands which we shall ask for her.

Now we further pray your honorable body, if you find it consistent with her record, to grant her a pension for the remainder of her life and any other favors which in your wisdom and generosity you deem just and politic.

JAMES H. BROWN,
Company C, Second Michigan (Tonganoxie, Leavenworth County, Kansas)

F. SCHNEIDER,
Late Colonel of the Second Infantry (Lansing, Mich.)

SYLVESTER LARNED,
Late Lieutenant Second Michigan Infantry Volunteers (Detroit)

• • • • •

The following letter from General O. M. Poe, colonel of Engineers, with headquarters at Detroit, though not necessary, completes the proof of identification and service:

Detroit, Mich., January 4, 1885
Dear Sir: I am this moment in receipt of a letter from Mrs. S.E.E. Seelye, of Fort Scott, Kansas, requesting me to write you and testify to her identity with one Frank Thompson, who served as an enlisted man in the Second Michigan Volunteer Infantry from the time that regiment was mustered into the United States service, in May, 1861, until the early part of April, 1863, a period of nearly two years.

I was colonel of that regiment from September 16, 1861, to the 29th of November, 1862, when I was appointed a brigadier-general of volunteers, my own regiment forming a part of my brigade until my final separation from it, on or about the 10th of April, 1863. I cannot recall just when "Frank Thompson" first came under my personal notice, but I distinctly remember that "Frank" was on duty as brigade mail carrier just preceding the battle of Fredericksburg, in December, 1862, and was my orderly in that battle. "Frank" continued on such duty until after we arrived at Lebanon, Ky., early in April, 1863. I have no personal knowledge of her movements after the 10th of April, when I relinquished command of the brigade, until I met her at the reunion of my regiment at Flint, Mich. in the autumn of 1884, where there was no difficulty about her identification with "Frank Thompson." I think I would have recognized her anywhere. My wife, who knew her in the army, and was with me at Flint, recognized her equally with myself. I would be perfectly willing to go upon the stand and swear that the soldier known as "Frank Thomson," of the Second Regiment Michigan Volunteer Infantry, and the woman now known as Mrs. S.E.E. Seelye are one and the same person. There is not the shadow of a doubt about it, and I know that my wife, as well as many officers of the regiment, would give the same testimony.

As a soldier "Frank Thompson" was effeminate looking, and for that reason was detailed as mail carrier to avoid taking an efficient soldier from the ranks. As a woman she is masculine looking. But a single glance at her in proper character caused me to wonder how I ever could have mistaken her for a man, and I readily recall many things which might to have betrayed her, except that no one thought of finding a woman in a soldier's dress. I don't think I could be deceived in that way again, even if, as was the case, the whole regiment was in ignorance regarding the matter.

As a soldier "Frank Thompson" did her duty to the best of her ability as long as she remained with the regiment

Please let me know if an affidavit is wanted from me and others, or if this is sufficient. There is plenty of testimony in this case.

O.M. POE
(Late) Colonel Second Michigan Volunteer Infantry